Extraordinary Praise for Lou

"*Dark Ride* is Lou Berney at his best. [An] actor at a theme park who finds his [path to help] abused children is both thrilling and [life?] affirming. The story of a man who finally stands for something after a lifetime of falling for anything will haunt you."

—S. A. Cosby, *New York Times* bestselling author of *All the Sinners Bleed*

"*Dark Ride* is a remarkable book written by Lou Berney, a storyteller I admire as a writer and cherish as a reader. *Dark Ride* effortlessly grabs you and does not let you go until the final page. I didn't want this book to end and it stayed with me long after I finished reading it. Lou Berney is a magnificent writer with talent to burn."

—Don Winslow, *New York Times* bestselling author of *City on Fire*

"*Dark Ride* is moving, deeply involving, funny, and breathless, and I loved every single page of Hardly's harrowing journey from stoner to sleuth."

—Lisa Unger, *New York Times* bestselling author of *Last Girl Ghosted*

"*Dark Ride* is a brilliant book from a master storyteller. Sometimes the hero you need is the person you least expect and Berney's novel takes you on a remarkable journey where you witness an unlikely stoner become the hero two children in trouble need."

—T. J. Newman, *New York Times* bestselling author of *Falling*

"I've been a Lou Berney fan for years, and *Dark Ride* is a cause for celebration. A suspense novel shot through with heart and soul, it has the feel of an instant classic. Through the journey of Hardly Reed, a lovable pothead turned amateur detective, Berney wrestles with a central existential question: what do we owe our neighbors, and what are we willing to give up to help them?"

—Steph Cha, bestselling author of *Our House Will Pay*

"*Dark Ride* is quite simply dynamite. Lou Berney lights the fuse on the first page and from there, the suspense builds to an utterly explosive climax. . . . . This is a story that grabs you by the throat, then reaches deep into your heart. It's a dark ride, yes, but one well worth the trip."

—William Kent Krueger, *New York Times* bestselling author of *The River We Remember*

"Lou Berney is such a talent, and he's at the top of his game here. Hardly Reed is a protagonist to root for—an affable stoner who just might be the one person who can save two children in danger. *Dark Ride* will grab your heart in chapter one and not let go until the final, searing page."

—Alafair Burke, *New York Times* bestselling author of *Find Me*

"Put your to-be-read pile to the side. A new book from Lou Berney should go to the top of your agenda."

—Lori Rader-Day, award-winning author of *The Death of Us*

Praise for *November Road*

"I am really enjoying a down-and-dirty thriller, *November Road* by Lou Berney. Cold, violent, and clever. You might enjoy it too."

—R. L. Stine

"Nothing less than an instant American classic. Haunting, thrilling— and indelible as a scar."

—A. J. Finn, #1 *New York Times* bestselling author of *The Woman in the Window*

"When people say they want to read a really good novel, the kind you just can't put down, this is the kind of book they mean. Exceptional."

—Stephen King

"Berney's emotional, empathic writing keeps the dynamic between these two lost souls intriguing, and it resonates on a larger scale, placed as it is against such a vivid backdrop. In the tradition of great historical fiction, Berney finds within an exhaustively covered setting his own nooks and crannies."

—*Entertainment Weekly*

"This superior novel from Edgar winner Lou Berney melds crime fiction with a tale about people reinventing themselves, played out during a cross-country automobile trip. . . . An emotional story about the power of love and redemption through sacrifice with the backdrop of a crucial historical moment."

—Associated Press

"Berney's gentle, descriptive writing brilliantly reflects these times of both disillusionment and hope. . . . Perfectly captures these few weeks at the end of 1963—all that was lost and all that lay tantalizingly and inevitably just beyond the horizon."

—*Kirkus Reviews* (starred review)

"Wistful and complex, Berney's confident portrait of a roadside America traumatized by Kennedy's death gives the novel literary heft, while the ticking clock of the mob closing in on the family to settle accounts lends a genre bite."

—*Library Journal* (starred review)

"Berney creates nail-biting suspense by placing Marcello's top hit man on Guidry's trail, the book's power derives from Charlotte, who finds hidden strength as she confronts unexpected challenges. This is much more than just another conspiracy thriller."

—*Publishers Weekly* (starred review)

"Berney bends his notes exquisitely, playing with the melody, building his marvelously rich characters while making us commit completely to the love story, even though we hear the melancholy refrain and see the noir cloud lurking in the sky. Pitch-perfect fiction."

—*Booklist* (starred review)

DOUBLE BARREL BLUFF

DOUBLE BARREL BLUFF

A Novel

Lou Berney

WM

WILLIAM MORROW

An Imprint of HarperCollinsPublishers

DOUBLE BARREL BLUFF. Copyright © 2024 by Lou Berney. All rights reserved. Printed in the United States of America. No part of this book may be used or reproduced in any manner whatsoever without written permission except in the case of brief quotations embodied in critical articles and reviews. For information, address HarperCollins Publishers, 195 Broadway, New York, NY 10007.

HarperCollins books may be purchased for educational, business, or sales promotional use. For information, please email the Special Markets Department at SPsales@harpercollins.com.

FIRST EDITION

Designed by Diahann Sturge-Campbell

Library of Congress Cataloging-in-Publication Data has been applied for.

ISBN 978-0-06-229248-3

24 25 26 27 28 LBC 5 4 3 2 1

For my aunts: Susan Berney, Mary Beth Berney, Janice Senseney, Rosemary Berney, Kay Senseney, Marjorie Harrigan, and Marge Berney

DOUBLE
BARREL
BLUFF

Chapter One

Of all the ancient wats near Siem Reap, with lotus flowers floating in secluded reflecting pools and stone ramparts broken to pieces by strangler figs, French's favorite temple by far was Banteay Srei.

Unlike Angkor Wat, Banteay Srei was designed to invite, not overwhelm, with no tower taller than thirty feet and grounds that could be explored in half an hour or less. The reliefs on the lintels and pediments were unusually delicate—carved by women, according to local legend—and a special kind of rose-colored sandstone had been used on the main buildings. When the early-morning sun was just right, like now, the gopuras and sanctuary were as rich and warm as a blushing cheek.

Seriously exquisite, French thought, gazing at the temple. Just perfect.

He and Ramos sat parked at the far end of the temple parking lot, in the old yellow Mercedes that Ramos had stolen earlier in the week. Theirs was the only car in the lot, along with the pair of *tuk-tuks* waiting near the ticket booth.

"Did you know, old chum," French said, "that in all of Angkor, all the various temples, no two apsaras are alike? Nuts, isn't it?"

Ramos didn't answer. He fired up what the locals called a Buddha: Cambodian weed spiked with a dash of opium.

"Apsaras are the celestial maidens you see carved all over the temples," French went on. "Thousands of them. Hundreds of thousands. And each and every lovely lady has a distinctive face, a unique expression. It blows one's mind."

Ramos held the smoke in his lungs for what seemed like an impossible amount of time. Finally he released it.

"Okay," he said.

Ramos! The dude lacked even a soupçon of personality. French often felt as if he were trying to have an intelligent conversation with one of the empty-eyed stone heads, streaked with bat shit, that guarded the temple gates at Prasat Bayon.

He checked his watch. Ten minutes had passed since they'd arrived. French decided to wait a few more minutes. The timing of this next stage was critical. He knew they wouldn't have this opportunity again.

They'd been following the woman since Thursday. Every morning at six-thirty, she hired one of the *tuk-tuks* waiting outside her hotel and spent a few hours sightseeing. She hit Angkor Wat on Thursday, Angkor Thom on Friday, Ta Prohm on Saturday. Today, finally, the woman's *tuk-tuk* had turned onto the highway and puttered north, past the Landmine Museum and into the jungle, toward Banteay Srei.

Banteay Srei was the most far-flung of Siem Reap's attractions. A lot of tourists skipped it, and those who didn't tended to visit after making stops at the closer, A-list temples. Until nine in the morning, Banteay Srei was almost deserted.

Perfect.

"We'll give our girl a few more minutes," French said.

Their *girl*. That's how French had begun to think of her, even though she was in her mid-forties or so, probably six or seven years older than him or Ramos.

Ramos took another hit of the Buddha, then passed it to French.

"Play it cool with your guy," Ramos said. "Be careful."

French gave him an innocent look. "Really, Mason?"

"Yeah." Ramos's expression didn't change. French had discovered that irony, no matter how thickly piled on, had little effect on Ramos. He was ridiculously literal, a mule pulling a cart.

Oh, well. French reminded himself that he'd recruited Ramos for his practical experience, not his sparkling personality.

French had met Mason Ramos back in February, in one of the grubby expat bars on Pub Street. The two of them were the only daytime drinkers in the place, both of them American and both blown by ill winds to the other side of the globe. French had abandoned the United States after the university revoked his tenure. He'd seen the move to Southeast Asia as a new beginning, a fresh start, but he'd been abroad a year now, his new novel remained unwritten, and he was almost out of money. Ramos, French learned after he bought him a drink, was from California, where a few months earlier he'd finished "a stretch."

French bought Ramos a second and a third drink. He hoped Ramos, with his spiderweb tattoos and heavy-lidded watchfulness, might be willing to share a juicy story or two about life in the Life. French was toying with the idea of writing a screenplay (commercial but literate: *Ocean's Eleven* filtered through a Proustian lens) and needed some inspiration.

As a muse, though, Ramos kind of sucked. His stories, vague and lacking concrete detail, managed to be both brief and tedious. On the other hand, he was a good listener. And sympathetic to the ordeal that French had gone through—the sexual-harassment committee back home, that lynch mob of shrill harpies and dick-less assistant provosts.

So what if French had slept with a few of his female students over the years? He was a young, attractive professor, and the relationships were always consensual. The women in question were *adults,* responsible for their own choices, and if one or two of them had mistakenly believed that sex with French might improve their grades, then that was *their* problem, not his.

"You don't want to spook him," Ramos said now.

"Ah. I'd better write that down."

Ramos considered. "Okay."

Ramos! French checked his watch again. It was past seven-thirty. It was time.

He got out of the Mercedes and strolled across the parking lot. Their girl's *tuk-tuk* driver squatted in the shade of a sugar palm, smoking a cigarette.

"So she didn't wait for me, did she?" French said, greeting the driver with a smile. "Typical. She went inside without me?"

The *tuk-tuk* driver squinted up.

"My lady friend," French explained. That was as specific as he could get, since he didn't know the woman's name. He didn't know anything about her except that she was from the United States, traveling solo, and—Bjorn had assured him—very, very wealthy. "The one you brought here? From the hotel? The American woman."

Their girl's *tuk-tuk* driver nodded warily. "Yes."

"Yes," French said. "But it's okay. You can go now. You don't have to wait for her. She can ride back to town with me. I have a car."

The driver shook his head. *No.* He wanted the fare back to town.

French was prepared for this. He took out a twenty-dollar bill. The driver eyed it.

"Chum reap leah," French said. Good-bye.

The driver hesitated, then shrugged, snatched the twenty, and mounted his motorcycle. He putt-putt-puttered away.

French's man, Chan, waited a few yards away, next to the only *tuk-tuk* left in the lot now. French gave him a discreet nod and returned to the Mercedes.

"Perfect," French told Ramos, "if I do say so myself."

"Okay," Ramos said.

Ten minutes later the woman, their girl, emerged from the temple gate. French took a final hit of the Buddha and handed it back to Ramos. Ramos licked his thumb and snuffed the burning tip. Together they watched the woman stop, remove her sunglasses, and scan the parking lot for her missing *tuk-tuk*.

She was dressed tastefully and expensively, in tailored linen slacks and a silk blouse the deep aubergine of Cambodian twilight. Dark hair, a long, aristocratic neck. French suspected that their girl was a babe, but he hadn't been close enough yet to make a definitive ruling.

"What's he waiting for?" Ramos said.

"Don't worry," French said.

He had faith in Chan, a sweet-natured kid, eighteen or nineteen years old, who mopped floors at the fleabag hotel where French was living. In his spare time, Chan drove a *tuk-tuk,* taking tourists on unlicensed tours of the Tonlé Sap fishing villages. When French said he needed someone to help with a practical joke, Chan had jumped at the offer. He had a wife and three children to support. French offered him more money than he'd earn in a month.

"He needs to make his move," Ramos said.

"Don't worry."

Right on cue, Chan walked over to their girl.

"Tuk-tuk?" he said, his palms open and a big cheerful smile on his face. French had coached him well. "Hello, madam! Need *tuk-tuk?"*

Their girl scanned the parking lot one last time, then nodded. She followed Chan to his *tuk-tuk* and climbed in.

"What did I tell you?" French said.

Ramos started the Mercedes. Chan's *tuk-tuk* pulled onto the highway.

"When?" Ramos said.

"What?"

"What did you tell me when?"

French looked at Ramos. It was like looking into an empty swimming pool.

"I told you my plan would work," French said slowly. "I told you it was a perfect plan."

Ramos considered. He nodded. "Yeah."

They followed the *tuk-tuk,* giving it plenty of space. A mile or so from Banteay Srei, Chan turned off the highway and onto a narrow dirt road. Ramos slowed and turned onto the dirt road, too.

French reached into the backseat for the masks—cheap plastic knockoffs of traditional Khmer masks that he'd bought at a stall in the central market. His was Hanuman, the heroic monkey general who led Rama's forces to victory in the *Ramayana.* For Ramos, French had picked a slack-jawed demon soldier with crooked fangs. Ramos, naturally, missed the irony.

The dirt road led into the jungle. They put on their masks. When they reached the clearing, a hundred yards in, Chan had already parked and was standing next to his motorcycle. He scratched his head and pretended, as instructed, to be lost. Their girl climbed out of the *tuk-tuk.* French didn't know if she bought Chan's act or not. At this point, of course, she didn't need to.

Ramos eased the Mercedes up behind the *tuk-tuk.*

This, French knew, was it. His Rubicon. The point of no return. The risk was enormous, but so was the potential reward.

Two million dollars. He would be able to start a new life. He'd finally have the life he deserved.

His heart pounded, but at the same time he felt strangely calm. His senses tingled and hummed. He could see the drop of dew on a blade of grass twenty paces away. He could hear the creak of sandal rubber when Chan shifted nervously from one foot to the other.

"You okay?" Ramos said.

French nodded. "Perfectly okay."

He wished he had some coke. Just enough to make sure he stayed on this fine, bright edge of awareness.

He pushed open the door of the Mercedes and stepped out.

"Good morning," he said. He lifted the gun Ramos had found for him. The gun, a small black automatic, felt heavier than French remembered. He realized that his palm was sweating.

The woman turned. If she was alarmed by the sight of a man wearing a monkey mask, pointing a gun at her, she didn't show it. But the lenses of her sunglasses were very dark. French couldn't see what was happening behind them.

"Drop your bag, please, and put your hands behind your back." He kept his voice relaxed, friendly. He wanted to maintain the right tone. Restrained. *Civilized*. "We aren't going to hurt you."

Their girl took a moment to consider. She remained unflustered.

"May I ask one question?" she said.

Before French could answer, Ramos stepped forward.

French saw the gun in his hand. "What is that?" he said, startled.

Ramos wasn't supposed to have a gun. French had been explicit about that. He wanted to avoid unnecessary bluster. The tone, again: restrained, civilized.

"I don't know," Ramos said. He glanced at French, then at the gun, then back at French. "It's Russian, I think."

"No, for God's sake, I mean what are you *doing* with it?"

"You are making a mistake," their girl said.

Ramos pointed his gun at her sternum.

"Stop talking," he said. "Do what he said or I'll put you in the ground."

Their girl dropped her bag and turned around. She put her arms behind her back. Ramos stuck the gun in the waistband of his jeans. French watched as he cuffed her wrists and gagged her with a *krama*, one of the checkered scarves almost every Cambodian wore.

It struck French then. *This is really happening.* He felt almost giddy with disbelief.

"Trunk," Ramos said.

"What?" French said.

He tossed the car keys to French. "Pop the trunk."

French unlocked the trunk of the Mercedes. Ramos gripped their girl's arm, tightly, and steered her over.

"Get in," he said. "Do it now."

"We're not going to hurt you," French said again. "This will be over before you know it."

He helped her climb into the trunk. She didn't resist. She settled on her side, knees tucked up, hands behind her back. Ramos slammed the lid of the trunk shut.

French stripped off his mask and used the sleeve of his linen blazer to wipe the sweat from his eyes.

This is really happening.

"What?" Ramos said.

"What?" French said. "Nothing."

French saw Chan still standing by his *tuk-tuk,* in what appeared to be shock. The kid was grinning with horror, one hand clamped to the top of his head, as if to keep it from flying off.

French walked over and gave Chan his most reassuring smile.

"It's okay," he said. "You did very well. Everything is going to be fine."

"No," Chan said.

"Yes. I promise."

"No."

Ramos walked over. He stood next to French, his mask still on.

"You weren't supposed to have a gun," French said. "I told you that. Do you remember what I told you about setting the right tone?"

"Yeah," Ramos said. He watched Chan, who was breathing rapidly, his shoulders rising and falling.

"Don't worry," French said. "He'll be fine. We can trust him."

French had made certain of that by paying Chan only half the money up front. And French would also explain to Chan that he was an accessory, now, to a very serious crime. If Chan went to the authorities, he'd end up in jail right alongside French and Ramos.

French put a hand on Chan's shoulder and squeezed it gently.

"I need you to calm down," French said, "and listen to me very carefully."

Chan managed to nod. He was still grinning with horror.

"Please stop grinning like that first. Okay?"

"Okay." But the kid couldn't do it.

"Everything is going to be fine," French said.

"He needs to keep his mouth shut," Ramos said.

French glanced over. "Really, Mason? You think so?"

He fired back up the reassuring smile and gave Chan's shoulder another squeeze.

"Chan, old chum," he started to say, but a shattering blast of heat inches from French's right ear sent him staggering sideways. Chan's head snapped back, and a spray of blood sizzled against the tin canopy of the *tuk-tuk*.

For a moment Chan hung suspended, neither rising nor falling, a man undecided. Finally his knees buckled. He sank, a slow droop, to the ground.

French, dazed, his right ear shrieking, turned to Ramos.

Ramos lowered his gun. "Yeah," he said.

Chapter Two

The black-and-white dropped in behind them when they turned onto Indiana Avenue. Bloomington PD.

"Make a right," Shake said. He pointed. "Right."

They turned right onto Seventh and swung up the north side of campus. The cop stayed with them. Shake, in the passenger seat, saw Jawad's eyes flick to the rearview; he saw his hands tighten on the wheel of the Kia Forte.

"Take it easy," Shake said.

"Yes," Jawad said.

"You understand what that means?" Shake said. "Take it easy?"

After working with the kid for two weeks, Shake always checked for errors in translation. Jawad knew a lot of complicated scientific terms, but past that his English was hit-or-miss. To be fair, Shake's Arabic was all miss. He only knew one phrase, *"Inshallah."* God willing. You could use it in just about any situation.

"Inshallah," Shake said.

Jawad nodded and seemed to relax. But then his eyes flicked again to the rearview.

"Easy," Shake said. He pointed again. "Left on Woodlawn."

Jawad sped up, slowed down, flipped on his right blinker, flipped it back off, and made a wobbly left. The Forte drifted toward the oncoming lane for a second, and Shake clenched.

He glanced in his side mirror. The black-and-white was still on them, fifteen feet back, a muscled-up Dodge Charger. Shake wasn't sure how he felt about cops in Dodge Chargers. The Dodge was an outlaw car, wasn't it? The *Dodge*. Shake pictured Junior Johnson hauling moonshine through the North Carolina hills in a '66 Coronet. Steve McQueen chasing down that black '68 Charger in *Bullitt*. Which, by the way, could only ever happen in the movies, a Mustang 390 GT fastback ever catching a 440 Magnum.

Shake remembered his first job as a professional wheelman. A quarter of a century ago, a bank in Arlington Heights, Illinois. The car he boosted for the job was a '71 Dodge Challenger, black on red, with a hood scoop and a hundred thousand miles on the odometer. Not exactly the perfect car for a discreet and reliable getaway. But Shake was young and dumb, just twenty years old, and that Challenger was so dangerous, so sexy, you felt like you'd committed a felony just by sliding behind the wheel.

Jawad had started to sweat.

"Jawad," Shake said, "the most important rule, any situation, is stay cool. You understand? That's the only rule. Stay cool."

"Stay cool," Jawad said, but high-pitched and panicky.

They hit a red light at the intersection of Woodlawn and Tenth. Jawad pounded the brakes, and they lurched to a stop. A woman dragging two toddlers entered the crossing. Shake figured that gave him a minute, so he clicked off his seat belt.

"Be right back," he said.

"What?" Jawad said, even more high-pitched and panicky.

Shake walked back to the Bloomington PD patrol car behind them. The cop was a woman, young, probably just a few years out of college. She looked up at him from behind mirrored shades.

"Can I help you, sir?" she said. Polite but all business. A ponytail pulled tight, her face pulled tight.

Shake leaned down. He considered what a new and strange and almost dreamlike experience this was for him—talking to a cop when he had nothing to hide, had committed no crimes, was just your average law-abiding American citizen.

"You're about to give the kid a heart attack," he said. He pointed his chin at the Forte, at the magnetic strip stuck to the trunk: STUDENT DRIVER.

"Which means he's about to give me a heart attack," Shake said. "And I bet you thought *your* job was dangerous."

A corner of her mouth untightened a little.

"Oh," she said. "Right. Sorry. I'm turning left here."

"Thanks. Then we'll be going straight."

Shake started to leave, then noticed the laptop mounted to the dash of the Charger.

"I remember police used to always drive Ford Crown Vics," he said. "Rear-wheel drive, like tanks. And they didn't have computers."

The cop waited for him to make his point. Shake realized he didn't have one.

"I guess times change," he said.

CHARLES SAMUEL "SHAKE" Bouchon: law-abiding American citizen. He'd been that for one year, three weeks, and change. Close to a personal best, and a streak Shake was determined to keep alive this time, come hell or high water.

"Left?" Karuna asked.

"Left," Shake said.

His final student of the day was a giggly, dark-skinned girl from India who, after only a couple of weeks, demonstrated all the makings of a first-rate wheelman: nerves of steel, excellent instincts, and a fanatical attention to traffic laws and regulations.

Most of the kids Shake taught were from other countries. The outfit he worked for specialized in international students attending the university. Driving lessons in other countries were expensive, so A-1 Excellent Driving could charge rates no American would ever pay. A pretty sweet racket, and perfectly legal.

Charles Samuel "Shake" Bouchon: perfectly legal. How do you like that?

Karuna's English was excellent, probably better than Shake's, and as they drove around Bloomington, she told him all about life in Mumbai. Shake learned that in India girls with dark skin were considered less desirable than those with lighter skin. Many girls, Karuna informed him, used special facial-whitening creams, though she herself thought such a practice was degrading.

"Do you not agree?" she asked him in her perfect, clipped accent.

"I do," he said.

Shake picked up a lot of information like that from his students. Facial-whitening cream in India, roasted guinea pigs in Peru, how in Uganda you never stepped *over* a pot on the ground, you walked *around* it. It was one of the things he liked about the job with A-1.

And he did like the job, believe it or not. It felt good to start with nothing and make something. A lot of the kids who signed up for driving lessons had never even touched a steering wheel before. Shake took it slow, he was patient, and the kids got better. Jawad, for example, would never be the world's greatest driver, but that afternoon Shake had finally taught him to check both ways before he pulled in to traffic and to stop running bicyclists off the road. Not bad for an honest day's work.

A guy playing Ultimate Frisbee decided to run a sudden slant pattern into the street. Karuna braked calmly and checked the mirror before she pulled around him.

"What was that?" Shake said.

She giggled. "That was staying cool!"

"Very good."

At the end of the hour, Shake dropped her and the Forte back at the office. He'd left his own car at home that morning. The June weather was perfect, and he liked the shortcut across the Indiana campus, past the massive limestone castles, the Gothic arches and bell towers. His favorite stretch was the winding path through Dunn's Woods, a miniature forest that in the summer was cool and peaceful. Autumn was even better, when the leaves turned and it was like the trees had gone up in flames.

Downtown he stopped at the organic market to pick up lamb chops and a finishing salt from Spain. Bloomington wasn't big, but there was a good food scene, and more than a few restaurants could have held their own in Los Angeles or New York.

The woman who owned the market knew that Shake liked to cook, so she dug out a little jar of hand-pressed olive oil, from a batch her partner had brought back from Crete.

Shake tasted it. "Name your price."

"Oh, don't be silly, hon," she said. "It's on the house."

That was Bloomington for you. Everyone was friendly. Everyone was *nice*. Even the guy who cut in front of Karuna had waved to her afterward. "Sorry!" he'd called.

Shake had been wary at first. What was the catch? But there was no catch. The nice was genuine. Before long he was dragging his neighbor's trash bin to the curb when she forgot to do it, he was smiling at people on the street for no good reason.

Some people might think that was weird, but Shake could think of worse ways to live. He'd lived some of them.

The woman who owned the organic market handed back his change.

"Don't take any wooden nickels," she said, "and say hi to your wife."

Shake walked the rest of the way home. He set out the lamb chops, opened a beer, and started the grill. The crepe myrtle along the back fence was starting to bloom, and the deck Shake was building, an hour or so every evening, was just about done. Next door the neighbor's golden retriever woofed at squirrels. Shake thought he might get up early tomorrow morning, before work, and drive out to Lake Monroe for some fishing.

He tapped his knuckles against the arm of his Adirondack chair. *Knock on wood.* That was from habit. For a long time after they moved to Bloomington, Shake had held his breath, braced for the other shoe to drop on this new, happy life of his. The other shoe, in his experience, always dropped.

But the weeks passed, the months, and now here he was already into his second June in southern Indiana. Shake's old life, the one he'd tried for so long to leave behind, had finally started to feel that way—left behind, shrinking steadily in the rearview mirror and just about to drop beneath the curve of the horizon.

He checked his watch. Almost seven o'clock. It would stay light for another couple of hours. Summer here was soft and balmy. People complained about the humidity, but Shake was from New Orleans. This wasn't humidity, not even close.

The neighbor's golden retriever was going nuts now, and all the dogs on the block had started barking along for moral support. Shake's neighbor wasn't home from work yet, so he figured he'd better check out the situation. The dog was a lover, not a fighter, and one time a testy blue jay had cornered him behind the woodpile.

Shake turned the grill down to medium, fished another beer from the cooler, and walked over to the stockade fence. The golden retriever sounded like he was about to chew through the neighbor's gate. Shake flipped the latch on his own gate and opened it.

A guy stood there, a big guy, eyeing the neighbor's gate. He had his hand on the latch but seemed less than thrilled by the idea of meeting the dog on the other side of the fence. He wore a purple velour tracksuit, the sleeves pushed up to his elbows and no shirt beneath.

Shake felt the world hesitate. The birds, the barking dogs, the pump of the blood through his own body. Nothing moved. A lazy drift of summer pollen froze in place, and so did the sunlight sparkling off it.

The big guy had a bald, bullet-shaped head and a face that looked like it had been used to break rocks. On his forearm was a crudely inked tattoo: a skull split in half by a battle-ax, with the words BEG FOR DEATH written beneath in Armenian.

Shake could read the Armenian because the last time they met, the guy had translated the words for him. He'd promised Shake that if their paths ever crossed again, he would make Shake do just that.

He noticed Shake now and grinned.

"Good," he said. "I find you."

Chapter Three

Stay cool. The first rule, the only rule.

Shake tried to remember that as he stared Dikran Ghazarian in the face.

Dikran Ghazarian, here and now, on a tree-lined street in Bloomington, on a soft summer afternoon.

Dikran Ghazarian, right hand to the *pakhan* of the Armenian mob in Los Angeles. And without a doubt the meanest, dumbest, most brutal thug that Shake—over the course of a career populated with mean, dumb, brutal thugs—had ever encountered.

Though, really, who was the dumb one here? *Shake* was. For becoming complacent. For thinking he could ever leave his old life behind in the rearview mirror.

Objects are much closer than they appear.

No one knew that Shake was in Bloomington. Who knew he was here? A couple of people, maybe, but people he could trust. People he'd thought he could trust.

Stay cool.

Dikran took a step toward him. He expected Shake to run. When Dikran came for you, that's what you did, you *ran*, as fast and as far as you could. It was the only sensible response. So . . . what the hell. Shake charged instead, shoulder down, and hit Dikran in the gut. It was like ramming a cinder-block wall, but Shake caught Dikran by surprise. Dikran grunted, stumbled backward, and tripped over a coil of garden hose. When he tried to use the trash bin for balance, the bin rolled out from beneath him, and down he went.

Now: Shake ran.

He took off across his backyard. Shake knew that Dikran was surprisingly quick for a guy his size, murderously nimble. Maybe, though, he'd have trouble hauling himself over the six-foot stockade in back. And maybe Shake would be able to get over the fence himself. He was forty-five years old, and the shoulder he'd used to ram Dikran had gone numb.

Shake didn't have a better plan. He just knew that he had to get Dikran away from the house.

Dikran bellowed. Shake grabbed the top of the fence pickets, pulled himself up, swung a leg over. Every dog in Bloomington was barking by now. Shake hoped someone would call the cops. That was a first, that hope, but he'd rather answer a few awkward questions down at the station house than have Dikran tear out his—

Something heavy slammed Shake between the shoulder blades and knocked him off the fence. He landed hard on the other side, bad shoulder first. For a second he just had to lie there, dazed, while he waited for the clouds to stop spinning. A tiny terrier yapped at him. Next to a tipped-over tricycle was the coil of garden hose that Dikran had nailed Shake with.

The tiny terrier tried to sneak in and bite him. Shake rolled over and pushed himself up. Dikran was already half over the fence, looking down at him.

"Don't move, asswipe," he said.

Shake moved. Dikran dropped off the fence and tackled him.

Shake groped around for . . . anything. He came up with a child's bike helmet. Pink, with molded plastic kitty ears. He swung the helmet, and one of the kitty ears caught Dikran just above the left eye. Shake scrambled away, and Dikran tackled him again, driving Shake into the fence. The post snapped, and the whole section of fence collapsed beneath them.

They were back in Shake's yard. Dikran had a hand clamped to Shake's ankle. When Shake tried to run, Dikran cracked Shake's leg like a whip and brought him down again.

"I say don't move!"

Shake knew he was as good as dead. But he needed to buy time, he needed to get Dikran away from the house. Where, he wondered, were the police when you needed them? He tried to kick Dikran in the balls with his free foot. Dikran swatted the foot away. He hit Shake in the kidney, a punch that felt like it traveled through Shake's body and out the other side.

The neighbor's terrier had followed them into Shake's yard. The little fucker was still trying to bite Shake. The other neighborhood dogs, Shake noticed, had stopped barking. The show was over. Shake was over.

Shake had always suspected that Gina could read his mind—she was usually that far ahead of him. So now, with no other options, he closed his eyes and tried to will a thought into her head.

Go!

She'd be home from yoga in a minute or two. She'd pull in to the driveway and get out of her car.

Shake concentrated. He put everything he had left into it, all his focus and energy. He gave it what he knew might be his last breath on earth.

Run!

He twisted hard and tried one more time to wrench free. Dikran slammed him back down, with so much force that the terrier yipped and darted away. Shake didn't understand why Dikran was waiting to kill him. The possible explanations weren't comforting.

Shake looked over his shoulder. Dikran squatted on his haunches, fists clenched in his lap. His ugly face was clenched, too, lumpy and knuckled and flushed, an expression Shake didn't recognize. Dikran had two basic expressions, malice and rage, and this wasn't one of them. A tear rolled down his cheek.

Shake was so surprised he didn't believe his own eyes.

A tear?

"I need your help," Dikran said. "Please."

Chapter Four

Shake sat up. Warily. This had to be a trap.

But what kind of trap? And why?

The tears were genuine. Another one slid off Dikran's chin. Dikran wiped his cheek with the back of his big fist, his right fist, the arm with the split-skull tattoo.

BEG FOR DEATH.

That was Dikran's style, not this. Dikran didn't set traps. He was the trap that other people set, the last sound you heard on earth, the sharp iron teeth snapping shut on your ass.

Dikran looked at Shake.

"Speechless," Dikran said. "Ha. First time in life for the asswipe and his smart mouth."

Shake didn't take offense. One, it was probably true. Two, it was the nicest thing Dikran had ever said to him.

Maybe this *was* a trap. But at least Dikran hadn't pulled Shake's arm out of the socket and beaten him to death with it.

Yet.

"What are you doing here?" he asked Dikran.

"I tell you already."

"All right. Why do you need my help?"

Dikran's face clenched even tighter. "She is disappear."

"She?" Shake tried to think. "Who?"

He pivoted and attempted to kick Dikran in the balls again. Dikran punched him again, this time in the knee.

"Stop it," Dikran said.

The pain made Shake's eyes water. "Shit," he said. "Yes. Okay."

"She is disappear." Dikran punched Shake's knee again. "You see?"

Shake wondered if he'd ever be able to walk again.

"Dikran," he said. "Stop. Okay. No. I don't see. Who's disappeared?"

Dikran's face unclenched suddenly, like a tire blowing and flapping to pieces on the highway. He let out a sob, so wet and pained that a couple of neighborhood dogs roused themselves again to howl along.

"She!"

Shake realized who he had to be talking about. Dikran was equipped with the soft, warm heart of a hammerhead shark. There was only one person in the world he cared about, only one person he'd ever cry for.

"Lexy?" Shake said, surprised yet again. Alexandra Ilandryan, the *pakhan* of the Armenian mob in L.A. and Dikran's boss. She'd been Shake's boss, too, off and on, when she hadn't been trying to kill him. And also his girlfriend years ago, off and on, sometimes even when she *had* been trying to kill him.

For a guy who'd never wanted anything more than the nice and simple, Shake's life had been awfully twisty, so many hairpins and switchbacks he'd lost track.

"Yes!" Dikran said. "She! She! Who do you think?"

Dikran and Lexy had grown up together, like brother and sister, in a tiny mountain village in Armenia. But Alexandra Ilandryan was *pakhan,* and Dikran refused to call her by her given name. He considered it disrespectful. It drove Lexy nuts.

"Start from the beginning," Shake said. "Tell me what's going on."

Dikran wiped his cheek again. He blew his nose onto the grass.

"Nine days ago," he said, "she leaves for her trip, like always. You know this trip."

Lexy was one of the most powerful players on the West Coast. The Russians gave her a piece of their action, and she was the only non-Mexican the cartels and La Eme would do business with. She moved around burn companies and crooked district attorneys like she was arranging flowers. Every summer, though, she took a break. For two weeks she went off the grid, by herself, to some far-flung corner of the world. All contact with her was prohibited. Not even her top lieutenants or most important clients were allowed to call, text, or e-mail her. The only exception she made was for Dikran. He worried obsessively about her, and if she didn't let him call once a day, he would've insisted on coming along with her.

Shake, when he and Lexy were together, thought she might make an exception for him, too.

Nope.

"What if I'm on my deathbed?" Shake had asked when he dropped her off at LAX. "What if your voice is the last sound I want to hear?"

Lexy laughed, a sweet, rising melody.

"Poor Shake," she said, "then I will weep for you when I return. I will put flowers on your grave."

"Eight days ago I call her," Dikran said. "We talk. All is well."

"Where did she go?"

"Someplace. Cambodia. Shut up and listen."

"Okay."

"Seven days ago I call her. We talk. All is well. Six days ago I call her. We talk. All is well."

"Dikran," Shake said. "Are you gonna cover this in real time? Because I'm gonna need a beer if that's the case."

"Shut up. Smart mouth. Five days ago I call her. We talk. All is well."

"I get it!" Holy shit. "When did it turn not so well?"

"Four days ago," Dikran said. "She does not answer. I try again, one hour later. She does not answer. All day, she does not answer. And never since! I call many times, every day since. She does not answer. Something bad is happen to her. I feel in my bone."

"You left her voice-mail messages?" Shake asked.

"Ha. How stupid am I, do you think?"

"On a scale of what to what?"

Dikran glanced over his shoulder, back at the house.

"You say you have this beer?" he said.

"No," Shake said. "How did you find me anyway?"

"I don't care."

"I do."

Dikran cocked his fist back again. "You care?"

"Okay, take it easy."

"Yes, I leave voice with mail!" Dikran said. "Stupid cockjob. I am in a mystery, why she is bring a man like you to her bed."

It was a legitimate question, but Shake didn't think Dikran—in a purple velour tracksuit, with a face that made small children burst into tears—was in a position to ask it.

"Did she take a bodyguard?" Shake asked. He knew Lexy's philosophy on personal security but thought he'd ask anyway.

"No. I tell her always, keep bodyguard by your side always, twenty-four/seven. You know what she says? She says, 'Dikran, you want to die? Then keep bodyguard by your side always, twenty-four/seven, till he cuts your throat while you sleep.'"

"She's fine," Shake said. He could think of a dozen good reasons that Lexy hadn't answered Dikran's calls. A hundred. Of course

Dikran wouldn't recognize any of them. He had the cognitive skills of the fence post lying broken in half next to them. "She hasn't disappeared. She's on a beach somewhere and doesn't want to talk to you. You ever wonder why she has to take a vacation every year?"

Dikran's lip curled, baring one sharp yellow canine. Now, *that* was an expression Shake knew well: rage with a malice chaser. Shake tensed.

But then Dikran fished a prescription bottle out of the pocket of his tracksuit and tapped a couple of pills into his mouth. He chewed and swallowed. His lip uncurled.

"Listen now with your brain, asswipe," he said. "I know how hard this is for you. Four days ago is fifth day of June."

The date meant nothing to Shake. "Okay."

"Fifth day of June!"

"So?" Shake said. And then the date clicked for him.

June 5 was the day, two decades earlier, when Lexy and Dikran had arrived at Port Newark in a metal cargo container—dehydrated and half crazed from three brutal weeks at sea, penniless and friendless. Lexy had told Shake that after they slipped ashore and past security, the two twenty-one-year-olds swore a promise to each other: They had survived Armenia, and now they would conquer America.

Lexy was the least sentimental person Shake had ever met. But June 5, he knew, was a holy day for her.

"Yes, asswipe!" Dikran said. "Now you see! Tell me a time, just once ever, when she and I do not talk on the fifth day of June. No matter where she is, what she does. I tell you, something bad is happen to her. She is in plane crash. She is lost in jungle or drown by ocean."

"Or she lost her phone charger," Shake said. "Or the Wi-Fi at her hotel is down."

"She has enemy. Many, many enemy."

True, but none who were willing to start a war with the Armenians. Even though Shake had to admit that it wasn't like Lexy to ignore the June 5 anniversary, the odds were still better than excellent that she was lying on a tropical beach right now, sipping a mimosa.

"The fifth day of June," Dikran said. He shook his head. "She would call me. She would find way."

Shake sighed. "Why do you need me? Have you talked to Narek? Is he still her number two?"

"No. Babikian now, since three years."

Shake didn't know Babikian. "Whoever. If Lexy's really in trouble, what can I do? I'm just a guy, Dikran, a driver. A retired driver."

Dikran grunted in resigned agreement. "You are just asswipe."

"Let's stick with retired driver, if you don't mind."

"You think I trust Babikian? The snake. You think he loves her?"

"Dikran . . ."

"You are just asswipe, I know this, but you love her, too. You do not betray her."

Dikran was talking about the three years Shake had done at Mule Creek, when he'd refused to dime Lexy out. Shake was surprised Dikran gave him any credit for that.

Dikran leaned closer. Shake tensed again, until he realized that another tear was sliding down Dikran's cheek.

"You must help me," Dikran said. "If we do not come for her, you and I, who comes for her?"

The odds were good, Shake told himself again, that Lexy was safe and sound. Probably she was just off cutting a multimillion-dollar deal in Indonesia, or on vacation in the Maldives, basking on some beach and sipping a cocktail. Maybe she'd called Dikran on their anniversary and he'd accidentally deleted her message. Maybe she'd told Dikran before she left that she'd be out of touch on the fifth.

Shake imagined Lexy's gentle sigh of exasperation when she got home and found Dikran worked into a lather.

Dikran, she would say. *Did you not remember what I told you?*

Oh, Dikran would say.

The odds were good that Lexy was fine. But they were still odds, Shake had to admit. That was the nature of gambling. The horses still ran the race, the dealer still turned over the river card.

If something bad *had* happened to Lexy, Shake knew it would be something very, very bad.

He decided he needed a drink. "So you want a beer?"

Dikran blew his nose onto the grass again. "Yes. Give it to me."

Shake started to stand. That's when he saw Gina. He hadn't heard her car. She'd come through the garage and crept up behind Dikran. She crouched behind a stack of the two-by-six cedar boards Shake was using for the deck.

She put a finger to her lips. *Shhhh.*

Shit.

"Wait!" Shake said. "No!"

"What?" Dikran said, turning, as Gina pulled the trigger on the nail gun and shot him in the head.

Chapter Five

Gina drove. Shake dialed. Dikran sprawled in the backseat, cursing and groaning and bleeding all over the stack of towels that Shake had wedged beneath his head.

The call went to voice mail. Shake dialed the number again.

Shake knew he should let it go. Marriage, he'd learned, was all about letting it go.

"Just curious," he asked Gina. "When was it you decided to pull the trigger? Was it when I said 'Hold on!'? Or was it the 'No, stop, don't!' that tipped the scales?"

"Don't worry, buttercup," Gina said. "Next time I come home and there's a homicidal Armenian trying to murder you, I promise I'll go back inside and have a cocktail instead. Cross my heart."

Gina, like Shake, had left behind a life far different from the one they now lived, and she had her own unhappy memories of Dikran. A few years earlier, he'd kidnapped her and sent her off to be killed.

"But he wasn't trying to murder me," Shake explained. "That's where the 'No, hold on!' comes in."

"Or you know what? Next time a homicidal person of *any*

nationality is trying to murder you, I will err on the side of caution. I'll make myself a manhattan, probably."

Shake leaned over and kissed her.

As long as he lived, Shake knew, he would never take this gift, this astounding luxury, for granted—that he could kiss Gina whenever he wanted, and she would kiss him back.

Her eyes, catching the light, were more green than brown, like polished glass you found on a beach. The nose of a Roman empress, dusted with freckles. A smile that could drop man or woman from a hundred paces. And Gina was even smarter than she was beautiful, hard as that was to believe. What Shake really couldn't believe was that he was married to her. Holy shit.

"You're so lucky," he said, "that you found a guy like me."

"Am I?"

"Or maybe it's the other way around. I get confused."

"So do I. I guess that means we're meant for each other."

Shake thought they probably were. They'd been through more ups and downs together, more flips, flops, and flying bullets, more bad choices (his and hers), more desperate comebacks, than any normal couple had a right to.

"I guess so," he said. He kissed her again.

"Please," Dikran groaned from the back. "Stop this or shoot me one more time for my misery. I am beg you."

"Shut up," Shake said. He got voice mail again. "We'll just go over there and hope he's home."

"Why don't we go to the ER?" Gina said.

"No!" Dikran said.

"Too many questions," Shake agreed.

"Not if we just dump him out front and honk the horn."

Dikran muttered something in Armenian.

"I know what that means, asshole," Gina said. "Or I can guess."

"Good," Dikran said.

Shake turned to check Dikran's status. The towels were almost soaked through with blood, but the only damage was a shallow three-inch gash across his bald scalp. Point-blank range, perfect aim, a hundred pounds of pressure per square inch, and the nail had basically bounced off Dikran's head. Shake's suspicions about the thickness of Dikran's skull had been confirmed.

"Keep the pressure on it," Shake said.

"Asswipe is doctor now."

"Take a left up ahead," Shake told Gina.

"Left? You sure?"

Shake looked at her.

She shrugged. "I'm just checking."

She turned left. The apartment complex was just ahead. It looked the same as most off-campus student housing in town, like the landlord lived in Florida and did maintenance once or twice a decade. The sagging balconies were crowded with charcoal grills, old lawn furniture, and sad plants. Most of the sliding glass doors were hung with sun-faded Hoosiers banners.

They parked close to Number 9, a downstairs unit. Shake went up alone and knocked. Jawad answered the door.

"Mr. Bouchon!" he said. Surprised, then confused, then worried.

"It's okay, Jawad," Shake said. "You're premed, right?"

"Yes!" Surprised, then confused, then worried.

"Your lucky day," Shake said. *"Inshallah."*

Chapter Six

Shake got Dikran settled on the futon sofa while Jawad went upstairs to borrow a needle and thread. Jawad's roommates, two skinny African kids in oversize IU basketball jerseys, played Xbox and kept sneaking glances at Gina. Gina rummaged around in the kitchen and found a bottle of cheap vodka. She poured Shake a shot and one for herself.

"Give to me," Dikran said.

"Say please or I'll put another nail in your stupid head," she said. Shake saw she'd brought the nail gun along, just in case. He was on board with that. He thought Dikran was telling the truth about Lexy, but that didn't mean Shake trusted him. Now or ever.

"Give me this vodka," Dikran said. "Pretty fucking please."

Gina tossed him the bottle. Dikran downed a third of it in one swallow. Jawad returned with the needle and thread, plus a first-aid kit and a lighter. He cleaned the gash on Dikran's scalp, then sterilized the needle with the lighter.

"Very difficult situation," Jawad told Shake.

"Yes," Shake agreed.

Jawad threaded the needle, then poked it through the flap of scalp. Dikran, checking his cell phone, didn't even flinch. Shake was the one who flinched.

"You see?" Dikran held up his cell phone. "No message from her still. No call. We must find her."

Shake watched Jawad work. He'd been worried the kid might doctor like he drove, but Jawad's hands were steady and he seemed to know what he was doing. More or less. Every now and then, Dikran would grunt and Jawad would say, "My apology, sir."

Shake went outside to sit with Gina on the patio.

"Just another summer evening in Bloomington," she said.

"I don't know how he found us."

"Let's start with why."

Shake had told her, back at the house, that Dikran wanted his help. Now he filled in the details.

Gina laughed. "Oh, my God."

"I know what you mean," Shake said. And then, after a second, he wasn't sure he did. "You mean it's crazy that he'd come to me."

She looked at him for a long time without saying anything.

"No," she said finally. "I mean it's crazy he'd think you'd ever do it."

Shake shifted in his lawn chair. "You hungry? I can order a pizza."

"You're going to run off to Cambodia with a guy who's tried to kill you twice. Or is it three times?"

"I don't remember," Shake said. "Just twice, I think. And I haven't decided anything yet."

She smiled sweetly, and he realized how badly he'd taken that curve. He hadn't taken it at all, in fact. He'd plowed right into the embankment.

"You'll let me know when you've decided?" she said. "If it's not asking too much. Just text me."

"That's not what I meant," Shake said.

"That's what you said."

Marriage was the best thing that had ever happened to Shake, but it was also, truth be told, complicated beyond belief. Shake had never been in a long-term relationship before, so he had to figure out everything on the fly. The little stuff, the big stuff. It was like studying for a chemistry test and getting a question on medieval history. And even if you knew the answer, you didn't know the answer. For example:

Question: When your spouse is in a bad mood, do you try to cheer her up?

Answer: It depends.

"What I meant to say," Shake said, "is that nothing's decided yet because I have not discussed it with you. Dear."

He waited to see how that landed. Gina had never been in a long-term relationship either. She was figuring out everything on the fly, too.

"Fine," she said. "Let's discuss how it could be possible that I married a man so stupid he thinks I'd be willing to discuss this."

"I won't be gone long. I just want to make sure Lexy's not really in trouble. I'll be back in a couple of days."

She glanced inside at Dikran, who'd taken off his velour track jacket and was now sitting bare-chested on the sofa, playing Xbox while Jawad stitched his scalp shut.

"Because what in the world could go wrong?" Gina said.

Shake could tell she was mad. When she was mad, her nostrils contracted. She took in oxygen but didn't release it.

"Is this about Lexy?" he said.

"Lexy?" she said. And then, "Lexy," in a soft purr, batting her eyelashes. Shake gathered that this was her impression of him. "You mean the old flame you never got over and would do anything for?"

"I got over her a long time ago," Shake said. "Long before I met you."

"The old flame who's always been so sweet to me?"

It was Lexy who'd ordered Dikran to kidnap Gina. Lexy had sold Gina to a sadistic strip-club owner in Vegas. There were extenuating circumstances—Gina had ripped off the strip-club owner, a business associate of Lexy's, to the tune of three hundred grand—but Shake knew better than to split hairs.

"Gina," he said. "I'd do anything for *you,* not her. But—"

He stopped himself, too late. Another curve missed, another concrete embankment plowed into. When it came to marriage, Shake was like Jawad behind the wheel of a car.

"But?" Gina said. "Oh, pumpkin. You were so close."

Shake went inside to retrieve the bottle of vodka from Dikran. He came back out and poured Gina another shot. He poured a double for himself.

"She's probably fine, but if Lexy does need help . . ." Shake shrugged. "I have to help."

Gina's nostrils contracted. "And why is that, exactly?"

Shake didn't know if he could explain it. He'd come to believe that people—if they wanted it enough, if they were willing to risk everything on a crazy gutshot-straight draw—could change in significant ways. Look at him. Look at Gina. But Shake also knew there were certain fundamental things about yourself you could never change, the parts that made you that self, whether you liked it or not.

He'd known Lexy for a long time. They'd been through a lot together. They shared a mutual appreciation for the value of that.

Shake remembered the last time he'd heard from Lexy—a year ago, right after he and Gina got married. Lexy had sent a wedding gift, brand-new his-and-her Audi S8 Quattro sedans. His and *her*—even though Lexy didn't care for Gina any more than Gina cared for Lexy.

Shake had called to thank her. And to tell her that Gina had donated her car to charity.

Lexy had laughed, that musical run of notes.

"Of course she did," Lexy said. "You chose your wife wisely, Shake."

"She's a friend," Shake told Gina now. He shrugged again.

She drank her shot. She slipped her flip-flops off and propped her feet on the arm of his chair.

"This is exhausting, isn't it?" she said.

Marriage. Shake smiled. "Someone should have prepared us."

She ran her bare foot along his arm. He squeezed her calf.

What Shake wanted, he wanted Gina to come with him to Cambodia. The thought of spending even a single night away from her was like a kick to the stomach. But Lexy was Shake's friend, not Gina's. His problem, not hers.

Most important, she'd be safe in Bloomington. Gina could, clearly, take care of herself, but Shake didn't want her anywhere near Dikran.

The patio door slid open, and Dikran stepped outside. Jawad had bandaged his head in what seemed to be a fairly professional manner. Dikran picked up the vodka bottle and finished it off.

"We go now," he told Shake.

"Give us a minute," Shake said.

"No. No time."

Gina picked up the nail gun. Dikran scowled and went back inside.

Shake looked at Gina. She looked at him. Finally she shrugged.

HE CALLED HER that night from Indianapolis. The drive from Bloomington had taken more than two hours because of traffic on

37, and they'd just missed the last flight that connected onward to Los Angeles.

"We have to spend the night here," Shake said.

"The Four Seasons?" Gina asked. "A king-size bed and a heart-shaped Jacuzzi tub for two?"

"The airport DoubleTree. Separate rooms, separate floors. And I plan to put a desk chair under the door handle."

"That'll stop him?"

"Probably not."

Shake watched as Dikran, across the lobby, reached the front of the hotel check-in line. He leaned down to sniff the platter of complimentary cookies, then started stuffing the cookies, all of them, into the pockets of his track jacket.

"I'll be careful," Shake said.

"Oh! That changes everything. Why didn't you say so before?"

"Sir," the desk clerk said to Dikran. "Excuse me."

"I excuse you," Dikran said. "Now, shut up and give to me more cookie."

"I'll be very careful," Shake said. "It'll be fine."

Chapter Seven

French added an extra splash of Jameson to his morning coffee and tried not to think about Chan. It was getting easier. Chan no longer haunted French's dreams, at least. He no longer stood there with a bemused smile on his face, half his skull blown away.

When Ramos shot Chan, French had gone numb. His brain had gone numb. Sensory information continued to flow, but he couldn't decipher it. The world around him jabbered away in a language French no longer understood.

He'd staggered to the edge of the clearing and crouched, hands on knees, as a heavy sludge of nausea spread over him.

"You all right?" Ramos said.

"We could trust him! He wasn't going to talk!"

Ramos shrugged. "You want to put your life on it?"

They'd driven back to the house in silence. Ramos moved the woman from the car to the room they'd prepared for her. French rolled a Buddha with trembling hands and quickly smoked it. The weed calmed the trembling; the opium blurred the horror he felt when he forced himself to answer Ramos's question.

No, French had to admit, he was *not* willing to wager his life against Chan's silence.

That didn't make him evil, French told himself. It didn't make him evil that he was finding it easier and easier to forget about Chan.

No. Chan's death, he could see now, had been inevitable. Fated, even. You had to have the right perspective. "The question is not what you look at," Thoreau had written, "but what you see."

Ramos walked in and poured himself a cup of coffee. "What did he say?"

"He said to sit tight."

"He said that yesterday."

French sighed. "I'm aware of that, Mason. Thanks."

"It's been four days already. We need to call her family. Call whoever."

"You need to be patient."

To be honest, though, French was starting to get antsy, too. Bjorn, whenever French pressed, just kept saying the same thing: "Soon."

"He's hanging us out to dry," Ramos said.

"He's not."

Most people assumed that the expression "hung out to dry" related to laundry. French, though, knew it came from the practice of skinning an animal and draping the meat on the branches of a tree.

No. No way. Bjorn knew what he was doing. He had not hung them out to dry. He just had several irons in the fire. Not only did he run a flourishing high-end prostitution ring, his distribution network also supplied most of the dope that the expat community in Siem Reap smoked, swallowed, and snorted. In addition to that, he owned several legitimate businesses, which he used to launder money from illegal timber-logging operations. When it came to the art of crime, he was the real deal.

"Four days with our cocks on the block," Ramos said. "That's a long time."

French agreed. Sequestered for four days with the world's dullest man was driving him to the edge of madness. It was like being trapped in an English-department faculty meeting that never ended.

"Be patient, Mason," French said again. "And don't mix your metaphors. Are we hung out to dry or are our cocks on the block?"

"What?"

French left the kitchen, hoping Ramos wouldn't follow, and moved into the parlor. The parlor was the only room in the rambling old wreck of a mansion where you could find a little sunlight, a pleasant breeze. It was also the only room that had survived an ill-advised remodel in the Swinging Sixties. The original crown molding remained, a beautiful old brass basket chandelier. On the mantel sat an ornamental elephant tusk that had to be a hundred years old.

The plumbing in the house was probably a hundred years old, too. French had expected more luxurious digs, but what was that old saying about real estate? Location, location, location. They were at the end of a long private road, three miles from the edge of town and a quarter of a mile from the nearest neighbor, hidden behind a garden that had been allowed, ages ago, to run amok. Bjorn knew what he was doing, French reminded himself. He knew what he was doing.

French settled into the leather easy chair by the window and closed his eyes. A second later he felt a shadow fall across him. Ramos. French sighed.

"I want to meet the guy next time," Ramos said. "The guy behind the job."

"I told you," French said. "He hired me, and I hired you. He deals with me, and I deal with you. That's the way it works."

"What's his name?"

"Please, Mason."

An enormous flying insect of some sort—beetle? cockroach?—buzzed through a hole in the window screen and landed on the arm of French's chair. Ramos picked up the insect with his thumb and forefinger. He pressed it slowly against the rusted wires of the screen until the shell cracked and the goo ran out.

"Four days with our cocks on the block," Ramos said.

French stood. "I'll take breakfast up this morning," he said.

"What?" Ramos frowned. "I'm the one does that."

Ramos insisted that it was safer if only one of them had contact with the hostage. But if they wore masks, what did it matter?

French needed a change of scenery. He'd had enough of Ramos to last a lifetime.

"Trust me," he said, "I think I can handle her."

At some point in the past, the attic had been finished out and converted to a maid's room. The half bath and the presence of only a single window—too high to reach, too narrow to squeeze through—made it the perfect place to keep their girl.

French put on his mask and unlocked the two double dead bolts that Ramos had installed. He knocked, opened the door, picked the tray back up, and stepped into the room.

The attic was hot and gloomy, but not much worse than the rest of the house. Their girl sat on the edge of her bed, her wrists cuffed in front of her now and secured to the iron bed frame with a heavy chain.

She lifted her chin, her posture perfect, and regarded French coolly. Her tailored slacks and silk blouse were a touch the worse for wear after four days, but somehow she still managed to look like she'd just stepped off the pages of *Elle*.

"Good morning," French said.

She looked away. When French had asked about it, Ramos said she never spoke to him, not a single word.

"Do you ever talk to *her*?" French had asked.

"Why would I?"

That was so Ramos. After four days of him, the woman would probably find French a breath of fresh air.

He set the tray on the floor—coffee in a paper cup, two croissants on a paper plate, a bottle of water—and took a seat in the metal folding chair across from her.

"So tell me," he said, "how did you sleep? I hope well, Veronica."

She turned her face back toward him, surprised at the sound of her name. They'd found her passport in her bag. Veronica Wagenseller, forty-four years old, from Moraga, California.

"I apologize for the accommodations," he said. "This isn't the way you wanted to experience exotic *Indochine,* is it? But look, really, if there's any way I can make you more comfortable, please just ask. Okay? I mean that, Veronica."

There it was, another ripple of surprise. Her eyes were a shade of gray that reminded French of polished pewter. She was even more attractive than French had suspected, with the pale complexion and dramatic cheekbones of a woman in an El Greco painting.

Or did he find her so attractive because of what she represented? Was she burnished by the glow of the $2 million Bjorn had promised him? Veronica Wagenseller of Moraga, California, was French's future. His golden goose.

"Would you care to wash up before breakfast?" he said.

She studied him and seemed to weigh the decision. French let the silence stretch. It was a tactic he used in the classroom, a way to draw shyer students into the discussion. Most professors abhorred a vacuum and rushed to fill it.

"Yes," she said. "Thank you."

"Of course."

French left her wrists cuffed, per Ramos's instructions, and unfastened the padlock. The chain that secured her to the bed frame was heavy and slick with grease, like something from one of Blake's dark satanic mills. French didn't know where Ramos had found it.

Veronica wobbled when she stood. French placed a hand beneath her elbow to steady her.

In the bathroom he handed her a bar of soap, a towel, a travel-size tube of toothpaste. Ramos refused to let her have a toothbrush. French thought that was crazy. Did Ramos really think a petite forty-four-year-old woman from the ritzy suburbs of San Francisco was going to make a shiv and shank him?

French waited outside the bathroom door until she was finished, then led her back to the bed and reattached the chain. He moved the tray from the floor to the chair so she could reach it.

"Croissants again, I'm afraid," he said. "But fresh and very good. The French might not have been the most enlightened colonial power, but they do know their bread."

She twisted the top off the plastic water bottle and drank until the bottle was empty. She tore a croissant in half. French caught her glance at his shoes: saddle-brown John Lobbs with double monk straps. He'd bought them the day he'd been awarded tenure. They'd cost a fortune, seriously more than he could afford, but women noticed a man's shoes. It was the one useful lesson his fuckup of a father had taught him. That and how to navigate a tricky staircase after half a dozen martinis.

She continued to study him as she ate. French hummed the Elvis Costello song "Veronica" to himself. It was one of his favorite oldies.

Is it all in that pretty little head of yours?
What goes on in that place in the dark?

"So, Veronica," he said when she'd finished the first croissant, "why don't you tell me a little about yourself?"

She watched him over the rim of the coffee cup. Her gray eyes were otherworldly. French felt for an instant as if she could see every thought in his mind, even the ones he kept hidden from himself.

"You are serious?" she said finally.

"Of course," French said. He was genuinely curious about her. Was she an heiress? Married to a billionaire? He'd Googled her name and come up with nada, not a single Veronica Wagenseller. He'd been surprised, but not too surprised. The rich valued their privacy and had the means to ensure it.

Bjorn said he didn't know much about her either. He just knew she had more money than God. Four million, the ransom they were going to demand, wouldn't even be missed.

"You are serious," she said again, though not a question this time.

"Yes," French said. "Let's make the best of a difficult situation. I want to get to know Veronica Wagenseller."

After a beat he saw the tension in her jaw soften. She took a sip of coffee, and then—there it was, like the first bloom of spring—she smiled.

French smiled, too, behind his mask. That was all it had taken: a gentle touch, a little patience. If Ramos were up here, he could observe and learn. Though if Ramos were up here, French knew, he'd probably ruin everything.

She set the coffee cup back on the tray, her fingers long and graceful.

"Okay," she said. "Good."

Chapter Eight

They flew out of Indianapolis at six in the morning but had to connect through Toronto and Hong Kong, with layovers in both airports. They didn't land in Siem Reap until almost three o'clock in the afternoon, Cambodian time. More than twenty-four hours of cramped coach seats and screaming babies and people banging into you as they lurched down the aisle to the bathroom. Shake didn't sleep a wink.

They deplaned on the tarmac in Siem Reap. Shake's first breath of Southeast Asia was like sticking his face into the steam from a bowl of hot soup. Now, *this,* he conceded, was humidity.

They took a shuttle to the terminal. Shake sent Gina a text: HERE. FINALLY.

She sent him a text back: MISS ME?

YOU COULD SAY THAT.

In the terminal they had to wait in line to buy visas. Dikran checked his phone and showed it to Shake.

"You see? Still nothing from her."

"No kidding?" Shake said. Dikran had been giving him updates every five minutes since they'd been on the ground.

"Other line is faster. We switch there."

"No."

"You are half-of-wit camel pussy." Dikran fished the prescription bottle out of his pocket and swallowed a couple of pills.

"What are those anyway?" Shake said. The last time he'd seen Dikran, a few years ago, Dikran's doctor had him on the testosterone patch for high blood pressure. The patch made Dikran even angrier, meaner, and more prone to senseless violence than he normally was. Shake wondered how long it had taken the doctor to discover that, and if he'd survived the discovery.

"Pills."

Pills. "Pills for what?" Shake said.

"For calming. Or maybe a bubble pops in my head. Doctor says this."

"Do they work?" Shake hoped so but was dubious.

"How do I know? Doctor gives to me, I take." He held up his phone. "Still nothing."

Shake sighed. "Can I have a couple of those pills?"

"No. They are for prescription only."

"I'm kidding."

"Ha-ha. See how you laugh when I put your head through this wall."

Maybe Dikran's chill pills did work. It was only the eighth or ninth time since they'd left Indiana that he'd threatened to put Shake's head through a wall, a window, or the fuselage of an airplane.

Or maybe the pills didn't work and Dikran was just waiting until they found Lexy before he killed Shake. The possibility had crossed Shake's mind, you better believe it.

Finally they reached the window. They bought their visas, changed money, and were waved out of the terminal by a soldier who looked like he was about fourteen years old. His automatic rifle was almost as tall as he was.

Here we go, Shake thought.

Outside, they were swarmed by sweaty guys who smelled like hair oil and cigarettes and tried to shoulder one another aside. Just like in Belize, Panama, Egypt—Shake figured it was pretty much the same outside every airport in the world.

"Hello! Hello!"

"Need taxi? Where you go?"

"*Tuk-tuk?* Moto? Discount for you, monsieur!"

Shake picked a driver at random. The driver shooed away the others and escorted them to what Shake supposed was a *tuk-tuk*—a motorcycle pulling a three-wheeled cart. They squeezed in, Shake facing Dikran and their knees pressed together. The driver kick-started his little four-stroke Honda Super Cub and waited for Shake to tell him the destination.

"You have it?" Shake asked Dikran.

Dikran grunted and handed Shake a scrap of paper. On it was scrawled the name Lexy was using in Cambodia—Veronica Wagenseller—and the address for the private villa where she was staying.

Shake showed the scrap of paper to the driver. The driver nodded, and they set off. The first stretch was on a modern highway, straight and flat, past enormous mass-market hotels with parking lots filled by Chinese tour buses.

Farther along, though, the view improved. The center of Siem Reap reminded Shake a little of New Orleans—the leafy side streets, the French Quarter balustrades and wrought-iron lanterns. But then they'd turn a corner and Shake would be looking at . . . what, exactly? A cluster of bell-shaped stone structures, eight feet tall and ornately carved, painted silver and peach and gold. They looked like giant Christmas ornaments from a Dr. Seuss book.

"What are those?" Shake asked the *tuk-tuk* driver.

"Stupa," the driver said.

That didn't help Shake any. "What are they for?"

The driver shrugged. "Stupa."

A dozen monks in orange robes, with shaved heads and shaved eyebrows, crossed the street single file. Heading the opposite way, a kid pushed a cart full of hairy, scary fruit that looked like feral strawberries.

Okay, Shake decided, maybe Siem Reap didn't remind him of New Orleans that much after all.

Traffic was unbelievable, mostly motorcycles, bicycles, *tuk-tuks*. One scooter carried an entire family—a woman holding a baby, three kids, and the dad balancing a toddler on the handlebars.

They crossed a bridge over a muddy brown river. At the edge of a park, a couple of old ladies sat next to wire cages filled with birds.

"Hey," Shake asked the driver again. "They're selling birds?"

"Make merit," the driver said. At least that's what Shake thought he said.

"Make merit?"

"Chinese eat bird," Dikran said, not taking his eyes off his phone.

"No, no, no," the driver said. "Make merit!"

"They're Cambodian," Shake said. "They're not Chinese."

"Snake, too," Dikran said. "Chinese eat anything."

The driver nodded. "Yes. Snake."

"See? What do I tell you?"

Make merit. Shake guessed that must have something to do with good karma.

"People buy the birds so they can set them free?" he asked the driver.

"Yes."

That was nice, Shake supposed, if you ignored the fact that the birds were free to start with and had to be caught before the whole making-merit process could begin.

The *tuk-tuk* pulled to a stop. The driver pointed toward a tall stone wall. Shake and Dikran made their way down a narrow lane and found, just before the lane dead-ended, an iron gate. Shake pressed the call button.

A few seconds later, the gate hummed open electronically and a young Cambodian guy emerged from the guard shack. The guard shack was almost as big as, and probably nicer than, Shake's house back in Bloomington. The villa in the distance was a jaw-dropper—an Asian Versailles. Shake had expected no less. Lexy's house back in L.A., on one of the bird streets above Sunset, was all swoop and glass, stark metal angles and concrete cantilevers. She had impeccable taste and defied stereotype in all other ways, but her house looked like it belonged to the bad guy in every eighties action movie.

"Bonsoir," the young Cambodian guy said. He was in his early twenties, with perfect skin, perfect teeth, perfect posture. His hair looked like it had been parted with a slide rule. "Welcome to Fleurs d'Angkor. How may I be of assistance?"

The afternoon heat was dense and damp, layered with exhaust fumes and the sweet, potent scent of frangipani.

"We're here to see your guest," Shake said.

"Where does she stay?" Dikran said. "Show to me now."

He took a threatening step toward the guy. Shake moved in front of Dikran to cut him off. The guy glanced at the BEG FOR DEATH tattoo on Dikran's arm, the skull split in half by an ax. Shake guessed that the gist of the message was pretty clear, even if you didn't read Armenian.

"Veronica Wagenseller," Shake said. "We're friends of hers."

Shake caught the question in the young guy's eyes before he asked it.

"Who, monsieur?"

"Veronica Wagenseller." Unless, Shake considered, Lexy was

using a different name. But that was the name she always used. She'd used it for as long as Shake had known her. "The woman who's renting the place."

The young guy shook his head. "Please forgive me, monsieur, but at this time we have no one in residence at Fleurs d'Angkor. We have had no one in residence for seven days."

Shake thought for a second this might be some kind of security protocol. You know, like if two sweaty, shifty, jet-lagged strangers showed up at the front gate, one of them with a BEG FOR DEATH tattoo on his forearm, the policy was to claim that no one was home—then call the fucking police.

But the young Cambodian guy seemed sincere. He seemed both sincerely pained to be the bearer of bad news and sincerely relieved that this, whatever it was, was outside his area of responsibility.

Dikran was frowning with confusion. "What do you say?" he asked the guy.

"She's not here," Shake said. "She was never here. She's staying somewhere else."

"No! This is the place. She writes the name down for me."

"Then she wrote it down wrong."

Of course she had. It made perfect sense, now that Shake thought about it, for Lexy to give Dikran a dummy address. She was on vacation, and the last thing she wanted was Dikran, or anyone else, showing up unannounced.

"No," Dikran said. "*You* are wrong."

"Do you want to find her or not?"

Shake wondered how many high-end villas there were in Siem Reap. A lot, probably. And maybe Lexy wasn't even in Siem Reap at all.

His head had begun to ache. He was tired and hungry and stiff from the flight. More than anything, he needed to hear Gina's voice.

"She does not lie to me," Dikran said. "Never!"

"She didn't lie to you. She just . . . maybe she changed her mind."

Dikran thought about it. He seemed like he could live with that explanation. Or at least not kill Shake because of it.

"We must find her!" Dikran said.

"Thanks," Shake told the young Cambodian guy.

The guy gave a little bow and backed away. The gate hummed shut. At the same time, a gleaming black Escalade squeezed into the lane and rolled toward Shake and Dikran. It nosed to a stop ten feet away, boxing them in.

Dikran grabbed Shake's arm.

"What is it?" Shake said.

"Not good," Dikran said.

Chapter Nine

Two guys got out of the Escalade. Shake was six feet tall, 175 pounds, but Dikran could just about wrap his entire hand around Shake's bicep. He squeezed, hard.

"Is Babikian," Dikran said. Lexy's new number two, Shake remembered. "Say nothing. You understand?"

"Let go of my arm. Yes."

"They must not know she is disappeared."

"Let go of my arm."

Dikran dropped the arm. The two guys swaggered over. Both were late thirties, lean and slouchy, heads a size too big for their bodies. They both wore fancy Italian suits and aggressively futuristic eyeglasses.

The guy in the lead had the bigger head, the more rolling swagger. Babikian for sure.

He barely glanced at Shake. Shake could live with that.

"Ghazarian," Babikian asked Dikran, "what the hell are you doing in Cambodia?"

"I ask you same question."

"And what's up with the old noggin, buddy?"

Babikian pointed to the spot on Dikran's head where Gina had shot him with the nail gun. In the center of the gauze bandage was a spot of dried blood.

"Is accident," Dikran said.

"Yeah?" Babikian said. "I thought maybe you finally had a brain transplant."

Babikian's flunky snickered.

Babikian had a big, white, wraparound smile, more teeth than seemed possible for a single human mouth.

Shake realized he did know Babikian. A few years ago, when Babikian was still middle management, he'd tried to get Shake to drive an ill-advised bank job he'd lined up behind Lexy's back. Shake said no. Not long after that, at the annual Christmas party Lexy always threw, Babikian was screaming at a scared young waitress who'd spilled his drink. Shake stepped in, Babikian took a swing, and Shake knocked him on his ass.

Shit, Shake thought. He hoped Babikian had forgotten all about that—and him.

"I ask you question," Dikran said. "Tell me what do you do here?"

"No. First, because none of your fucking business," Babikian said. "You're an ant, Ghazarian, and I don't explain myself to you. Second, we have a meeting on Friday in Phnom Penh, Alexandra and me, with some very important people."

Babikian never stopped smiling, the exact same smile the whole time. It was as if the bottom of his face were painted on.

"Huh," Dikran said. "I think maybe you just do this. Explain to me, I mean."

Shake thought that was a pretty good shot. Babikian ignored it.

"Now, go back inside and tell her I'm here," he said. "Yeah, yeah, I know she's on vacation for another couple of days. But I need to talk to her. We need to get our shit together for this meeting or we all look bad."

"You will see her," Dikran said, "when *she* needs, not you. I am ant, maybe, but do you forget? She is *pakhan*."

"I remember, buddy," Babikian said mildly. "She's the *pakhan* right now."

Right now. His threat landed. Dikran took a long, deep breath. But—or *and,* Shake wasn't sure which—he didn't blow.

"I will tell her you say this," Dikran said.

Babikian's smile remained painted on, but Shake could tell *that* threat had landed, too.

"Ghazarian." Babikian studied him. "I think there's something going on here. I think there's something you're not telling me."

"No," Dikran said. He shrugged, but not convincingly.

Babikian's flunky snickered. Babikian turned to Shake.

"Hi, asshole," Babikian said, still smiling. "And who the hell are you?"

"Nobody," Shake said.

"Nobody. Ghazarian, who's the asshole?"

Dikran tried another casual shrug. It was casual like he'd been hit by a Taser.

"My friend," he said.

Babikian's smile got even bigger. Shake thought he might have another set of teeth behind the first one, like moray eels did.

"Your *friend,*" he said. He turned to his flunky in astonishment. "Did you hear that, Jeff? Ghazarian has a *friend.*"

The flunky snickered. Shake was getting tired of it. Was that all Jeff was good for? Drive the car and snicker?

"Dikran," Babikian said. "Between you and me. That's the worst lie you've told so far. You have a *friend*? You. *You?* A good lie has to have at least a grain of possibility, buddy."

Babikian nodded to his flunky. Before Shake could even blink, the flunky had a gun out and pressed to Shake's cheek.

Okay, maybe the guy could do more than drive the car and snicker.

The flunky kept the gun against Shake's cheek and reached around behind Shake with his free hand. He grabbed Shake's butt cheek.

"I've been working out," Shake said. "Can you tell?"

"Shut up, smart mouth," Dikran said, before he remembered whose side he was on for the time being.

Babikian's flunky grabbed the other butt cheek and found Shake's wallet. He handed it to Babikian. Babikian pulled the driver's license and tossed the wallet away.

"Charles Samuel Bouchon of Bloomington, Indiana," Babikian said, reading. He looked up at Shake. "Where the hell is that?"

"Nowhere," Shake said.

"Shoot him," Babikian said. "No, wait."

"It's in southern Indiana," Shake said quickly. "About an hour from Indianapolis, straight down Highway 37. Indiana University is there."

"Shut up," Babikian said. He studied Shake the way he'd just studied Dikran. "I know you. Why would I know you? Why would I know a Charles Samuel Bouchon of Bumfuck, Indiana?"

Shake knew it was just a matter of time now. He might as well get it over with.

"I'm the driver," he said.

"Wait. I remember now. You're the getaway driver."

"That's what I just said."

Babikian's smile got even bigger. "Shake Bouchon," he said. "That's right. Lexy's little pet. The asshole pussy who sucker-punched me next to the Christmas tree."

"You punched first."

Babikian started to answer but then stopped and turned to

Dikran. "Wait," he said. "Shake Bouchon. Isn't this the asshole pussy you hate so much?"

Dikran shrugged again. Third time was not the charm.

Babikian took another look at Shake's driver's license and then flicked it away.

"Ghazarian," Babikian said, "I'm gonna find out what's going on. I will, buddy. You can bet your bottom dollar."

"You are always man of your word," Dikran said, in a tone that indicated just the opposite.

"Shoot them both," Babikian said. "No, wait."

He nodded at his flunky, who tucked the gun away and yawned.

Babikian hadn't stopped smiling, not once.

"It's not the first punch that counts, asshole," he told Shake. "It's the last one."

Chapter Ten

Shake waited till the Escalade had disappeared before he picked up his wallet. It took him a while to find his driver's license, beneath a bush with lethal-looking blade-shaped leaves.

His heart continued to bang against his ribs. You never really got used to almost getting murdered; the spark never went out of that experience.

Back on the main road, Shake flagged down a *tuk-tuk*.

"A nice hotel," Shake told the driver. "Nice but not too expensive. And not one owned by your uncle."

The driver nodded, and they set off. Shake checked to make sure the Escalade wasn't tailing them.

"Ha," Dikran said. "Babikian. He is smart, he thinks. The snake. But I pull his wool. You see?"

"You pulled his what?" Shake said.

"His wool. From his eyes."

"Over his eyes."

"Yes."

"No. You didn't."

"He is like toy in my hand."

"No."

Dikran knew it. He stewed.

"You think Babikian will make a move if he finds out Lexy's missing," Shake said.

It wasn't advanced calculus. Probably Babikian was just waiting to grab power. At the first opportunity, the first sign that Lexy's guard might be down . . .

"The snake," Dikran said. "Yes. He waits in the grass. But I say this. If he betrays her, the sky will rain blood!"

Shake leaned his head back and closed his eyes. It seemed like just yesterday, didn't it, that he'd been sitting in his backyard, drinking a cold one and getting ready to prep a salt-and-garlic paste for the lamb chops. And not caught in the middle of a potential mob war, the forecast calling for a heavy rain of blood.

It *was* just yesterday.

They drove through a park. At the edge of the park was an elegant old French Colonial building with a peaked roof and wooden balconies. The Victoria Angkor. A pair of stone dragons guarded the entrance.

Inside, the lobby of the hotel was all cool marble and dark teak, the kind of place, 150 years ago, where you would have sipped a gin fizz after bagging an elephant.

Dikran looked around. "I need to move my bowel."

Maybe this, Shake considered, was how Dikran planned to kill him—just by being Dikran.

"I beg for death," Shake said.

"What?"

"Nothing. Go move your bowel."

"Stupid cockjob."

Dikran stalked off to find the men's room. Shake went to the front desk and asked for two rooms, in separate wings of the hotel if possible.

While he waited for the desk clerk to code the key cards, Shake thought about how easy it would be to walk out of the hotel, catch a *tuk-tuk* back to the airport, and buy a seat on the first flight out. By the time Dikran finished moving his bowel, Shake could be halfway to Hong Kong, headed back home.

He savored the fantasy for a moment, then scooped up the key cards and took a seat in a leather armchair. He'd started to doze off when Dikran shook him awake.

"Get up, cockjob," Dikran said.

Shake handed him one of the key cards. "Go get some sleep. I'll see you in a few hours."

"No! We must find her!"

Shake stood. "I need to sleep for a couple of hours first. I can't even see straight."

Dikran huffed and puffed, growled and glowered. Shake let him.

"I give your way this time," Dikran said finally. "But listen to me. If we do not find her because you are lazy, you will not beg for death. Do you know why?"

Shake had a pretty good idea it would have something to do with his tongue being yanked from his head and then used in a way God had not intended. He headed toward the elevator.

"I'll see you in a few hours," he said.

EVEN THOUGH HE was exhausted, Shake had a hard time getting to sleep. It was morning in Bloomington, and his body thought he should be up and about, out making hay.

Now what?

He didn't know where to start. He was no detective. He never even watched detective shows on TV. They were too predictable. The killer always turned out to be a minor witness the cops had talked to early in the show and then forgotten about. And the motive for murder was always overly complicated, like the killer was the dead guy's long-lost sister and now she was hooked on bath salts.

In Shake's experience, motives were usually a lot more straightforward than that. Or there wasn't much of a motive at all—the dead guy just happened to stick his nose in the wrong place.

Yeah. In real life that happened all the time.

The alarm buzzed about five minutes after he finally managed to drop off. He got up, took a hot shower, and shaved. His room looked out over the park. Shake stood on his balcony, the heat easing as the sun set, and watched the birds lifting up off the trees. He'd never seen so many birds—wave after wave of them, filling the darkening sky.

He ordered coffee and eggs from room service, then pulled up the Web browser on his phone. His search for "luxury villa siem reap" returned links to half a dozen property-management companies. Shake wrote down the phone numbers even though he was dubious that Lexy would be staying at a place you could find with Google.

The room-service waitress was dressed like an old-timey Parisian newsboy, in culottes, suspenders, and a beret. Shake wondered how she felt about having to wear that getup.

He tipped the waitress big, ate his eggs, and considered his options. Shake knew that if he was going to make any headway in Cambodia, he needed a fixer, someone local who spoke the language, literally and figuratively. Unfortunately, there was only one guy Shake knew who might be able to hook him up.

He strapped himself in for the long haul and dialed.

"Let me ask you something, Shake," Quinn said after half a ring. Like he'd been expecting Shake's call, like the conversation was already well under way, even though Shake hadn't talked to him in almost a year. "If you had an opportunity to change the world, Shake, the very course of history I'm talking about, how fast would you say yes?"

"No."

"Just hear me out. Can you get to D.C. by Monday? You'll need a suit or two. What are you, a thirty-eight long? And a decent tux."

"I'm in Cambodia," Shake said, hoping that would get Quinn's attention.

It did. "What? Did you say Cambodia?"

Quinn was a retired CIA spook who Shake had met in Belize, a silver-haired Casanova and bullshitter extraordinaire. He always had at least one scheme on the front burner, two on the back. Shake, against his own better judgment, had been drawn into one of those schemes. It was a miracle he'd survived, both the scheme and Quinn.

"Cambodia!" Quinn said. "My old stomping ground. I was there ten minutes after the Vietnamese pulled out in '89. All right, maybe a few minutes *before* they pulled out, if we're keeping this off the record. I was back a few years ago, too, wrapping up a business venture with an old buddy of mine."

"I'm in Siem Reap. I could use a little help."

"You're there on vacation? You and the missus? I'm hurt you didn't invite me along. But here's my advice: See Angkor Wat at least twice, once in the morning and once at sunset. And you like French food?"

"I'm not here on vacation."

Shake told Quinn why he was there. Quinn knew Lexy by reputation. He was quiet for a long time after Shake finished. A long time for Quinn was one, two seconds.

"Did you think maybe she's just with some fella?" he said. "Cuddled up in a secret love nest somewhere, doesn't want to be disturbed?"

"Yes."

"Yes, you thought that?"

"Yes, I thought that."

"But you think something's hinky, or else you wouldn't be in Cambodia, would you? All right. Settle down."

"You know anybody here who might be able to give me the lay of the land?"

"Damn it."

"What?"

"This business I mentioned up top, here in D.C. I'm wrapped tight for another two weeks at least. Otherwise I'd be on my way to the airport as we speak."

"That's too bad," Shake said.

Quinn laughed. "Same old Shake."

"So do you know anybody in Siem Reap?"

"Sure. The old buddy of mine I just told you about, he runs that town. A heavy hitter, if you know what I mean. If anyone can get you on the inside track, he's the one."

Shake hesitated. Another old buddy of Quinn's, back in Belize, had pointed a shotgun at Shake and almost pulled the trigger.

"What's his name?" Shake said.

"Ouch."

"What happened?"

"What? No. That's his name. Ouch. Just the one word, like Elvis."

Shake grimaced. He didn't want to know how you got a nickname like Ouch. He could guess.

"You know anybody else?" he said.

"It's not what you think. That's his real name. That's a real name in Cambodia." Quinn paused. "I'm not saying he's a pussycat. He's a formidable hombre, I'll be candid with you. Former Khmer Rouge, if you really want to know."

"Aren't those the people that killed all those people?"

"They've been reformed. Hell, the prime minister of the country used to be Khmer Rouge."

"Great."

"Like I said, though. If it goes down in Siem Reap, Ouch will know about it. Just . . . mind your p's and q's around him."

Shake decided to take his chances. He didn't have much choice.

"Can you put me in touch with him?"

"Of course I can put me in touch with him. Where are you staying, so he knows where to find you?"

"How about you just give him my phone number?"

"Shake."

Shake moved back out onto the balcony. He sighed and told Quinn the name of the hotel.

"One more thing," Quinn said. "Watch your step in Cambodia. It's not like here at home. You can't trust anybody."

That sounded to Shake just like back home. "Except your old buddy," he said.

"No! Jesus! Have you been listening? He can help you maybe, but I wouldn't trust him to pass the salt. Don't trust anybody! I don't know how to explain it any clearer than that."

"Okay. I got it."

Quinn was silent again. Five seconds this time, ten. A world record.

"It's a peculiar place," Quinn said, "Siem Reap is."

"Peculiar how?"

"Just peculiar. I mean, you think Suryavarman picked that spot for his temples by accident? He's the fella who built Angkor. That jungle was sacred for five thousand years before he even showed up. Ask anyone. Sometimes you get a feeling when you're there, like you've got one foot in this world and the other one somewhere else."

"What time is it in D.C.?" Shake said. "You're getting mystical on me."

"'There are more things in heaven and earth, Horatio, than are dreamt of in your philosophy.' That's Shakespeare."

"Tell your buddy to get in touch with me," Shake said. "As soon as possible."

"All right. But watch your step out there, you understand me? First sign of trouble, get on an airplane and come home."

Quinn saying that. Quinn, who just shrugged in Belize when he found out that a natural-gas billionaire with limitless resources was trying to kill him. Who saw the sunny upside of the most hopeless situation. Who always wanted in on the action, whatever the action might be.

Shake knew he was in trouble. "Thanks," he said.

Dusk had turned the sky a deep, ripe purple. The lamps in the park flickered on, and another wave of birds billowed up out of the trees. The sound the birds made was strange, the shrill squeaking of wet leather. A second later Shake realized they weren't birds—they were bats. Hundreds of them, maybe thousands, gathering and swirling and shredding the moon to pieces.

Chapter Eleven

Normally Gina scooted straight home after work on Fridays. The six-o'clock class at her favorite place was for beginners, and Gina—in yoga as in life, she was the first to admit it—bored easily. Plus, Shake knocked off early on Friday, and she didn't want to be doing yoga, or anything else, when she could be with him.

She'd never tell him that, of course.

He knew it anyway, of course.

This Friday afternoon Gina had no reason to scoot straight home. Her husband was in Siem Reap, Cambodia. An empty house awaited her, with only the lonely creak of her own footsteps to keep her company.

Okay, she could be a little melodramatic. Gina was the first to admit that, too.

Judith, the receptionist, poked her head into Gina's office.

"Yvette called to cancel!" she said.

"That's fantastic!" Gina said.

And it was. Historically, Yvette just blew off the appointment without notice and showed up two days later, blazed out of her mind and full of rambling excuses. A phone call ten minutes ahead of time was a major breakthrough.

Gina volunteered for a nonprofit called Heads Held High. It provided counseling and coaching to girls in their late teens and early twenties who . . . what? Gina couldn't remember, exactly, the euphemism they used on the brochure and the Web site. Girls, basically, who needed to get their shit together and get it together fast.

Back in San Francisco, before Indiana, Gina had run her own boutique venture-capital firm. It had been fun at first, a rush whenever one of her long-shot ponies finished in the money. After a while, though, the whole thing became a grind—the stacks of research, the meetings, the meetings about meetings. Now she got to do something that mattered, or at least didn't feel like work.

At Heads Held High, Gina helped the girls study for the GED, taught them networking and time-management strategies, gave them tips on what to wear to job interviews. A bra? Yes! A T-shirt that said GET ON DOWN THERE, IT WON'T LICK ITSELF? Maybe not!

Mostly, though, Gina sat the girls down and gave them advice about life. Her basic message was, *Get your shit together!*

You hate when your unemployed, meth-smoking boyfriend borrows your car and then forgets where he parked it? Well, *get your shit together* and dump his loser ass! Or: You hate slinging drinks and getting groped by old coots at that skeezy casino on the Kentucky border? Well, *get your shit together and find a new job!*

"But it's complicated," some of the girls would whine, with a certain kind of shy, sly smile they hoped would make Gina nod with sisterly understanding.

Yeah. No.

"It might be *hard*," Gina would say. "But it's not *complicated*. Big difference. So get your shit together and stop making excuses."

The girls didn't like that. Naturally. But most of them kept coming back. They got that Gina got them. The other volunteer counselors at Heads Held High, sweet ladies all, came from loving families, nice neighborhoods, good schools, and happy childhoods. Gina came from exactly none of the above.

"I guess this means you can go home early now," Judith said.

To an empty house. To the lonely creak of her own footsteps. To the vacant pillow next to her, the scent of Shake's aftershave still on it.

Yeah. Well. The next morning Gina decided she was done with the self-pity and strolled over to the Starbucks by campus. She liked it during the summer months, when most of the students had gone home and you could have your pick of the leather chairs.

This morning Gina took her chai tea latte over to a chair next to the window. The window faced west, so she couldn't enjoy the warmth of the sun, but that was fine. Gina had weightier grievances to bear at the moment.

She wasn't mad that Shake had run off to Cambodia. Infuriated, maybe, and exasperated, but not mad. How could she be mad? Shake was Shake. Shake would always be Shake. If there was a right thing to do, no matter how potentially dangerous, he did it, and he did it without thinking twice.

It was infuriating. It was exasperating. Yes, granted, Gina herself was alive right now—enjoying a chai tea latte—only because Shake was a good guy in a world full of bad and worse. But . . . whatever. She stood by her central thesis.

Think twice every now and then, before you do the right thing! Would it kill you?

Though what really infuriated Gina, what really exasperated her, was how much she loved that about Shake—that he did the right thing *without* thinking twice about it.

She listened to the hiss of steam and the chuckle of the espresso machine. On the wall opposite her was a big map of Bloomington, marked with locations from the old movie *Breaking Away,* which had been filmed here in the seventies. A year ago she and Shake had been lounging around in bed, a hotel room in midtown Manhattan, watching TV. They'd just come back from Cairo, those crazy two weeks, and were trying to decide where they wanted to live. They had enough money, thanks to Gina's investments, to go anywhere in the world they wanted. Fiji? Curaçao? And then *Breaking Away* came on. Shake couldn't believe Gina had never seen it, or even heard of it.

"It's one of the best movies ever made," he said. "It won an Academy Award, I think. Or it was up for one."

"Is it funny or sad or exciting or what?"

"It's all that! It's about friendship and family and growing up. It's about the people who worked in the quarries, how the things they built don't belong to them anymore. It's about falling in love for the first time, then realizing you're an idiot."

Gina peered at the screen. "Is that Dennis Quaid? He looks like he's barely out of high school."

"It was one of his first movies."

"Look at how short his shorts are! Did you have shorts like that back then?"

"Just watch the movie, okay?"

She grumbled and groused, but by the end—when the underdog, undersize townie guys came from behind to beat the rich douchebag college boys in the big bicycle race—Gina was crying her eyes out.

"What did I tell you?" Shake said.

"There," she said.

"There?"

"Let's move there."

"Bloomington, Indiana."

"Bloomington, Indiana."

Because . . . why not? It was a place unlike any other they'd considered, unlike any other place either one of them had ever lived or visited or even imagined visiting. Which made it the perfect place. If you really wanted to change your life, you needed to go all in. It was hard, but not complicated.

Shake had nodded. "Let's do it."

Gina was so exasperated with herself. Shake had barely been gone two days, and already she missed him so much it hurt.

Why hadn't he asked her to go with him to Cambodia? That, more than anything else, made her the grumpiest. He should have begged, bullied, and wheedled. He should have said whatever it took to convince her that even a few days apart would be the death of him.

Her phone rang. Shake.

"Hi!" she said. "I'm up at the Starbucks by campus. Want to meet me downtown for lunch?"

He was quiet for a beat and then, "Very funny."

"Oh, wait. You've been gone for two days, haven't you? I'm so stupid. I didn't even notice."

She heard what could have been a yawn, or a groan, or both.

"It's only been two days?" he said.

She tucked her legs up beneath her. She remembered the first time she'd heard Shake's voice. He was trying to talk his way out of an inopportune traffic stop, just one wrong word from the cop looking in his trunk and sending Shake away for the rest of his life. Gina was amazed at how calm Shake had stayed. She thought she might have fallen in love with him at that very moment.

Or the moment she'd first seen his eyes, clear and wry. Gina had felt a little guilty when circumstances demanded that she roofie him and cuff him to a bathroom pipe.

"What time is it there?" she asked him now.

"Eight at night."

"Eight at night today or tomorrow? Or yesterday?"

"One of those."

"Come home."

"I want to. Believe me."

"But you can't."

"Not yet."

So beg me! Gina wanted to say. *Bully me! Do whatever it takes to get me on the next freaking flight to Cambodia!*

But she'd never say that. She'd beg to be begged over her own dead body.

"So have you found her yet?" Gina said. "The ex-girlfriend you can't let go?"

Shake wisely, Gina thought, let that one go.

"No. I'm getting ready to start checking with every property company in Siem Reap that rents high-end villas. Do you know how many property companies in Siem Reap rent high-end villas?"

"Lots? Lots and lots?"

"Did I mention it's about a hundred and five degrees out?" He yawned or groaned again. No, definitely a groan this time.

"Do you even know what name she's using? You'll have to hope someone remembers her."

"Lexy? They'll remember her."

Gina remained silent and let him grasp the magnitude of the mistake he'd just made.

"What I mean," he said, "I mean . . ."

"Stop."

"Okay."

Gina tapped two fingers against her lips. Shake always knew when she was thinking and let her do so in peace. It was one of the things Gina loved about him.

"Why does she go on these trips every summer?" she said.

"To get away," Shake said.

"From everything."

"Yeah. The job, L.A. Dikran. Everything."

Gina put aside her personal feelings about Lexy for a moment and tried to imagine herself into Lexy's life. What was it like to run the Armenians? Lexy was the first female *pakhan* in the history of the outfit, and Gina guessed that her ride to the top had been a bumpy one. Staying there probably wasn't any easier. Even the snootiest, most cold-blooded witch in the world—which Lexy definitely was, by the way—would have to become a version of herself that the other versions might not even recognize.

Gina knew all about that. It's how she got through her teenage years without stepping off a highway overpass. And what made her so good, later, at the fine art of the con.

Who do I need to be today?

"Yes," Gina said, "I think she wants to get away from *everyone.*"

Shake was quiet for a long time. "From herself, too."

If she were Lexy, Gina thought, she might want to pretend for a couple of weeks every year that she was someone else. Someone she used to be, or someone she could have been.

She let Shake think. It was only fair.

"So check places I *wouldn't* expect her to stay," he said.

"See?" For a second they weren't three thousand or however many miles apart, separated by however many oceans and continents. They sat in the same room, her arm around his neck, his hand on her leg, scheming together like always. "That wasn't so hard, was it?"

Chapter Twelve

'll talk to you later," Shake told Gina.

"Try to be safe."

"Always."

She laughed and laughed, like Shake had just said the funniest thing ever, then hung up.

A second later Shake's phone dinged. And then dinged two more times. Three texts from Dikran.

ARE YOU WAKE YET.

WE MUST FIND HER.

CALL ME ASSWIPE.

The phone buzzed as he was holding it. Shake answered.

"Hello, asswipe," he said, as instructed.

There was a moment of confused silence on the other end of the line.

"I have wrong number," Dikran said.

"No you don't," Shake said. "What do you want?"

"What do I want? What do I want?"

"Calm down."

"We must find her!"

"I need to do some digging."

"What digging?"

"You want me to explain? You want me to spend ten minutes explaining when I could be doing it?"

"Where are you? I will help with digging."

"I'll call you in a little while."

"No! Listen to me! You—"

Shake killed the call and turned his ringer off. Following Gina's advice, he threw away his list of high-end property-management companies. He pulled up TripAdvisor, the bane of his existence when he'd owned a restaurant in Belize and was at the mercy of every dipshit who left a bad review. Skimming through the list of hotels in Siem Reap, he ruled out youth hostels, backpacker guesthouses, and bed-and-breakfast joints— Shake doubted that Lexy wanted to get away from clean towels or private bathrooms. He ruled out five-star resorts and anyplace that seemed like it would have a Chinese tour bus parked out front.

That left the boutique hotels. There were fourteen viable candidates, including the one he was sitting in right now. Shake took a shot—why not?—and called down to the front desk. No luck. Veronica Wagenseller wasn't a guest at the Victoria Angkor.

He went back to TripAdvisor and started working his way through the list. It took him twenty minutes to call the remaining hotels. Eleven places said no on Veronica Wagenseller, and three didn't answer the phone. Those three hotels, Shake saw when he checked the TripAdvisor map, were all by the river, clustered along a road called Wat Nhek.

He checked the time—almost nine—and took the elevator downstairs to the lobby. The bellhop out front whistled over a *tuk-tuk* for him.

The driver drove Shake through the center of town, down a

street lit by neon bar signs and strands of colored bulbs strung overhead. All the signs were in English, and the bars had names like Angkor What? and Fun Fun. Most of the people on the sidewalks were foreigners, ruddy-cheeked men with big bellies and booming voices. Shake saw a few stumbles here and there, but he could tell that the night's party hadn't ramped up yet. Wispy Cambodian women in sarongs stood outside the restaurants, fanning themselves with menus.

At the end of the block, a cop kept an eye on the action. He wore a tall peaked cap and a uniform shirt with enough gold braid for a four-star general. The cop somehow managed to both smile and remain stone-faced at the same time, a trick Shake had noticed that a lot of Cambodians could pull off.

The *tuk-tuk* driver stopped in front of a hotel called the Golden Moon. Shake paid him and climbed out. The Golden Moon didn't look big enough to be a hotel. It was just a two-story French plantation house. Once Shake threaded his way past the *tuk-tuk* drivers loitering by the curb, though, he saw that behind the main house there were several small, individual cottages, tucked in among the banana trees.

Shake rang the bell of the main house and waited. After a minute he tried the door. It was unlocked, so he stepped inside.

The deserted lobby was tiny compared to the Victoria Angkor's and hadn't been updated in a while. But the place had a faded, comfortable charm—black-and-white checkerboard tile, rattan chairs, an iron birdcage elevator. A ceiling fan with wooden paddles shaped like flower petals turned slowly overhead.

Shake took another look around. Never in a million years would you guess that the *pakhan* of the Armenian mob was staying here. Which, if Gina was right, was probably the point.

The reception desk was just that, an old wooden desk. Shake

opened the top drawer and pulled out a three-ring binder. He flipped through photocopies of passport pages until, on the very last page, he found Lexy gazing serenely back at him. And handwritten in the margin next to the photo: *"Veronica Wagenseller, Bungalow Three."*

Shake waited a few more minutes, to see if a desk clerk would turn up. When one didn't, he borrowed a ballpoint pen and a paper clip from the desk and headed back outside. He followed a stone path that led to the bungalows. Bungalow 3 was at the far edge of the grounds, so close to the river that Shake could hear the murmur of water.

The lights in the bungalow were off. Shake peered into a window, but it was too dark to see anything. He knocked. He knocked again. He knew it was too much to hope for, that Lexy might open the door, but he hoped it anyway.

Nothing.

The bungalows were spaced for privacy, each one behind a six-foot wooden lattice covered in bougainvillea. The next bungalow over was thirty feet away, and its lights were out, too. If he worked fast, Shake decided, he shouldn't have a problem.

He twisted the metal clip off the ballpoint pen, pulled apart the paper clip, and got down on his knees. He couldn't remember the last time he'd picked a lock. The dead bolt was an old one, sticky as hell, and the paper clip kept slipping out of his fingers when his hands started to sweat.

He took a deep breath and tried again. Nice and easy. He felt a little give finally. A little more. He almost had it. Almost. And then—*pop.* The paper clip snapped.

"Shit," he said.

"Hello," a voice behind him said.

Shake tensed. He turned and saw a Cambodian woman standing

there watching him. Next to her was the biggest dog he'd ever seen—like a rottweiler pony. The dog was watching Shake, too. It cocked its massive head and growled.

Shit.

"Hello," Shake said.

The woman had her head cocked at the same angle the dog did. "Wow," she said, "you're in a lot of trouble."

Chapter Thirteen

Shake started to stand, but the giant rottweiler barked at him, a slobbery concussive blast that made Shake's ears ring. Shake stayed on his knees.

"Why don't we discuss this?" he asked the Cambodian woman.

She kept her head cocked to the side as she studied him. She was in her late twenties or early thirties, Shake guessed, with a round face and dreadlocks down to her shoulders. She wore a tie-dye skirt and a Flaming Lips tank top. Her cheeks were pierced, one silver stud in each.

"Quite a bit of trouble," she said again. "Wow."

Shake didn't need to have it repeated. The giant rottweiler had him cornered. Shake's only chance, maybe, if he couldn't talk his way out of this, was to bust through the wooden lattice and hope he made it to the river before the dog brought him down like an impala on the savanna.

He started to ease himself up again, more slowly this time. The giant rottweiler barked again, even louder and with even more slobbering. Jaws slapping together, teeth clacking—it was bad, like the sound of bones crunching, like wet flesh tearing.

"I bet he's really a sweetheart, isn't he?" Shake said.

The Cambodian hippie chick had both hands on the leash, holding tight. "She."

"She."

"No. She's the dog from hell, actually."

Perfect.

Shake remembered what a cellie of his at Mule Creek had told him once—that the way to deal with a dog, you balled up a fist and then stuffed the fist in the dog's mouth, down the dog's throat, as far as you could stuff it.

That had seemed like terrible advice to Shake at the time. It seemed like even worse advice now.

"Listen," he said. "I know what this looks like. But this isn't what it looks like."

The hippie chick appeared puzzled. Shake didn't blame her. He was dying to hear this himself.

"It is, I guess," he said, "what it looks like. I'm trying to get in. But not to steal anything. A friend of mine is staying here. I can't get hold of her, and I'm worried. No one was at the front desk, so . . . You can call the cops, I understand why you'd want to do that, but maybe just think about it for a second, okay?"

"Oh," she said. "I don't mean you're in trouble like that."

Shake wondered what else she could mean. Did she plan to skip the cops and just let the dog have him?

"You don't?" he said.

There was a slight lag before she answered, like she was downloading the bits and bytes of a satellite transmission and reassembling them into a complete image. Or she was high.

"No," she said. She shook her head, and the small silver bells braided into the tips of her dreadlocks tinkled. "You're a good person. I can feel that. You've got a very positive energy. Your energy feels like a groovy old Hammond B-3 organ. Like a lot of the old

American soul bands used to use? Do you know 'Last Night' by the Mar-Keys?"

Shake tried to figure out if she was for real. He thought she might be.

"Booker T. Jones," he said.

"Yeah? Can you feel it, too?"

"Not really. But thank you."

"But *that*." She pointed to a spot a few inches above Shake's head. "Where your aura blends with the universe. It's not blending properly."

Her English was perfect, with a hint of a British accent threaded through it.

"My aura?" Shake said.

"It's all swirly and tangled and darkish green. Like, *really* dark-ish green? I think it means you're in quite a bit of trouble."

The trouble, Shake wanted to tell her, was that she'd taken one hand off the leash to point to his aura. The dog from hell had realized this and was tugging closer and closer to Shake, with a big scary smile on its, her, face.

"Your dog," he said.

It took a moment for the transmission to reach the hippie chick.

"Oh. Queenie! Chill!" She grabbed the leash with both hands and heaved the rottweiler back a few inches. "She's not mine," she told Shake. "I'm just babysitting for Jacques. He owns the hotel? My name's Mitch, by the way."

"Mitch?"

"Just call me that. You can't pronounce the Khmer."

"Okay," Shake said. "Mitch, I'm going to stand up now."

He rose to his feet. Carefully. The rottweiler barked again, bones crunching and wet flesh tearing. Mitch heaved her back a few more inches.

"Queenie! Chill! I mean it!"

Shake wanted to get the hell away from that dog, but he thought he'd better find out if Mitch knew anything about Lexy.

"So you work here?" he said.

"I'm the manager. The manager and the receptionist and the handyman and— Queenie! I'm everything, actually, when Jacques is on holiday."

"The woman who's staying in this bungalow. Veronica Wagenseller. Do you know her?"

"Yeah. She's been here, like, a week and a half? Really unusual eyes and a complicated energy?"

"Gray eyes."

"I told her, 'Wow, you've got a complicated energy,' and she just laughed. She's got a really musical laugh."

Gray eyes, musical laugh. Complicated. That was Lexy.

"Have you seen her lately?" Shake said.

"Do you know that feeling? When you're at the sea and you jump in the water and it just takes your breath away it's so cold? And then you're in this other world, this entire new far-out world beneath the surface. That's what her energy reminds me of."

"Have you seen her lately?"

Mitch thought about it. "No, now that you mention it. Not since last week, I think. Shall I fetch the key?"

"The key?"

She shrugged. "You've got a really positive energy. I trust you. I'll be back straightaway."

She dragged the giant rottweiler off. Shake couldn't believe his luck. He decided that first thing in the morning he'd better go down to the park and set a few birds free. It was the least he could do.

A few minutes later, Mitch was back, with a key and without the dog. She unlocked the door to the bungalow. Shake stepped inside and turned on the light.

Everything in the living room seemed right. No chairs knocked over, no broken vases. Shake moved into the bedroom. It seemed right, too. On the table next to the neatly made bed, he saw a paperback book. *Un Américain Bien Tranquille.* Graham Greene, Shake knew, was one of Lexy's favorite writers.

The clothes hanging in the closet, various shades of purple, definitely belonged to Lexy. The scent was hers, too.

Shake looked for her purse but couldn't find it. He did find a leather jewelry case. Inside were a pair of diamond earrings, a couple of rings, and, on a thin silver chain, an Orthodox cross so ancient and delicate it looked like a melting snowflake. The cross had belonged to Lexy's great-grandmother, who'd been killed during the genocide in Turkey. *"Medz Yeghern,"* the Armenians called the genocide. The Great Crime.

Mitch followed him into the bedroom.

"D'ya think perhaps she hired a car and drove down to Sihanoukville or Phnom Penh?" she said. "Usually guests tell us if they're going away for a few days, but not always."

Shake slipped the cross into his pocket for safekeeping. He knew Lexy would never leave town without it.

"Do you remember anything unusual that happened several days ago?" he said.

"Unusual?"

"Like somebody hanging around the place. Or a car parked somewhere it shouldn't have been. Anything at all. Any small thing."

"Let me think."

She pursed her lips. The silver studs in her cheeks heightened the effect. Shake noted that she wasn't wearing a bra under the Flaming Lips tank top and looked away. He walked over and picked up the Graham Greene paperback.

"Sorry," Mitch said. "No. What's your name, by the way?"

"Shake."

"I thought it might be something like that. I'd love to read your past lives."

"Maybe some other time."

"It'll blow your mind, how cleansing the process can be. Sometimes you have to make peace with your past lives before you can properly inhabit the one you have now."

Shake showed her what Lexy had been using as a bookmark: a square of embossed paper with official-looking stamps, handwritten dates, and a passport-size photo of Lexy in the bottom corner.

"You know what this is?" he said.

"That's a tourist pass for Angkor." She leaned closer. "It expired a couple of days ago."

"Is Angkor close? Can you walk there?"

"No, not really. It's ten or fifteen minutes by moto or *tuk-tuk*."

Shake had hoped so. "Mitch," he said. "You want to do me another favor?"

"Sure."

He led her outside, back through the banana trees and out to the street. The *tuk-tuk* drivers were still loitering. Shake waved them over and showed them the tourist pass with Lexy's photo on it.

Almost right away a guy pointed at the photo and nodded.

"You remember her?" Shake said.

"*Baat.* Yes."

"You drove her out there?"

"Yes."

That seemed to be the outer limits of the guy's English.

"Can you ask him what I asked you?" Shake asked Mitch. "If he remembers anything unusual?"

She nodded, then said something to the guy in a language that sounded to Shake like a cat trying to claw its way up a stainless-steel refrigerator.

The guy answered. He and Mitch went back and forth for a minute.

"He says he drove your friend on Sunday morning," she told Shake. "Out to Banteay Srei. That's the far temple, at least half an hour from here. But he says he didn't bring her back."

"He didn't bring her back? Is that unusual?"

And then Shake noticed the *tuk-tuk* driver who'd driven him to the Golden Moon, sitting five feet away and watching Shake like a hawk. The jet lag was making Shake stupid. He answered his own question before Mitch could.

"It's unusual," he said. "Because they want the fare going back."

Mitch nodded. "He says he was waiting for her. Outside the temple while she was inside looking around? But then a man in the parking lot paid him twenty dollars to bugger off without her."

Whatever slim hope Shake had been holding tight to—that maybe, just maybe, all this was only a dumb mix-up and Lexy was somewhere safe and sound—that hope slipped away and went flapping off, like a bat into the black Cambodian night.

"And then you left?" Shake asked the *tuk-tuk* driver. He looked at Mitch. "And then he left?"

"*Baat.* Yes. I go." The *tuk-tuk* driver was starting to look nervous. He said something to Mitch in Khmer.

"He says the man who gave him the money was the woman's friend. Her best friend. He says what was he supposed to do?"

"Tell him it's all right," Shake said. "He didn't do anything wrong."

It wasn't hard to piece together now, how the grab went down. Probably the guy who paid off Lexy's driver had a partner with a cab or a *tuk-tuk*. So when Lexy came out of the temple and saw that her ride had abandoned her . . .

Shake wished there were a little flex in the driver's story, wished he could spot another possible conclusion or two. There wasn't, though. He couldn't.

"What did he look like?" Shake asked the driver. "The guy who paid you?"

Mitch asked the question in Khmer, then translated the answer.

"He was a *barang*," she said. "A foreigner. He spoke English and had blond hair."

"Did he have a car?" Shake said. "Was he alone? Ask him if he remembers anything else at all. If that's exactly the way it happened."

Mitch asked the *tuk-tuk* driver. Shake watched the guy's face. Gina was the ace liar in the family, but Shake wasn't bad at spotting one. That's how, without any other real talent for the game, he survived at the poker table. If someone tried to bully him on the turn and the river card, Shake could usually flip that double-barrel bluff around and pull the trigger.

But Cambodians. Shake wasn't sure that a smile here meant what it meant back home. He didn't know what the guy's smile was really telling him.

"He says no," Mitch said. "Nothing else. He says he's telling you everything he knows."

Shake decided to believe him. The *tuk-tuk* driver waited to see if Shake had any more questions. He did, but none the guy would be able to answer. Now that Shake knew for sure that someone had grabbed Lexy, the burning question was *why*? In other words, had what happened to Lexy been a hit or a straight grab?

Shake gave the *tuk-tuk* driver five bucks for his trouble. His mind started working.

Maybe he was ignoring the evidence because he wanted Lexy to be alive, but it seemed to him that a straight grab made the most sense here. A hit, why not do it right in the temple parking lot? If you wanted to take out someone as dangerously connected as Lexy, you'd do it the first chance you got, right? You wouldn't run the risk of moving her somewhere else first—you'd pull the trigger and start running before the shell casings hit the ground.

Mitch was frowning. "This is really dodgy. What do you think happened? We should call the police."

Shake remembered what Quinn had told him about the Cambodian police.

"Do you trust them?" he asked her. "The cops?"

She nodded uncertainly. "Well . . ."

"Yeah."

"I don't understand. I've never heard of anything like this happening to a tourist. Who would do something like this?"

That was the question, Shake thought.

Babikian, maybe. He was the obvious choice, since the history of organized crime was the history of the number-two guy making a move on number one. Shake couldn't see it, though, Babikian ordering a hit or a kidnapping. The real power in the Armenian outfit was behind the throne—the Board, a group of old, old-school guys who picked the *pakhan* and didn't stand for any shenanigans. It was highly unlikely that Babikian would run the risk of pissing them off. Even Lexy handled them with care.

The Russians? La Eme? They were the only two organizations in Los Angeles with the same juice, ambitions, and lethal reach as the Armenians. But the Russians were more business partners than rivals—Lexy had helped make them a lot of money over the years—and La Eme's interests were completely separate from Lexy's. Neither outfit, as far as Shake knew, had any reason to stir up the status quo.

That left . . . who? A small-time crew trying to make a name for itself? A wildcatter? Shake knew there were a couple of those out there, highly skilled and highly selective professional kidnappers who spent months picking a target and planning, who pulled down

$10, $20 million per job. But why would a professional kidnapper pick a hard target like Alexandra Ilandryan, when you could walk down the street in Hong Kong or Manhattan and bump into a dozen real-estate or hedge-fund tycoons?

"I don't know who would do something like this," Shake said.

One thing was for sure, he decided. Whoever had kidnapped Lexy either knew exactly what they were doing or they really, really didn't.

Chapter Fourteen

Bjorn told French to meet him at the open-air café across from the Old Market. He was, as usual, late. French knocked back a few bottom-rail gin and tonics while he waited and watched heat-stunned American tourists in L.L. Bean wrinkle-free travel gear stagger through the maze of stalls. Finally, at half past seven, a smoke-colored Porsche 911 pulled up to the curb. The GT3 coupe that Bjorn drove retailed for $150,000. French had looked it up.

Bjorn breezed into the café. This evening he was wearing a shawl-collared cardigan that came to his knees and a knit beanie that was more turban than hat. The outfit would have made most dudes look like Gloria Swanson in *Sunset Boulevard,* but Bjorn pulled it off. He was half Khmer and half Swedish, with the best features of both: glossy black hair and cheekbones from Dad, eyes as clear as an arctic fjord from Mom. He'd been named after both a Swedish tennis star and a famous Khmer singer of the 1950s. His full name was Khat Bjorn Borg Sinn Sisamouth.

"Frennnnch," Bjorn said, drawing it out. He spoke flawless surf-hipster American, thanks to an elite boarding-school education at Thacher in the Ojai Valley. "What's bumpin', *m'ijo?*"

His default expression was the shit-eating grin to end all shit-eating grins, as if he'd just had sex with two women at the same time. Which, French knew, was a distinct possibility. The first time he saw Bjorn, at a bar in the French Quarter called the Foreign Correspondents' Club, he'd been feeding cocktail olives to a pair of Australian bikini models.

French stood. Bjorn gave him a bro hug and slid into the booth.

"What are you drinking?" Bjorn asked. Before French could answer, Bjorn called over the waitress. "You have that Jura I like? Yeah? Awesome balls. Bring me a double, ice on the side. And some nibbles for me and my boy."

Bjorn's drink of choice was a thirty-year-old scotch, from a remote island in the Inner Hebrides, that sold for six hundred dollars a bottle. French had looked that up, too.

"So, Bjorn," French said. "We need to—"

"One minute, dude. I gotta take a leak."

He slid back out of the booth, the tail of his cardigan flowing after him. Bjorn spent more time in the men's room than anyone French had ever met. French had discovered, eventually, that Bjorn wasn't (just) doing blow in there. He was primping, styling, gazing upon his own reflection in the mirror.

That night at the Foreign Correspondents' Club, French and Bjorn had struck up a conversation when the two bikini models stepped out onto the balcony to share a joint.

"So, dude," Bjorn had asked French. "What's your story? What brings you to our fair city?"

This wasn't long after French had arrived in Cambodia, when Siem Reap, with its romantically seedy allure, still seemed rich with possibility.

"I'm here," French had said, lifting his glass, "for adventure."

Bjorn gave him a fist bump. "Bingo is his name-o."

They hit it off. French discovered that Bjorn, only twenty-five years old, owned two of the hottest restaurants in Siem Reap. When the bikini models returned from the balcony, Bjorn gave French his number.

"I've got to bone out right now, but hit me up next week," Bjorn had said. "We'll get a drink and kick it."

And so they did. Kicking it became a more or less regular thing. Eventually French learned the full extent of Bjorn's illicit, and highly lucrative, activities.

"How can I get in on that?" French had joked more than once. And then, a couple of weeks ago, Bjorn had glanced around the bar where they were drinking, to make sure no one was eavesdropping.

"So heads up," he'd whispered to French, "I might have an opportunity for you."

"What kind of an opportunity?" French said.

Bjorn explained that he had a "slant" on a "primo" score. Bjorn had found out about a rich ("as fuck") female American tourist staying alone at a small hotel on Wat Nhek. No security, no bodyguards. Bjorn and French would split the ransom fifty-fifty.

"The . . . *what*?" French said. "The *ransom*? You mean you're talking about a—"

"Easy," Bjorn said. "Keep it wolf, dude. Be cool."

French couldn't believe what Bjorn was proposing. He lowered his voice to a whisper.

"You want me to help you with a *kidnapping*?" he said.

"Dude," Bjorn said, "it's a layup. Trust me, I've done it before. It's not like in the movies. This is *Cambodia*. This kind of shit is a day at the office. No fuss, no muss and some nice, quick bank."

"It's absurd," French had said, to himself as much as to Bjorn. It *was* absurd, wasn't it? And then, just for the hell of it, he asked, "How much bank, exactly?"

"Two million."

French licked his lips and played it cool. "Two million dollars."

"Yeah. We rake four million and cut it five-oh five-oh."

Two million *each*? French licked his lips again. "Huh," he said.

"But we snooze, we lose. There's a clock on this one. We have to jump, pronto. Like, *yesterday*." Bjorn grinned his shit-eating grin. "So you down for it, my brother?"

It was completely absurd, the thought of helping Bjorn with a kidnapping. A *kidnapping*. What had stopped French from telling Bjorn no that night? A thousand times no! French even now wasn't entirely sure. He supposed it had been the thought of what awaited him, the life he'd be forced to resume, if he turned the offer down. Siem Reap was cheap by Western standards, but French was broke by any standard. He could borrow money and return to the United States, but . . . return to *what*, exactly? A shitty apartment in Queens or Oakland. The constant scramble for adjunct courses at bad community colleges. The rejection letters from publishers. The smirks and scowls of former colleagues when they spotted him skulking around at MLA.

French couldn't live that life again. He refused to do it.

Bjorn returned, now, from the men's room. He took a sip of his scotch.

"So everything's coolio back at the ranch?" he said.

"Actually, no," French said. He'd rehearsed his speech on the way over. He'd rehearsed the calm but stern look he gave Bjorn now. "We've been waiting five days, Bjorn. Almost six, now. There needs to be . . . I feel very strongly there needs to be movement. We have to move ahead with the plan. Not soon, *now*."

Bjorn reached for the plate of nem chian that the waitress had brought. He nodded.

"Real talk," he said.

"If we don't move ahead now—"

"Make the call. Yeah. Let's get this party started."

"Make the call?" On the way into town, French had worked up

a detailed and thorough case. He hadn't expected Bjorn to agree before he had a chance to present opening arguments.

"Go for it," Bjorn said. "Chick's ripe now. Her *people* are ripe. Trust me, dude, her people are flipping out by now."

"Ah," French said.

"Right? They'll be all, 'Four million? No problem!' You know what I'm saying? We've softened up the beaches."

French wanted to laugh. Of course Bjorn knew what he was doing. Because of the time that had passed, their girl's family would be frantic, desperate, malleable. French had let Ramos get into his head. French was going to take great pleasure, when he got back to the house, in telling Ramos, *I told you so.*

"Right," French said. "I see."

"Keep the first call short. Keep the leash tight, you feel me? Don't even mention the numbers. Tell them you'll hit them up again later." Bjorn motioned for the waitress to bring him another scotch. He slid the plate of nem chian toward French. "Dude, get in on this. These are the best spring rolls in Cambodia. Maybe not the best. You want another drink?"

"Anyway, just so I understand," French said, "when I call, I should . . ."

But Bjorn was already sliding out of the booth again.

"Be right back," he said. "Gotta take a leak."

"I TOLD YOU SO," French said. Ramos sat at the kitchen table, cleaning his gun. French waited. "Did you hear me?"

"Ripe?" Ramos said.

"Primed. Teed up. Her family must be worried sick by now. They'll pay the ransom right away, without any argument. You see?"

"Okay."

"It's an astute psychological strategy." French couldn't find his mask. He checked the top of the fridge. There it was. "I thought you'd be happier that things are moving forward now."

Ramos looked up at him. "Where you going?"

"Upstairs."

"Upstairs."

French wondered how much Buddha Ramos had burned while French was in town, or if he was just being purposefully dense. French had taught students like that.

"I'm going upstairs to get a phone number from our girl," French said. "And the name of a person to call. So we can move forward and make the ransom call?"

"She's not a girl," Ramos said.

"What?"

"She's not a girl."

French sighed. "Yes, I know. She's a *woman*. It's just a figure of speech, Mason. I'll try to be more politically correct."

"She's merchandise," Ramos said. He went back to the oily pieces of his gun. "Don't forget."

FRENCH KNOCKED AND entered. Veronica was sitting with her back against the wall, gazing up at the narrow window across the room. The moon was fat and full tonight, and the light that filled the attic gave every surface a sharp, silvery edge.

"Good evening, Veronica," French said. "I hope I'm not disturbing you."

She smiled, shyly. "No."

French smiled back, but . . . the stupid mask. It was a serious annoyance. He wished he could ditch it. How likely was it, really, that the authorities would track him down on the basis of some crude, sketch-artist likeness? Twenty-four hours after Veronica's husband or family paid up, French would be ten thousand miles away from Cambodia, lost in the anonymous urban sprawl of São Paulo or Buenos Aires.

"Glad to hear it." He pulled the metal folding chair closer to her bed and sat down. "How was dinner?"

"Fine."

But French saw the flicker of a frown. "What is it?" he said.

"It is nothing."

She had a touch of an accent and a charmingly formal aversion to contractions. French guessed she might be from Eastern Europe originally, maybe Russia. Though Wagenseller—that was a German name, probably.

"You can tell me," he said.

She hesitated. "Your partner. He frightens me."

Now French frowned. Fucking Ramos. "What did he say to you? Did he . . . he's treated you with courtesy, right?"

"Yes, of course. And no, he says nothing to me. But . . . his way he looks at me. No. I will say it is his way he looks *through* me."

French relaxed. He knew that look. "Don't worry. You get used to it. And he's not my partner, by the way. He works for me, so you have nothing to worry about. He's my . . . associate. That look you're talking about. Do you know those giant stone bodhisattva faces at Prasat Bayon, the ones with the empty eyes? He reminds me of one of those."

Her laugh was like fingers dancing across the keys of a piano.

God, she was a total babe. After six days of confinement, six days without a proper shower or even a brush for her hair, Veronica managed somehow to look even *more* lovely than she had that first morning outside Banteay Srei.

French preferred his women fresh from the oven, in their late teens and twenties, shiny and smooth and rosy-cheeked. What man, if he was being honest, didn't? But there was something about Veronica, a vulnerability in her eyes, that he found deeply attractive.

"So you were telling me earlier about your life in San Francisco," French said. "How did you end up with your own venture-capital firm?"

"Tell me first. How you became a professor in the university."

French sighed. "That. Well. I suppose you could call that an accident of sorts."

"An accident?"

"I published a novel when I was only twenty-two. With one of the big houses. My book was . . . I'll just say that one critic, a major one, called me the voice of my generation. I had such ambition. So many . . . *plans.* You know? But then I sort of . . . I lost the thread."

"The thread?"

"Of the story. The story of my life."

"The future is seldom what we expect it will be."

"Exactly. We create narratives about ourselves. *For* ourselves. We believe in them deeply, and then—*whoops!* We discover we're imprisoned in an entirely *different* narrative, one we didn't even choose for ourselves. We think, 'Hold on! This isn't right. Promises were made!'"

She mused. French sensed in her a kindred spirit, a woman who at some point in her life had found herself lost in the dark woods.

"Have you read Dante's *Inferno*? There's a line at the beginning. It's much more evocative in the Italian, but basically it says . . ." French caught the flicker of another frown. Veronica was easy to read. "What's wrong?"

"May I ask a favor?"

"Of course."

"It has been so long since I have seen the sky, or smelled the breeze. May I? For a few moments only? Please." And then she looked down quickly, to hide what French suspected was a tear.

He didn't see the harm of letting her look out the window. Ramos would probably flip if he found out. But he wouldn't find out, and screw him anyway.

"If you call out or try to attract attention," French warned her, "you should know we're far from civilization. No one will hear you, and that'll be the end of it."

"I will not call out." She looked up at him earnestly again. "You have my word."

"Okay, then."

He unshackled her from the chain and led her to the window. She had to stand on her toes to see out.

"The moon," she said.

"Beautiful, isn't it? Though not much of a view from here, I'm afraid."

She took a deep breath. "This mountain. To the north?"

"The west."

"Do you know how it is named?"

It wasn't much of a mountain, really just a jungle-covered hillock a mile or so from the house.

"I think the locals call it 'Baksaei.' The Bird. Because do you see?"

He pointed. The summit was oddly shaped, like the curved beak of a parrot.

"Yes, I see," she said.

Her arm brushed his. French felt strangely nervous, like he was fifteen years old again, at a sophomore mixer in the school cafeteria, about to ask Katie Duffy—the blond ice goddess of North Shore Country Day—to slow-dance.

"What will happen to me now?" Veronica said. "How long will you keep me here?"

French remembered why he was here. He took the ballpoint pen and pad of paper from the inside pocket of his blazer. He remembered with some sheepishness that no, he was not at a sophomore mixer in the school cafeteria.

"I need a telephone number, Veronica," he said. "Someone we can call, someone in your family, so we can . . . negotiate your return. You understand?"

She understood. "I will write it for you, if you will help me."

He held the pad for her while she—awkwardly, because her hands were cuffed—wrote down a number.

"Your husband?" French asked casually. She wasn't wearing a ring, but you never knew.

"No," she said. "An old friend. He will give you what you want."

"Very good. Thank you."

French reached for the pen.

"Wait," she said. She looked up at him. It was almost impossible to tell where the moonlight ended and her otherworldly gray eyes began. "You have a kind heart, I believe."

French liked to believe so. Women often believed so, which was the important thing.

"I try my best," he said.

"So I must ask one more favor."

"What's that?"

"You can see, how uncomfortable this is for me."

She lifted her hands to show him the handcuffs, how raw and red they'd chafed her slender wrists.

"I'm very sorry about that," French said. "I can bring you some lotion tomorrow."

"But tonight. Will you unlock me? For a few moments only?"

"I don't know," French said. Again, though, what was the harm? He gave her a friendly nudge with his elbow. "What's in it for me?"

Veronica picked up on his tone. She gave him a playful poke in the ribs with the ballpoint pen.

"It will be a surprise, perhaps," she said.

French smiled. He reached into his pocket for the key to her handcuffs, then stopped. He could hear the muffled thump of footsteps on the stairs. Ramos. *Shit.*

"Please," Veronica said. "For only one moment."

Ramos rapped on the door.

"You done?" he called. "You get it?"

French grabbed Veronica's elbow and hurried her back to the bed. He looped the greasy chain back through her arms and over the links of the handcuffs. He snapped the padlock shut.

"I'm sorry," he whispered to Veronica. "Next time, I promise."

Chapter Fifteen

Shake decided some leg stretching would do him good, especially after the day—the two days?—he'd had. He asked the Cambodian hippie chick, Mitch, if he could walk back to the Victoria Angkor. She said sure and gave him directions.

"I do remember something oddish, actually," she said as he was about to take off. "It was six nights ago. I remember because six nights ago the moon was a waxing crescent."

Shake realized she was waiting for him to say something, like, *Yeah, of course, the waxing crescent.*

"Yeah, of course," he said. "The waxing crescent."

"Absolute worst time to read past lives. I don't even take appointments, or I'll make a total bodge of it. I had a dream that night. Natalie Wood was in it. The actress? And she was topless. She was topless and had devil horns."

Shake smiled politely. He didn't want to hear about her dream. There was nothing more boring than listening to somebody else's dream.

"Okay," he said.

"There were flames everywhere. I was drinking a martini, so I don't think it was supposed to be, like, hell. And Rock Hudson was there, too, I think?"

"Interesting," Shake said. "But what about the oddish thing that happened that night?"

The lag between transmission and reception was longer than usual. Mitch cocked her head. Her tiny silver dread bells tinkled.

"What do you mean?" she said.

He realized what she was telling him. "Your dream. That's what you were talking about?"

"It had a really insistent energy. That's why I remembered it. It was like the dream was saying, 'Look at me! Pay attention!'"

"I better get going," Shake said.

"I'm not saying it means anything. My dream. A lot of times dreams *don't* mean anything. But you never know."

"You never know."

Shake headed back to the hotel. After a couple of left turns, the neighborhood began to change. The streetlights disappeared, and the streets were in rougher shape, littered with big chunks of crumbled asphalt and puddles of oily water. The signs were in Khmer, not English, and the shops sold motorcycle chains and used teakettles, not paintings of Angkor Wat at sunset.

A guy stacking charcoal bricks looked at Shake. Not unfriendly, but wondering. Shake shrugged. *You and me both,* he thought.

Shake walked until he reached a cluster of the big Dr. Seuss bells he'd seen earlier. *Stupas,* he remembered. These were less festive than the other ones, the paint on the concrete peeling and faded. The place made Shake think of the cemeteries in New Orleans and Cairo, where the dead rested aboveground and not under it. Maybe it was the same here.

He followed, as Mitch had told him to do, a gravel path that led between the stupas. The moon was full, but the stupas were seven, maybe eight feet tall and blocked most of the light. Shake was just starting to think how this would be a good spot to get jumped when he heard, behind him, the scuff of footsteps.

He turned and saw, trotting toward him, two wiry Cambodian guys with big, bright smiles. *Shit.* Shake silently apologized to the hippie chick for not taking her diagnosis of his aura more seriously.

The first guy came in low, swinging at Shake's knee with what looked like a sawed-off piece of rebar. Shake dodged, and the rebar just clipped him. Here came the second guy, with a flying kick that nailed Shake in the sternum. The guy's feet were bare, but—mother of God—it was like getting hit with a shotgun blast. Shake went down hard, barely able to breathe.

The first guy kicked Shake in the ribs. Shake scooped up a handful of gravel and whipped it at him. The guy cursed and kicked Shake in the stomach. That took care of whatever air Shake had left in his lungs.

The first guy said something to the second guy in Khmer. The second guy cocked his bare foot back again, aiming for Shake's face. Shake could see the grime beneath the yellow toenails.

And then the foot was gone. The guy was gone. Shake heard a surprised grunt. He struggled up onto an elbow in time to see the guy with the yellow toenails smack face-first into a concrete stupa.

Dikran stood where the guy had been a second before. He hitched up the pants of his purple velour tracksuit and rolled his shoulders, getting loose.

Shake had never imagined a scenario where he'd be glad to see the dumb, murderous beast, but here, against all odds, it was.

The first Cambodian guy was just as surprised to see Dikran. He took a step backward and sized Dikran up. He took another step backward.

Dikran glanced over to see if the second guy had any fight left in him. Didn't look like it. His face had left a bloody smear on the side of the stupa, and he was crawling away as fast as he could.

"You make a mistake," the first guy said in English, so quietly that Shake wasn't sure if he was talking to Dikran or himself.

Dikran cupped a hand to his ear. "What do you say?"

The first guy feinted once, feinted twice, and then fired a kick at Dikran's head. The kick was impressive, just a snap and a blur, but Dikran caught the guy's foot as nonchalantly as you'd pluck dandelion fluff out of the air. He stomped on the guy's other foot, pinning it to the ground, then started to pull him apart like a wishbone.

The guy screamed. Shake winced. Dikran dropped the guy, who tried to stand but collapsed instead. He crawled away after his partner, dragging himself off into the darkness.

Shake climbed to his feet. His sternum ached, and he still couldn't breathe very well. All in all, though, it could have been worse. It would have been a *lot* worse, he knew, if Dikran hadn't shown up.

"You followed me from the hotel?" he asked Dikran.

"Yes," Dikran said. "Because I trust you no percent."

Shake had a feeling that the guys who'd jumped him weren't your garden-variety muggers. Best guess, they worked for Quinn's buddy Ouch. Who, as Shake had feared, wasn't as much of a buddy as Quinn thought he was.

"Not that I'm looking a gift horse in the mouth," he told Dikran, "but you could have stepped in a little sooner, you know."

"And I am right. You betray me."

"I didn't betray you. I followed a couple of leads on my own. If you think—"

Dikran covered the ground between them in two long strides and clamped a hand around Shake's neck. He lifted Shake onto his toes.

"Dikran," Shake said. Or tried to say. Dikran's grip was tight, getting tighter.

"Do you remember what I tell you will happen?" Dikran said. "If you betray me?"

Shake dug a hand into his front pocket and discovered that the muggers had missed Lexy's cross. Thank God. Shake pulled out the cross and held it up.

Dikran's big bald head turned. He stared for a second, then snatched the cross away and dropped Shake.

"How do you have this?" he said. "The cross of her *tatik*? Why do you not tell me sooner, stupid cockjob?"

"I don't know." Shake felt like his throat was stuffed with sand and broken glass. "Maybe because you were too busy trying to strangle me?"

"Do you find her?"

"No."

Dikran scoffed. "You think I try to strangle you? If I try to strangle you, I don't try. You are dead already. Take my word from me."

"I didn't find her, but that's from the hotel where she's been staying."

Shake told Dikran what the *tuk-tuk* driver had said. He wasn't sure how Dikran would take the news that Lexy had been kidnapped. He was an unstable compound in the best of circumstances. Shake felt like Roy Scheider in that one movie from the seventies, maneuvering a truck loaded with nitroglycerin across a rickety jungle bridge.

"You lie," Dikran said.

"I'm telling you what the driver said. He said some sketchy foreign guy paid him twenty bucks to take off and leave Lexy behind."

Dikran grabbed Shake by the throat again and slammed him against a stupa.

"You lie," he said.

He slammed Shake against the stupa again, even harder. Shake didn't see stars, but he heard the Bee Gees begin to sing the chorus of "To Love Somebody."

Dikran released his grip on Shake and dumped him next to the stupa. He fumbled frantically in his tracksuit pants and pulled out his phone. "To Love Somebody," Shake realized, was Dikran's ringtone.

"It is not her," Dikran said, scowling at the caller ID. He clicked the talk button. "Who are you? Why do you want me?"

Shake tilted his head back against the stupa and closed his eyes. He took a deep, deep breath. After a few seconds, he opened his eyes. Normally Dikran was a noisy breather, grunting and panting like the first prehistoric fish that dragged itself up onto land. This was the first time Shake had ever heard him go completely silent.

Shake scrambled to his feet. "Give it to me," he said.

He grabbed the phone away from Dikran and pressed it to his ear.

"Did you hear me?" a man's voice on the other end of the line said.

"Say it again," Shake said. "I've got a bad connection."

"We have your friend," the man said. "Do exactly as I say, or she dies."

Chapter Sixteen

Is she all right?" Shake said into Dikran's phone.

"She's fine," Lexy's kidnapper said. An American accent. "She hasn't been harmed. Now, listen to me carefully."

He sounded nervous, which made two of them. Shake reminded himself of the most important rule: stay cool.

Shake moved back down the gravel path, trying to clear the stupas and get a better cell phone signal. Dikran followed right behind, wild-eyed.

"No problem," Shake told the kidnapper. "You're the one in charge here."

"That's right. Yes."

Shake reached the street. He found a spot, in front of something called Your Bright Future International School, where Dikran's phone pulled down two out of five bars. Better than nothing.

Shake waited. "I'm listening," he said finally.

"What?"

"You said to listen to you carefully."

"Yes. If you ever want to see her alive again, you'll do precisely as I say. Do you understand?"

There was something buttoned-up about the way the guy spoke. *You'll do precisely as I say.* Like he should have an English accent but didn't.

"Yeah," Shake said. "I got that."

Dikran looked like he was about to make a lunge for the phone. Shake gave him a warning glare. Dikran backed off. He fished around for his bottle of chill pills, shook a couple into his hand, and swallowed them.

"Don't involve the authorities," the kidnapper said.

The guy seemed to be reading a form letter he'd downloaded from the Internet. The authorities? He'd kidnapped the *pakhan* of the Armenian mob. Did he really think her people would ever involve the authorities?

"No authorities," Shake said. "What do you want?"

"I'll be in touch later, with additional details. That's all for now."

"Hold on. We're not done yet."

"I beg your pardon?"

Shake had never negotiated with a kidnapper before, but he'd been involved in plenty of standoffs. Sometimes you had to back down, but you never wanted to bend over.

"I said we're not done yet. I need to know she's all right. I need to know she's alive."

Dikran looked like he was about to have a heart attack. He punched the wall of Your Bright Future International School and then downed another handful of chill pills.

"No," the kidnapper said. "That's not . . . I told you. I'll be in touch when—"

"You need to give me proof she's alive, or all this is just a waste of time." Shake kept his voice relaxed, conversational, like they were a couple of guys just shooting the shit, talking cars or baseball. "You're wasting my time, I'm wasting your time. Nobody wants that."

Static again. It stretched on and on. Shake worried that he'd pushed too hard, too far.

"Fine," the kidnapper said.

"Good. Okay." Shake realized he was sweating through his shirt. "Now we're making progress here."

"I'll text you a photo of her."

"That's not good enough. I want to talk to her. I want to see her."

"You want to . . . what? No. That's unreasonable."

Sure it was, but Shake was curious to see how far the guy would go. He was curious to see if the guy would bend over.

"You'd do the same," Shake said. "If you were in my shoes."

"I told you, she's perfectly fine."

Shake tried to remember what it was called, when Gina talked to her friend Lucy in Cartagena. Gina could see Lucy right there on her laptop screen. Lucy would show off the shoes she'd just bought or the new tattoo on the inside of her wrist.

"So prove it," he said. "We can do it with the computer. With the video-talk thing."

"Zoom?"

That was it. Zoom. "Three minutes. That's all I'm asking for."

Silence. Then: "I'll call you in twenty-four hours with further details."

The call went dead.

Dikran had been breathing down Shake's neck. Now he grabbed Shake's arm and spun him around.

"Tell me," he said. "Does she live still? Will they show her to us?"

"I don't know," Shake said. He was wondering why the kidnappers had contacted Dikran and not Babikian. "We'll know in twenty-four hours."

Dikran cupped Lexy's cross in his palm and stared down at it.

"She is *pakhan*!" he said. "Who would do this thing?"

That was still the question. "I don't know."

"When I find these men, how will I kill them? Which small bone will I break first? How slow will I . . ."

Dikran's voice trailed off. His eyes got misty. At first Shake thought he was just savoring it, the vision of the pain he planned to inflict on Lexy's kidnappers. But then Shake saw the sweat beading along Dikran's brow, the flush of pink in his cheeks.

"How many pills did you take?" Shake asked.

Dikran began to sway a little—side to side, front to back. Shake slapped the bottle of pills out of his hand before he could pour more of them into his mouth.

"I feel very relax," Dikran said.

"Get it together."

"Hello."

Shit. "Dikran, look at me."

A minute before, the street had been deserted. Now, though, Shake saw a Cambodian cop down on the corner, watching them stone-faced from beneath the brim of his peaked cap.

"We have to get out of here," Shake said.

He looped Dikran's arm around his neck. When Dikran leaned into him, 280 pounds of deadweight, Shake staggered and they both almost went down.

"I am wrong," Dikran said. "You do not betray me."

Now there were two cops. Shake wondered if anyone in Siem Reap had ever been mugged and arrested on the same night.

"Walk," he said.

"You are brother of my blood. Do I ever tell you this?"

"One step at a time."

One slow step at a time, they headed up the street, away from the cops. Shake's knees started to burn from the strain of holding Dikran upright, and his shoulder felt like it was being gradually dislocated. He tried not to think about his old buddy Whelan, who years ago had been crushed to death beneath a boosted Corvette when a jack failed.

Dikran was trying to pat Shake's head but kept missing.

"You are blood of my brother forever."

"Great."

"We will save her. Yes? Tell me this, and I will believe you."

When they got to the intersection, Shake saw a *tuk-tuk* headed their way. He waved it down.

"We'll save her," he said, and tried his best to believe it himself.

Chapter Seventeen

Shake's head hit the pillow and he was out, just like that. He didn't wake until a little after dawn, with a spooky mist steaming up off the river and the sun just a weak pulse on the horizon. A few minutes later, his phone rang. Gina.

"So what's up, buttercup?" she said. "How's Cambodia working out for you?"

"Fine." He decided not to mention that he'd already been mugged in a Buddhist cemetery and that Dikran had tried to strangle him. He told himself he didn't want to worry her. "Everything's fine so far."

"You're such a bad liar."

He wasn't, not really. Just compared to Gina.

"Do you know people sell birds here?" he said. "Live birds, I mean. You buy them so you can set them free. It's good for your karma."

"Don't try to change the subject."

"Someone grabbed Lexy."

"Kidnapped her? Are you serious?"

"I wish I wasn't."

Silence. Shake knew that Gina was tapping two fingers against her lips.

"Who in the world would be crazy enough to kidnap her?" she said.

"That's what we've been asking ourselves."

"Well. What's that saying?"

"You reap what you sow?"

"Or karma's a bitch when you're a bitch like Lexy. That works, too. When will you be home?"

"Be home?" Shake said.

He waited. The line had gone dead. He called her back.

"I've got pretty good reception," he said. "Where are you?"

"I'm right here."

He could hear the anger in her voice, each word like the sound a cleaver made when it snapped through bone.

"Did you just hang up on me?" he said.

She hung up on him again. He called back.

"Do you need me to explain why I just hung up on you?" she said.

"No." Shake had figured it out. "Listen . . ."

"If it's a kidnapping, let the stupid Armenians deal with it!"

Shake would love nothing better.

"It's not that simple, unfortunately," Shake said. "If . . . hello?" He called Gina back. "Stop hanging up on me, please."

"I thought we were finished with shit like this," Gina said. "Isn't that why we moved to Indiana? To be finished with shit like this?"

"We are finished with shit like this. This is . . . an exception."

"Really? An exception? That's the leg you want to stand on right now?"

Someone began pounding on the door of Shake's room. Shake didn't have to guess who it was.

"Hello?" Gina said. "Did you hang up on me? Oh, my God."

"I'm here."

The pounding on Shake's door continued.

"Are you wake yet, asswipe?" Dikran bellowed. "Open the door now, or I will break it with your head."

Shake guessed the effect of Dikran's chill pills had worn off.

"Can I call you back?" he asked Gina.

"Oh, my God," she said, and hung up on him again.

Shake sighed and opened the door. Dikran shoved past him.

"Why do you sleep, stupid cockjob?" Dikran said.

"I thought I was brother of your blood."

Dikran looked like he'd just been given a surprise colonoscopy. "What do you say?"

"Brother of your blood forever. That's what you told me."

"No. Never!" He stalked to the other side of the room and then back again. He was wearing Lexy's cross around his neck. "It is Babikian. The snake. He does this to her."

"I don't think so," Shake said.

"Yes! You are blind."

"The board Lexy reports to. The board or whatever you call it."

Dikran eyed Shake suspiciously. "The *khorhurdy*. What does this matter?"

"Those old guys wouldn't be happy if Babikian pulled something like this without their go-ahead, would they? They'd come down on him hard."

"Ha! He would be puddle of grease. He would bleed from every—"

Dikran stopped to think. It was like watching a cruise ship turn around.

"You see?" Shake said.

"Heh."

"So I don't think Babikian would try to pull something like this."

"But maybe he thinks they will never find out. The *khorhurdy*. He is—"

"A snake. I got it. But would he risk his own ass like that?"

"What do you know?"

"I'm asking you."

The cruise ship continued to turn. Slowly, slowly.

"You are right. He is a coward. He is a . . . *accountant*." Dikran spit out that last word like it was even worse to be an accountant than a snake. "But . . . but . . ."

"I know," Shake said. "We still can't trust him. Lexy doesn't trust him. That's why she convinced the kidnappers to call *you*, not him."

Because she understood that if Babikian found out about the kidnapping, if he took charge of negotiations, he'd have a juicy and relatively risk-free opportunity to grab power. All Babikian would have to do, really, was nothing. Talk the talk, let the clock run out on Lexy's life, and move into the corner office. Even a coward, even an *accountant*, would be tempted by that play.

"Babikian must not find out," Dikran said.

"That's right. Now, go back to your room, get some rest. There's nothing we can do until the people who grabbed her call back tonight."

"No. I wait where you are in my eyes."

Fucking hell, Shake thought. "You're not staying here for the next twelve hours. Go back to your room. Go downstairs and get breakfast. I have to call my wife back."

Dikran ignored Shake. He pulled open the sliding door and stepped onto the balcony. Shake gave up. He went into the bathroom and brushed his teeth. When he finished, Dikran was still gazing out over the park.

"This life you live now, in Indiana," he said. "Is boring, yes? House. Cat. Wife. Go to job. Come home from job."

"I don't have a cat."

"Every day is the same day. No thrill."

"Like getting jumped and kicked in the chest in Cambodia is a thrill?"

Dikran grunted. He fingered Lexy's cross pensively. "I would have a cat," he said. "Maybe two cats, different color each one."

Shake didn't know what to say to that. "No one's stopping you," he said.

"There are prostitutes in Indiana?"

"Please get out of here and leave me alone."

"Many birds this morning," Dikran said. "Flying home to their trees. Come see."

"Those are bats."

"Heh?"

"They're bats, not birds."

Dikran stepped back inside and slammed the sliding door so hard the glass rattled. He yanked the drapes shut.

"Fucking place," he said.

There was a knock. Dikran moved toward the door, but Shake cut him off and checked the peephole. In the hallway stood a hotel bellhop. Shake opened the door.

"Hello, monsieur," the bellhop said. "I have a message for you, please."

The bellhop presented, with both hands, a business card. Dikran hip-checked Shake out of the way and snatched the card. Shake grabbed it back. Embossed on one side of the card was a single word:

OUCH.

Quinn's buddy. Shake flipped the card over. On the other side, someone had scribbled a message by hand:

"Six-thirty p.m. Friendly Fireplace."

"You know what this is?" Shake asked the bellhop.

The bellhop nodded. "Yes. I will tell you where, monsieur. I will give you the address."

Shake ran a thumb along the edge of the business card. Why did Ouch want to meet with him, after everything that had gone down last night? Shake could see a couple of possibilities. Either Ouch had changed his mind and decided to help Shake or he was planning to kill Shake himself and dump his body in the river.

Dikran was glaring at the card. "What is this?" he said.

"A gamble," Shake said.

Chapter Eighteen

Ramos didn't mind the mornings. Mornings in Cambodia were all right. It was the rest of the day that put him on edge. When the heat was like a plastic bag over your head and your sweat stank like rotten fruit.

Nights were the worst. At night Ramos always felt like someone was creeping up on him, breathing down his neck, even when the street was empty. Cambodians believed in all kinds of crazy shit. Demons, spirits. Maybe the world was like a mirror and over here on this side the crazy shit was real.

This morning Ramos got up early, before French was awake, and drove the Mercedes into town for a massage. His favorite girl was still on the clock. She was his favorite girl because she liked it rough.

"Let's go," he said. He didn't know if the girl spoke English or not, but she figured out what he meant and followed him to one of the little rooms in back.

The girl beat the shit out of him. She used her elbows, her knees, her feet. The other girls didn't know how to give a real Thai massage. They didn't get that a real Thai massage was supposed to hurt.

Ramos tipped her good. His mother had cleaned rooms at a hotel on the Sunset Strip. If some rich *pendejo* didn't tip, the family didn't eat.

When he got back to the house, French was still asleep. Ramos poured himself a little whiskey and sat at the kitchen table, in a wooden chair that creaked whenever he shifted his weight. The wallpaper in the kitchen was a pale green and a dark yellow like mustard. It was decorated with drawings and words both. The drawings were skillets and dishes and what Ramos thought must be a meat or a coffee grinder. The words were words like "Fish," "Spaghetti," and "Soufflé." Each word was in a fancy kind of printing, but the fancy printing was different for each word. "Fish" had a lot of curlicues. "Spaghetti" had letters that looked like they were dancing. "Soufflé" was cartoon balloons. It was like someone had made wallpaper by cutting words and pictures out of different books and magazines.

"What are you doing, Mason?"

Ramos looked up. French was awake. Yawning.

"Nothing," Ramos said.

"You're just sitting there staring at the wall. You realize that, don't you?" French laughed and hit the Jameson. "Oh, my God, you remind me *exactly* of Bartleby the Scrivener."

"Who?"

Scrivener. Ramos didn't know what that was. His first fall, at Salinas Valley, there'd been a punk on the block everyone called the Screamer. El Chillón.

"Bartleby is the title character in a short story by Herman Melville. He's completely passive, an empty vessel staring at the wall all day. All he ever says is, 'I would prefer not to.' My very first year of teaching, I assigned that story to my freshman lit class. I can't believe I'm just now making the connection."

French used to be a college teacher. He talked about it all the time. He said all the college girls had been hot for him. One time,

French said, a college girl had come to his office after class, closed the door, and dropped her dress without saying a word.

"When are you meeting him tonight?" Ramos said.

"Seven."

The once or twice Ramos had been on a college campus, the girls were wearing jeans, not dresses. Jeans or sweatpants. Sweatpants with a word like "Juicy" or "Pink" or "Bruins" written on the butt. The girls had smiled at Ramos as they walked past, even though they didn't know him or anything about him. A couple of them said hi. Because it was a college campus, Ramos guessed. A college campus was like a petting zoo.

French fired up a joint. He took a pull and handed it to Ramos.

"I think it went well last night," he said. "Don't you?"

"What?"

"Mason. The *call*. I kept them on their heels, I think."

"They were wearing sweatpants," Ramos said. "Sweatpants and jeans."

French was unwrapping the croissants Ramos had brought back from town. He stopped to look up at Ramos.

"What?" he said. "Who was wearing sweatpants and jeans?"

"The college girls I saw."

"When? Mason, I'm at a loss here."

He always called Ramos by his first name, like French was the teacher and Ramos was his student. Ramos was still on the fence, how he felt about that.

"I'm going with you," Ramos said. "To the meeting."

"Mason. *Mason*. What have I told you?"

Not much, so far. French said the guy behind the job was connected. That's how the guy knew the woman was rich. They were going to ask for four million. French's end would be one million. Ramos would get half of that, five hundred grand.

That was good money, enough to get Ramos the fuck out of

Cambodia. He didn't know if French knew what he was doing. He didn't know if the guy behind the job knew what he was doing. But Ramos had done jobs for less money with people who he was sure didn't know what they were doing.

A buena hambre no hay pan duro, Ramos's mother always said. When you're hungry, no bread is stale.

"Scores are like family, *carnalito.*" That's what Ramos's brother told him once. "Sometimes you don't get to pick and choose them."

French cut up a mango and put it on a plate. Barely nine o'clock, and already Ramos could feel it starting. The plastic bag over his head, his sweat smelling like sweet, rotten fruit. He stood.

"I'll do it," he said.

"That's all right," French said. "I'll take her breakfast up this morning."

"I'll do it."

Ramos waited until French stepped aside.

"Fine," French said. "For fuck's sake, Mason."

Ramos put on his mask and took the tray up to the attic. The woman watched him. She didn't say a word. It was like she had a mask on, too.

Downstairs, French was still in the kitchen. He was making coffee and studying the chessboard on the counter. A couple of days ago, he'd moved the chessboard from the living room into the kitchen so he could play chess with himself while the coffee brewed.

"Well?" French said.

"Well what?"

"How is she? I want to make sure you're treating her with courtesy."

The chess set that came with the house was a nice one, with polished wood pieces. Ramos had learned to play with chess pieces made from toilet paper, spit, and glue. An old head down for five to ten at Mule Creek had taught him the basics.

"I'm going with you tonight," he told French. "To meet the guy behind the job."

French sighed. He sighed like he did sometimes before he gave a big speech.

"Let me make this as clear as I can, Mason," he said. "The person who is organizing this operation is very influential."

"Connected."

"That's right. Connected. So you can understand, I *need* you to understand, that he has to be careful. He has to take certain precautions. He won't talk to you. He'll talk only to me."

"Okay," Ramos said.

"Okay?"

Ramos went to the drawer next to the sink, where he kept his piece. He made sure there was a round in the chamber. He always did that, ever since thirteen years ago when his brother dry-fired during a stickup and took a shotgun blast to the face.

Ramos tucked his piece in the waistband of his jeans.

Behind French's head the words on the wallpaper were "Chicken," "Fruit," and "Quiche." The drawings were a big fork, a chef's hat, and a teapot.

"He can talk to you," Ramos said. "I'll just listen."

Chapter Nineteen

Saturday night after she talked to Shake, Gina turned off her phone, stuck it in a drawer, and polished off a bottle of red wine. She binge-watched half a season of *The Real Housewives of Somewhere* and just generally luxuriated in her own righteous fury. It was even better, that last part, than a warm bath.

Sunday morning, when she turned her phone back on, she saw that Shake had left four voice mails. A good start, she conceded, but she was still too mad to call him back. She'd give him another day or two to mull over the consequences of his actions.

The weather was perfect, bright and warm, so Gina decided to hit the farmers' market at City Hall. She hoped the walk downtown would do her headache good. Though since when, Gina wondered as she squinted against the morning light, did a single bottle of wine, spread out across the course of a long evening, give her a hangover? She used to be able to party like a rock star. No. She used to be able to party like the whole band.

She strolled over to the farmers' market. She and Shake came here almost every weekend in the summer, to buy fresh squash and soak up the local color. There was an Amish farmer who looked like he'd just ordered Noah to build an ark and a sweet old lady who sang Janis Joplin songs while she played an accordion.

Gina wandered around for a few minutes, then gave in and called Shake back. She got one ring, and then the call went to voice mail, which meant . . . did Shake just check his caller ID and dump her off?

She thought about throwing her phone into the fountain. Instead she just jammed it back into her purse and bought some strawberries from the Amish farmer. All the benches were taken, so she found a place to sit on the steps of City Hall.

"Fucking hell," Gina said.

She ate a strawberry and looked around at the children and the families and the panting dogs, at the earnest college kids handing out flyers for good causes and the experimental dance troupe warming up, at the booths selling heirloom tomatoes and paleo-inspired baked goods.

A few steps down from Gina, a pair of attractive thirtyish women were laughing and sipping smoothies. They wore Lululemon tanks, big sunglasses, Adidas Superstars. If you happened to walk past and didn't know better, you'd think Gina was one of them.

She *was* one of them, she supposed. This was her life now.

And that was cool. That was great. This wasn't like San Francisco, where she'd been bored out of her mind by the woman she'd become. That woman didn't have Shake.

Occasionally, yes, she still thought about her life before San Francisco, before Shake. Gina hadn't loved that life. Well, some of the time she'd loved it—the risk, the rush, the sheer pleasure of never knowing, from one minute to another, what was going to happen next. Anything could happen next! Gina wouldn't have been human if she didn't occasionally miss that.

She was missing it now, she knew, mostly because Shake was off in Cambodia without her. What was it she'd said to him earlier? *I thought we were supposed to be finished with this shit!* Yeah, well, *she* was finished with it. And Gina wasn't completely sure how she felt about that.

At least the Amish strawberries were awesome. Gina ate another one.

"Yo, Ms. C!" A girl in line for the paleo-inspired baked goods waved to Gina and then hurried over. It was Yvette, wearing a T-shirt that said FOUR FINGERS IN THE PINK, ONE IN THE STINK!

"Hi, Yvette."

"Guess what, Ms. C? You know how you're always all up on me about that job I have?"

Slinging cocktails and getting groped by old coots at the skeezy casino on the Kentucky border.

"I'm not all up on you about anything, Yvette," Gina said. "I'm just telling you that you need to be all up on *yourself*."

"Uh-huh. Anyway, Ms. C, I did it! I finally quit! Two days ago. I told my boss I was *out*."

Gina gave her a congratulatory hug. She wanted to say something about the FOUR FINGERS IN THE PINK T-shirt, but hey, Rome wasn't built in a day, was it?

"That's awesome, Yvette!"

They sat and chatted for a while, and then Yvette gave Gina the side-eye.

"Ms. C," Yvette said, "you look like you got some heavy shit on your mind."

"I'm fine, Yvette, but thanks for your concern."

"Well, you know what you tell us, Ms. C." She lifted her chin and did her Gina impression. "'It's hard, but it's not *complicated*.'"

Gina gave her the finger.

"Oh, Ms. C, I forgot! I signed up for that other thing you're always all up on me about."

"The GED? That's awesome, Yvette."

"Well, I'm *gonna* sign up for it, soon as I can make some money. You know what he said? My boss at the casino when I quit? He said I don't get my last check 'cause I didn't give him two weeks' notice."

"I'm sure we can figure something out," Gina said. It only cost a hundred bucks or so for the online GED prep courses, another seventy to take the test itself, and Heads Held High had a special "scholarship" fund for situations just such as this.

On the other hand . . .

Gina looked over at the women in the Lululemon tank tops, chatting and laughing. One of the women noticed Gina. The woman hesitated, then smiled and waved at her. As if to say, *You're one of us, aren't you?*

Not this morning, Gina decided. This morning she was going to take a break from her new self and have some old-fashioned fun.

"You want a muffin, Ms. C?" Yvette said. "My treat."

"What's his name?" Gina said.

"Who?"

"Your boss at the casino. And how much does he owe you?"

THE TERRA SPLENDIDA Hotel and Casino was about two hours east of Bloomington, tucked into a not-so-splendida strip of industrial wasteland on the Indiana side of the Ohio River. It wasn't quite as skeezy as Gina had anticipated, a four-story concrete box with copper-tinted windows that looked like the headquarters of a failing regional health-care network. Maybe, once upon a time, that's what it had been.

The parking lot, at eleven thirty on a Sunday morning, was

almost full. Gina found a spot and thought about how she might take down Yvette's boss. She'd changed into slacks and a tailored blouse before she left Bloomington, which gave her multiple options. Potential investor? Representative from the state gaming board? Trophy wife with a gambling problem? She decided to play it by ear, like she always had.

Inside, she threaded her way past the slot machines and card tables, through the blue haze of smoke and quiet desperation, until she spotted an unmarked door near the back of the casino floor. A big, sweaty bruiser in a too-tight suit stopped her when she tried to open it.

"I'm here to see Dominic," Gina said. She realized she didn't know if that was the boss's first name or his last name. Yvette hadn't said.

"You have an appointment?" the bruiser asked.

"He's not expecting me." An understatement, Gina knew. "Tell him it's an urgent matter and no thanks, I'm not going to explain it first to his big, sweaty bruiser."

The bruiser flushed red. He turned his back to Gina so she couldn't hear what he mumbled into his walkie. Gina looked up at the bubble camera mounted on the ceiling above them and gave it a wave. After a second the bruiser lowered his walkie and jerked his head at an empty pai gow table.

"Wait over there," he said.

Gina took a seat. A few minutes later, the unmarked door opened and another guy in a suit came out. This one, though, had a much nicer suit and was no sweaty bruiser—he was young, lean, and so good-looking that he managed to pull off the scruffy little goatee, the slicked-back hair.

"You're an upgrade," Gina said, standing, "but I'm still not going away until I get Dominic."

The guy smiled at her, amused. It was a good smile. Gina's

mother had called smiles like that, bright and full of confidence, "panty droppers."

"You got him."

"You're the boss?" In Gina's previous life, she'd spent a fair amount of time in casinos, strip clubs, and bars. The dudes in charge tended, as a rule, to be sour old lizards on their second or third marriages and their third or fourth bypass surgeries. When they smiled, you didn't want to drop your panties—you wanted to run and hide.

"I'm the general manager," he said. He held out his hand. "Dominic Price."

Gina shook his hand. "My name's Gina. You're less lizardy than I thought you'd be."

"I try my best. How can I help you, Gina?"

She called an audible and decided that the direct approach, with this guy, might be more fun than coming in sideways.

"I'm with a nonprofit in Bloomington, Heads Held High. We help girls . . . I can't ever remember the official line. Basically, we help girls get their shit together."

"Okay."

"And you stole two hundred and fifty bucks from one of them."

He lifted an eyebrow. "Did I?"

"Give or take."

"What's the girl's name?"

"Yvette Berry."

"Ah." He nodded slowly, like that explained everything. *"Yvette."*

He was really young. Twenty-three or twenty-four, Gina guessed. And *really* good-looking. She wanted to run her finger along his jawline, just to make sure it was real and not made out of marble.

"You should lose that goatee," she said. "It's either passé or cliché, I can't decide which."

He smiled again. "What would I do without you?"

Was he actually trying to flirt with her? Gina wanted to advise him, confidentially, that he wouldn't know what to do *with* her.

"You can't keep Yvette's paycheck just because she didn't give notice," she said. "That's bullshit, and you know it."

"She told you that?"

"She didn't need to, Dominic. I know bullshit when I see it."

"No, I mean she told you that's why I didn't pay her?"

Gina tapped two fingers against her lips, thinking. She recognized that it was just like Yvette, being Yvette, to leave a few important details out of her story.

"He said, she said," Gina said. "Let's not get started."

"Her last day on the job, she got pissed off at a customer and dumped a tray of margaritas on his head. I had to comp his room, his meals, pay for the dry cleaning. And then on her way out of the lot, she clipped our beverage supervisor's Kia. Took off the whole back bumper."

All that, Gina had to admit, was just like Yvette, too.

"Well, that's your problem," she said. "And your beverage supervisor's. He's got insurance, I bet. And oh, please, you comp rooms all the time. That doesn't cost you—"

She stopped, surprised, because Dominic had taken out his money clip. He peeled off three hundred-dollar bills and handed them over.

"Have a drink with me," he said.

"It's not even noon yet."

"I won't tell if you don't."

"How old are you? Twenty-four?"

"Twenty-three."

"And you've been the GM here how long?"

"Let's have a drink and talk about it."

"I just want to know how long you've been the GM," Gina said. "I didn't ask to hear your life story."

He laughed. Gina guessed this was a new experience for him—a woman who could resist those baby blue eyes, the jawline, that smile.

On cue, a couple of cute young bunnies walked slowly past, checking him out. And then they checked out Gina, her shoes and bod and hair, the way women always check out the woman with a guy like him.

He ignored the bunnies. "You're something else," he told Gina. "You know that?"

"Sure do." She held up her hand to show him her wedding ring. "And happily married, for your information."

"I just want to have a drink with you, Gina," he said. "I didn't ask to hear your life story."

Now she laughed. He wasn't bad at the back-and-forth. Most guys this good-looking just stared dumbly at the ball as it bounced past them.

Gina took her phone out. Shake still hadn't called back. She sat down and waved over a cocktail waitress.

"What are we drinking?" she asked Dominic.

"Is this a test?"

"Sure is."

"Four Roses small batch," he told the cocktail waitress. "Neat."

The waitress left. Gina looked around.

"So who owns this joint?" she said.

"A group out of Louisville."

"I see. An organization. An outfit."

He shook his head, amused. "Nothing like that. You've seen too many movies."

No, Gina had seen too much of the world and knew how it

worked. A small casino in flyover country—profitable but not big enough to attract unwanted attention—was a primo place to park ill-gotten gains.

But she didn't care about that, one way or the other.

"So how long?" she said.

"I've been GM for eighteen months."

"You don't want to get stuck somewhere like this. You have to keep moving. Keep moving up."

"What do you have in mind?"

"Nothing. This is just general life advice. I can't hold your hand."

"Go ahead. You can hold my hand."

Gina laughed. He was too much.

No, really, he is *too much,* a quiet but insistently annoying voice in her head said. *All* this *is too much.*

The waitress brought their drinks. Gina took a sip. The bourbon had a nice mellow burn.

"Don't worry," he said. "I plan to."

"Keep moving up?" Gina didn't doubt it. "Who picks the music?"

The song playing on the casino floor was Dwight Yoakam's "A Thousand Miles from Nowhere."

"I pick it," he said. "You like this one?"

"It's all right." Dwight Yoakam was one of Gina's all-time favorites.

"Want to dance? Or is that something else you don't do on Sundays?"

She set her drink down on the pai gow felt and stood. "I have to go," she said.

"Give me your number."

"Nope."

"Let's have dinner tonight. I'll come to Bloomington."

"I'm busy."

"Just business. You can tell me more about your nonprofit. I'm looking for a good cause."

"Ha."

"Meet me on the square at nine. The one by the courthouse, right?"

"Thanks for the drink," she said, and headed for the exit.

Chapter Twenty

A little after six, Shake and Dikran took the elevator downstairs and grabbed one of the *tuk-tuks* waiting outside the hotel. The sun was just starting to go down. As the driver drove them along the edge of the park, Shake saw the bats still hanging from the branches of the trees, fat and heavy like fruit.

He'd been calling Gina back all day. No answer. Either she was pissed at him and asleep, since it was still early in the morning back in Indiana, or she was pissed at him and busy boxing up his clothes and hauling them to the curb. Toss a coin.

Dikran glowered at the endless silent flow of bicycles all around them. Locals pedaling to and from work at the hotels, bars, restaurants.

"What's wrong with you?" Shake said.

"Say it," Dikran said.

"Say what?"

"You are no brother of my blood."

That again. "Give it a rest."

"Say, 'Dikran, I admit this. I am no brother of your blood.'"

"Fine. I am no brother of your blood." Shake waited a beat, until Dikran relaxed. "Even though I did save your life."

"You lie!"

"You would have OD'd if I hadn't stopped you. You'd be a cold, dead Armenian right now."

Dikran rummaged through the pockets of his velour tracksuit. It took him a second to remember that his chill pills were history. "Fuck!"

"You know about the Bushido code, right?" Shake said. He'd learned about the Bushido code from Quinn, back in Belize. "That's what the warriors in Japan lived by, the samurai. I save your life, you're in my debt for life."

"But I save *your* life first. Ha! When those men try to kill you. How do you feel now, asswipe? When I turn over a table on top of you?"

"When you turn the tables on me. Those guys weren't trying to kill me."

"No. They were nice men."

"I didn't say they were nice."

They turned onto a street lined with bars. The neon signs began to flare one by one as they drove past, like a fuse that had been lit.

"Already in this country and you have make enemy. Explain this to me. Why you have so many enemy, in every place you step your foot." Dikran started ticking them off on his thick fingers. "The two nice men I save you from here. Babikian. Dick Moby in Las Vegas. And what is his name in Panama? The rich man. Ziegfeld."

"Ziegler."

Shake had always thought of himself as a guy who kept his head down and tried not to ruffle any feathers. But as Dikran ran through the list, he had to face the question. Why *had* so many people over the years wanted him dead?

"Ziegler," Dikran said. "Yes. And the Russian, long ago. You remember? And the other Russian. Who else?"

"That's it. You got them all."

If you didn't count Dikran himself. And an antiquities dealer in Cairo. A Belizean drug lord. A convict who'd escaped from prison just so he could hunt Shake down. A natural-gas billionaire who now served in the U.S. Senate. A freckle-faced ninety-pound girl named Meg. She'd been, by a long shot, the most dangerous of them all.

"It wasn't my fault," Shake said. "Not usually. Not always."

"We have a saying of Armenian," Dikran said. "'If a duck smells like shit . . .'"

"I have a saying of English," Shake said. "The longest year of my life was the two days I spent with you in Cambodia."

While Dikran was working his way through that, inch by inch, the driver let them out at the end of Kingdom Street. Shake was far from home, but he recognized the Friendly Fireplace right away. Paint scabbing, neon sputtering, a broken window patched with duct tape and cardboard—it was the kind of stone-cold dive bar where lowlifes nursed cheap drinks and planned intricate schemes. Shake, back in his own low-life days, had spent a fair amount of time in joints just like it.

Inside, the place was grimy and grim, with a fake log flickering in a fake fireplace. There were only a few customers, all of them foreigners like Shake and Dikran and all of them drinking alone. Expats, Shake guessed, not tourists. One porky guy in a Bayern München soccer jersey had fallen asleep with his head on the bar. Another guy was shooting pool like he wanted to murder the cue ball.

Shake was about to tell Dikran to grab a booth when he noticed the framed oil painting behind the bar. It was big, close to eight feet long, the colors dingy from decades of cigarette smoke.

Shake walked over to get a better look. And then moved even closer. The painting was a crazy, acid-trip version of hell: flames, topless women with devil horns. One of the devil girls, a brunette, was waist-deep in a cauldron full of fire. A handsome devil guy with a lantern jaw stirred the fire with a pitchfork. He seemed like he knew how to use that pitchfork. The devil girl was smiling, her chin tipped up and her eyes rolled back.

The bartender was a foreigner, too, a woman in her sixties with a steel-gray buzz cut. She tossed a napkin onto the bar.

"What'll you have?" she said.

"Is that Natalie Wood?" Shake said, pointing to the devil girl in the cauldron. "The one getting . . . cooked?"

The bartender glanced over her shoulder. "Cooked hard. Yeah. The blondes are Jayne Mansfield and Marilyn Monroe."

"And that's Rock Hudson. With the pitchfork."

"Some famous artist painted it back in the sixties, that's what they say. To pay off his tab. I don't remember his name." The bartender contemplated the painting. "I guess he wasn't that famous."

The dream that the hippie chick had described to Shake, when he'd asked her if she remembered anything strange—it was this painting, to a tee.

"Why do you stare?" Dikran said.

Shake told him about Mitch and her dream.

"Are you brain damage?" Dikran said. "Why do you not tell me this before?"

"Why would I?"

"Maybe this girl has a gift." Dikran rapped a knuckle against his bullet-shaped head. "A girl I know in Armenia, she has blood of the Gypsies. She has a gift. She tells me I will go to America one day."

"The girl I'm talking about doesn't have any gift," Shake said. "She's been to this bar, is all. The painting popped up in her dream. That's how dreams work."

Shake studied the painting for another few seconds. That had to be the only explanation. He wondered, though, what a woman like Mitch had been doing in a joint like this.

The bartender yawned. "I got all night," she said, "but I don't got all night."

Dikran smacked his hand on the bar so hard the guy shooting pool scratched and glanced up. The sleeping German guy stirred.

"Where is this Ouch man?" Dikran said to the bartender. "Tell me now!"

The bartender eyed him coldly. "I don't know who you're talking about."

"You do. Tell me now, or they will hear your scream a hundred years from here."

Shake saw the bartender's hand drop beneath the bar. If this dive was like the dives he'd frequented in L.A. and New Orleans, that was where the bartender probably kept a Mossberg pump or something equally destructive.

"Sorry," Shake told her. "Give me a minute."

He grabbed the sleeve of Dikran's tracksuit and dragged him away from the bar.

"What do you do, asswipe?" Dikran said. "We are waste time!"

"Go outside."

"Heh?"

"Go the fuck outside and wait for me."

Dikran rolled his shoulders, getting loose. "So. You give me order now?"

"Listen," Shake said. "Don't be an idiot, and let me handle this. I can handle this better than you, and you know it. You know it somewhere in that idiot brain of yours, or I wouldn't even be here."

Shake waited to see how that went down. The bartender waited to see if she'd need to shoot both of them, or just Dikran after he finished tearing Shake's head off his neck.

Finally Dikran nodded. Not much of a nod, just a twitch of his concrete-block chin, but there it was. He walked out of the bar.

"A beer," Shake told the bartender. "Draft."

She poured him the beer.

"I told you," she said. "I don't know nobody named Ouch."

Shake set the business card on the bar. The bartender glanced at it, then pulled a bottle of whiskey from the rail and poured him a shot to go with his beer.

"What's that for?" he said.

"Luck."

Chapter Twenty-One

The bartender pushed through a swinging door marked EM-PLOYEES ONLY and disappeared. Shake sipped his beer and waited. He waited some more.

The pool player finished a game and made his way over to the bar. He had to pick between Shake and the German guy drooling in his sleep. He picked the stool next to Shake.

They sat and waited together.

"Where'd she go?" the pool player said finally.

"Got me," Shake said.

"The bartender."

Shake glanced at him. "Yeah."

The pool player continued to gaze straight ahead, at the painting of hell, his expression neutral. That, and the kind of shoulders you got from doing a few hundred pull-ups a day, made Shake think the guy had done a stretch or two. Probably a pretty good percentage of the people who walked through the door of the Friendly Fireplace had.

"American?" Shake said.

"Yeah."

"How do you like it over here?"

The pool player thought about the question for a long time. "It's cheap."

"How's the food?"

The pool player turned his head a little, just enough to square Shake up in his peripheral vision.

"You got a problem with me?" he said.

Shake had been a law-abiding citizen for too long. He'd forgotten that in a place like this striking up a friendly conversation could get you stabbed.

"Nope," Shake said.

The pool player picked up a cardboard coaster. Angkor Beer. He tapped the edge against the counter.

"It's cheap," he said.

"The food?"

"Yeah."

Shake's phone rang. He took it out. Gina, finally calling back. Before Shake could answer it, though, the bartender returned. She pointed to the back of the room. A Cambodian man in a Hawaiian shirt had slipped into a booth. Shake walked over and sat down.

"Thanks for meeting with me," he said.

Ouch nodded. He was sixty, maybe sixty-five, with a bull neck and pitted cheeks. He looked like a meaner, Cambodian version of Manuel Noriega.

"So," he said. "Shay Bouchon. I've heard you were a very sexy food driver."

His voice was filled with helium, the accent tough to penetrate.

"Pardon me?" Shake said.

"I made some calls. You understand. I'm very careful. This is why I am a sexy food businessman."

Not sexy food, Shake figured out. *Successful.*

Ouch slid Shake's passport across the table to him. Shake

hadn't realized it was gone. The guys who jumped him must have grabbed it before Dikran showed up. So that was why Ouch had sent them.

He noticed that a dead-eyed Cambodian kid had slipped into a booth on the other side of the bar and was watching Shake. He was younger than the guys who had jumped Shake. They were probably still recovering from their encounter with Dikran.

"Sorry about what happened to your guys," Shake said.

"Oh, don't worry about that, Shay." Ouch lifted a hand and flicked the thought away. "Those weren't my guys. They just work for me sunshine."

Sunshine. *Sometimes.*

"Quinn said you might be able to help me," Shake said.

"Quinn. He is . . ."

"Full of shit? Piece of work? Pain in the ass?"

Ouch smiled, just a little, giving Shake a glimpse of one gleaming white incisor.

"So tell me, Shay. How can I assist you?"

"Last week someone grabbed a friend of mine."

"Grabbed?"

"Kidnapped. She went out to visit one of the temples and never came back."

"One of the temples here? Angkor?"

"Here. Yeah. But not Angkor. A temple called Banteay Srei. I don't know if I'm saying that right."

"Banteay Srei. Yes. But it's impossible that she was kidnapped. Tom Gone!"

The bodyguard kid slid out of his booth, came over, and handed Ouch a cell phone. The whole time the kid didn't take his dead eyes off Shake, not once.

"Tom Gone killed his first man when he was nine years old," Ouch said. "*He* is one of my guys."

Ouch began to scroll through the phone. "No," he said, "I was right. Nobody has been kidnapped here, Shay. If somebody had been kidnapped here, I would know about it. There must be some other explanation."

"There's not," Shake said. He told Ouch about the call from the kidnappers.

Ouch stared at Shake. "This makes me very unhappy, Shay."

Shake could understand why. Siem Reap was Ouch's turf. You didn't grab someone here unless you asked his permission first.

"Me, too," Shake said.

"Very, very unhappy."

"That's why I'm hoping you can help me."

"Tom Gone!"

Ouch snapped his fingers, and the kid handed him a notepad and pen.

"Please give me the name of your friend," Ouch told Shake.

Shake hadn't forgotten Quinn's warning: *Don't trust anybody.* There was nothing to stop Ouch, for example, from going straight to Babikian after he talked to Shake. But how could Ouch help Shake find Lexy if he didn't know he was looking for her?

"Alexandra Ilandryan," Shake said.

Ouch smiled again. And then he laughed. His laugh was like a sledgehammer breaking rocks.

"Tell me the truth now, Shay. What's the name of your friend?"

"Did you know she was in town?"

A long moment floated by. Ouch took out a pack of Juicy Fruit. He unwrapped a stick of gum, stuck it in his mouth, and started chewing so violently that Shake thought he was going to dislocate his jaw.

"I knew that, yes, of course," Ouch said. "Of course. But . . ."

He seemed even unhappier than he'd been before, the blood rushing to his face and darkening his pitted cheeks. Shake guessed what Ouch was thinking. The Armenians would hold him responsible for this, for Lexy getting grabbed in his own backyard.

That was good. That meant it was less likely Ouch would contact Babikian.

Ouch popped another stick of Juicy Fruit into his mouth. They were in the same boat, Shake realized, Ouch and him, blown by unlucky winds into a storm they wanted no fucking part of.

"The Armenians don't know she's been grabbed yet," Shake said.

"No?" Ouch said.

"No. So, for now, I think . . ."

"Yes. Yes, yes, yes. You make excellent scent, Shay." Ouch wrote a number on the notepad, ripped out the page, and handed it to Shake. "This is my private phone. I assure you, I will investigate this matter very closely."

"I appreciate it," Shake said.

Ouch stood and followed his dead-eyed bodyguard out through a door in back. Shake returned to the bar. The German guy was still sleeping. The pool player was almost to the bottom of his beer.

"How much I owe you?" Shake asked the bartender.

"On the house," she said.

The phone on the wall rang. The bartender answered it, listened, held the receiver against her chest. She looked at Shake, then over at the pool player.

"One of you named Ramos?" she said.

The pool player poured down the last swallow of beer. "That's me."

Shake pulled out his wallet and put down a five for a tip. He took one last look at the painting Mitch had dreamed about, the topless devil girls having such a swinging time in hell, then headed for the door.

Chapter Twenty-Two

French argued, pleaded, threatened. He calmly explained why Ramos couldn't come to the meeting with Bjorn. If Ramos spooked Bjorn and Bjorn backed out of the deal now—with millions of dollars so close they could almost smell it—they'd lose everything.

Ramos just shrugged. "That's why he won't back out. He'll lose it, too."

French wanted to slam his head against the wall. It would be more pleasant, and more productive, than trying to reason with Ramos.

Finally, with the meeting only an hour away, French convinced Ramos to compromise. Ramos would go to the Friendly Fireplace but remain invisible. He'd get there before French and Bjorn arrived, station himself at the bar, and pose as just another anonymous expat boozer. A role, French could have pointed out, Ramos was born to play.

"What if I can't hear?" Ramos said.

"I'll pick a booth near the bar. It's a small place."

"Not that small."

"You'll be able to hear. I'll make sure."

In fact, French planned to make sure Ramos *didn't* hear a word of the conversation. He needed to understand his place in the food chain.

Ramos took the stolen Mercedes and headed into town. French waited thirty minutes, then hopped on the ancient Vespa Sprint he'd bought for three hundred bucks when he first got to Siem Reap. When he reached the outskirts of town, he pulled over and called Ramos's cell phone to make sure he was in place.

No answer. No answer! French looked up the number for the Friendly Fireplace on his phone.

"I'm trying to reach one of your customers," French said. "His name is Ramos."

"Hold on," said the woman who'd picked up.

French waited. He was only a few blocks from the bar. It was almost seven o'clock.

"Yeah."

"Mason? Why aren't you answering your phone?"

Silence. Then, "Oh. Yeah. Battery's dead."

"Of course it is."

"Why's that?"

French practiced his yoga breathing. He inhaled slowly through the center of his nostrils and exhaled a long, soft "Ahhhh" sound.

"Are you ready? Are you in position at the bar?"

"Yeah. I'm here."

"Remember. You're invisible. It's essential you understand that."

"Yeah."

The line went dead. French kicked the Sprint until it sputtered back to life. A few minutes later, he pulled up to the Friendly Fireplace. Inside, Ramos was at the bar as instructed. French tried to catch his eye and give him a nod, but Ramos continued to stare straight ahead at the kitschy Frank Bowers painting of hell behind the stacks of highball glasses.

French ordered a martini and carried it to the booth farthest from the bar. A moment later the door opened and Bjorn breezed in. He was wearing cargo shorts and a tuxedo jacket with tails. French tried to keep up with Bjorn's handshake, a rococo series of fist bumps, knuckle taps, and thumb pops.

"What ho, baller?" Bjorn said. "Be right back."

He breezed off to the men's room. French finished his martini. He was about to get up and order another one when he saw Ramos heading across the bar toward the booth.

"What the hell are you doing?" French said.

Ramos slid into the booth next to him. "That's the guy?" he said.

"Get back to the bar! He'll be out any second!"

"The guy's a goof."

"You're supposed to be invisible. And he's not . . . *shit.*" French put a hand on Ramos's shoulder and gave him a shove, a gentle one. Ramos didn't budge. It was like he was bolted down. "Mason, for God's sake, you're going to screw this up for us."

Ramos looked at him. "Don't do that again," he said.

"I need a drinky-drinky, stat," Bjorn said, back from the men's room. He sat down before he seemed to notice Ramos. "Hey, *m'ijo,* what's crack-a-lackin'?"

"I'm afraid there's been a tiny misunderstanding," French said. "This is . . . he's working with me."

"Coolio," Bjorn said. He held out a fist for Ramos to bump. "I'm Bjorn."

Ramos ignored Bjorn's fist. *"No soy su hijo,"* he said.

"Hmm?" Bjorn had swiveled around to wave at the bartender. *"Lo siento,* dude. My bad. You want something to drink?"

"No."

"Respect. Tequila?"

"We've been sitting on her seven days. That's a long time."

"Mason," French said.

"Real talk," Bjorn said. The bartender made her way over. Bjorn ordered a bottle of Gran Patrón Platinum for the table.

"Our cocks've been on the block seven days."

This was going to be a fucking disaster. French knew he had to regain control of the situation and shut Ramos down. He lowered his voice, another old trick he used in the classroom.

"We made the call," he said, "but there's an issue. We need to discuss it."

That got Bjorn's attention. More or less.

"What kind of an issue?" he said.

The bartender brought the tequila and three shot glasses. French waited until she left.

"Her friend, the one I spoke with, wants proof that she's okay. He wants to Zoom with her. He's very insistent."

"He's freaked," Bjorn said, nodding. "That's why we put them on ice for a while. So they're all, 'Oh, shit, oh, shit, oh, shit!'"

The man on the phone, Veronica's friend, hadn't really seemed freaked. But French wanted to keep the conversation focused.

"So should we do it?" he said. "The Zoom?"

"I guess." Bjorn poured shots for each of them. "But keep it tight again. Let the dude talk to her for a second, tell him the number we want, then bounce. Bottoms up."

He downed his shot of tequila. French followed suit.

"You guess?" Ramos said.

French maintained his smile through sheer force of will. Fucking Ramos.

"So what are the risks?" French said. "The pros and cons of the Zoom thing?"

"No risk. Here. I was gonna hook you up with this anyway."

Bjorn reached into a pocket of his cargo shorts. French felt Ramos tense beside him. Bjorn pulled out an oversize smartphone.

"This bitch has awesome video," Bjorn said. "True 4k. And it's totally wiped. I've got a boy here in town works for me, he encrypted the *shit* out of it. Basically, this phone doesn't *exist*, na'mean?"

"Will they be able to trace us?" French said.

"No. My boy will set up a burner account for us. He can bounce it around the world, the IP or whatever. He'll use some little old lady's IP who lives in Reseda."

French gave Ramos a pointed look. *See? I told you so.*

"What about the other phone?" Ramos said. "The one we've been using."

"Oh. Yeah. Just dump that in the river. No worries."

"No. I mean what about it. Was that one wiped, too?"

"What? Yeah." Bjorn set the new smartphone on the table and reached for the bottle of tequila. "Absolutely. Do we want some limes? Some salt?"

Ramos downed his shot and let Bjorn fill him back up. Ramos downed that one, too. French started to relax.

"I gotta take a leak," Bjorn said. "Back in a flash."

"It's our cocks on the block," Ramos said. "Not yours."

"We should probably be going." French, pinned between Ramos and the wall, gave Ramos a nudge. "Thanks for the drink."

"We want a bigger slice," Ramos said.

Bjorn had started to slide out of the booth. He slid back in.

"You want a bigger slice of the four mil?" he said.

French panicked. He'd told Ramos that their share of the ransom would be one million and that Ramos would get half of that. It wasn't a lie. Well, it was a lie—their share was *two* million—but a lie in service to the partnership, intended to promote harmony.

If Ramos found out that French was going to clear a million more than he thought . . .

"Bjorn gets three million, Mason," French said quickly, "as previously discussed."

He glanced at Bjorn and put as much spin on that last phrase, *as previously discussed,* as he dared. To his relief, Bjorn didn't miss a beat.

"I get the three mil," he said, "because this is business, dude. And *I* brought this business to *you*. That's the way this shit works."

Ramos picked up the bottle and poured himself another shot. "We want two million, not one."

"We've already agreed to his terms, Mason," French said.

"I didn't agree."

"But you agreed to *my* terms."

French glanced again at Bjorn, for encouragement. Bjorn didn't take his eyes off Ramos.

"Do you know who I am, dude?" he asked Ramos.

"You're the one doesn't have his cock on the block."

"Why don't we discuss this tomorrow," French said. "Let's focus right now on the—"

"I dig your home slice, French," Bjorn said. He reached for the tequila. "He's no bullshit, all biznuts."

"Two and two is fair," Ramos said.

"All right. I'm down with that."

"Wait," French said. *Fuck.* "Wait. Let's just . . ."

Bjorn grinned his shit-eating grin. Of course he was down with it. He was still getting his original two million.

"You get a million now," Ramos told French.

Yes. *Fuck.* As opposed to the one point five that French had been guaranteed five minutes ago. Ramos, the idiot, had just cost French half a million dollars.

What could he say, though?

"Great," French said.

Bjorn slid out of the booth. "I gotta take that leak, brohans. Did we decide? Limes? No limes?"

The smartphone on the table began to buzz. The three of them stared at it.

"Shit." Bjorn laughed. "I must have given you the wrong one."

He searched the pockets of his cargo shorts and produced a second smartphone. He powered it up and checked the screen.

"Okay. Yeah. Now you're coolio." He handed the new phone to French. "You're good to go."

Chapter Twenty-Three

The kidnappers called a little after eleven o'clock. The guy Shake had talked to earlier gave him fifteen minutes to find a computer. Shake tracked down a hotel employee with after-hours access to the hotel's business center and logged into the Zoom account he'd set up earlier in the day. He came in just under the wire, with about a minute to spare.

"Wait out in the hall," Shake told Dikran, who was standing so close to him that he could barely move. The "business center" was about the size of a closet, with a desk, a single chair, and an iMac.

"No," Dikran said.

Shake noted how ominously direct that answer was—no "asswipe" or elaborate threat. He decided this wasn't a battle he was going to win.

"Fine," Shake said. "But squeeze over there, up against the wall, so you're not on camera. You can see the screen from there."

He checked the iMac to make sure Dikran was out of the frame and studied his own face for a second. *Jesus,* Shake thought, *when did I get so old?* The last few days had not been kind to him. He had bags under his eyes and creases everywhere. The hair on his temples seemed to have more silver threads than he remembered.

"What time do they call?" Dikran said.

"Keep your mouth shut, all right? No matter what you see or hear."

Dikran grunted. Was it a yes grunt or a no grunt? Shake clicked a button and the screen filled with the face of an angry green monkey, its teeth bared and nostrils flared. Shake focused on the eyes behind the mask. Blue eyes with pale lashes.

"Can you see me? I can see you."

It was the same guy Shake had been talking to on the phone. The mask muffled his voice, but Shake was almost certain.

"I see you," Shake said. "Where is she?"

The frame tilted as the guy in the mask pulled back. He was using a camera phone. Shake could make out, behind the guy, what looked like a kitchen counter, the corner of a wooden cabinet, a wall with patterned green wallpaper. Shake couldn't see what the pattern was.

"Not yet," the guy said. "First, I want to present our terms. They are nonnegotiable, and I won't repeat myself. Do you understand?"

"Thanks for agreeing to this Zoom thing, by the way. I appreciate it."

That seemed to throw the guy. "You're welcome."

"All right. Let's hear it."

"If you want us to release Veronica unharmed, then—"

The guy stopped. Shake hadn't caught himself in time, the flinch of confusion, and the guy had noticed.

"Go on," Shake said.

Veronica? Shake knew that was the name on Lexy's fake passport, but why would the kidnappers be using it? Why would . . . ?

"What's wrong?" the guy said.

Holy shit. Shake finally understood what was happening. He understood why, during the first call, the kidnappers had warned him not to contact the authorities.

Holy shit. Was it possible the kidnappers didn't know they'd grabbed the *pakhan* of the Armenian mob? How was that possible?

Shake had suspected all along that he was dealing with amateurs. Now he was sure of it. That made him *more* worried for Lexy's safety, not less.

Dikran, as usual, was struggling along, a beat behind. Shake could see him scratching his head.

"Who?" Dikran said.

"What?" the guy in the mask said.

Off-screen, Shake punched a fist toward Dikran. *Shut up!*

"Nothing," Shake said. "Nothing's wrong. Tell us what we need to do to get Veronica back."

Shake understood how Lexy must have played the mix-up. Once she'd realized that the kidnappers didn't know who she was, she made sure to keep it that way. If they figured out that they'd accidentally fucked with the Armenian mob, the kidnappers wouldn't send Lexy back with a polite note of apology. They'd kill her on the spot, cover their tracks, and then run as fast and far as they could.

"Is there someone there with you?" the guy in the mask said.

"Veronica?" Dikran said. "What is this person?"

Shake calmly tried to kick Dikran. "There's no one else here."

"I hear someone!" the guy said. "I warned you about contacting the authorities. If—"

"It's not the authorities," Shake said. He grabbed a pad of paper next to the iMac and scribbled furiously. "It's her brother. Veronica's brother. He's like a brother to her. I had to bring him into this. You understand that."

"What?" Dikran said, his confusion growing. "I am no brother to such a person."

Shake tore the page off the pad and shoved it at Dikran.

"They think that's who she is keep your mouth shut you idiot."

"This is unacceptable," the guy said. Shake braced for the screen to go dark, but it didn't. He could see the guy thinking, his pale lashes blinking.

"Tell us what we need to do to get her back," Shake said. "I'm listening."

He glanced over. Dikran was squinting his way through the note Shake had written.

"Four million dollars American," the guy in the mask said finally. "You have twenty-four hours to make a bitcoin transfer to our account. I'll provide you with the details five minutes before the transaction."

Shake wasn't exactly sure what a bitcoin was. Gina had explained it to him once—some kind of Internet currency that couldn't be traced.

"Forget it," Shake said.

"What?"

"And no wire transfer either. It's got to be cash. Otherwise what's to stop you? We send you four million dollars, and it disappears down the rabbit hole. We never hear another word from you. We never see her again. Veronica."

The guy stiffened, like he was offended. "That won't happen. You have my word."

Shake let that hang there for a second. He hoped the guy could hear how stupid he sounded.

"The only way this works," Shake said, "we do it old-school. A straight swap, in person."

"In person?" the guy said. "Absolutely not."

"I bring the four million—cash or gold, whatever you want—and you bring Veronica."

"I don't think you appreciate what's at stake here. You understand that you're haggling with your friend's life in the balance?"

"I'm not haggling," Shake said. "You said four million, I said I'll get you four million. I'm just trying to make sure everybody walks away from this happy."

The guy shifted in his seat. He was trying to find a hole in the argument.

"What's to stop you?" the guy said.

"Stop me?"

"If we meet in person for the exchange. What's to stop you from setting some kind of a . . . an ambush?"

"How am I going to ambush you? I'm just a guy, and it's your home court. And why would I do that? I want her back. You can have the money. I don't care about the money."

"Heh," Dikran said. He looked up from the note Shake had written. "I understand this now."

"What did he say?" the guy in the mask said.

"Nothing," Shake said. "What do you say? It's got to be a straight swap, or we don't have a deal."

"Then I suppose we don't have a deal."

The guy held Shake's gaze and didn't look away. Shake relaxed a little. Every decent poker player knew that if a guy stared you down, he was probably bluffing.

"Just think it over, all right?" Shake said. "Now let me talk to her, like we agreed."

The guy hesitated, then the frame jerked and blurred, flaring when the camera caught an overhead light. Shake scribbled furiously again, tore off another sheet, and shoved it at Dikran.

"Please please keep your fucking mouth shut OK???"

A second later the frame steadied and there was Lexy, in medium close-up from the shoulders up.

Dikran sucked in his breath. Shake studied her. She looked like shit, but like shit for Lexy was still pretty great.

When she saw that it was Shake on her screen, she arched an eyebrow. Shake couldn't tell if she was surprised or amused. Maybe both.

"Hello, Veronica," he said.

"Nice to see you, Shake."

Shake knew they didn't have much time. "How you holding up? What can you tell me?"

"Ah." That languid shrug was the first thing Shake had fallen for, all those years ago. "I sleep for maybe only twenty minutes at a time, then I wake from the darkness."

She was telling him she was about twenty minutes from the temple, the place she'd been grabbed. But twenty minutes in which direction? Shake knew she wouldn't be able to say. She'd been blindfolded or in the trunk of a car—that was the darkness she was talking about.

"I've always been a heavy sleeper myself," he said. "I can sleep through anything. Car horns, sirens."

"For me the quiet is best. Only the wind in the trees."

So they had her somewhere secluded.

"They treating you all right?" Shake said.

A hand was gripping her shoulder. Shake didn't think, judging by the angles, that the hand belonged to the guy holding the camera phone. That meant at least two kidnappers were in the room with her.

"Both of them, yes," Lexy said. So two kidnappers.

"What else can you tell me? We're worried about you."

"Ah." She shrugged again. "Do you remember what I have always said, Shake? How today life is like—"

"That's enough," a gruff voice to Lexy's right said. The guy with his hand on her shoulder. "Let's go."

The guy in the monkey mask squeezed into the frame from the left, his head right next to Lexy's.

"So you can see," he said to Shake, "Veronica's very much alive and well. Are you satisfied?"

"Dikran is with you?" Lexy asked Shake.

"He's here."

"I would like to say hello. If this is permitted?"

Shake saw the hand on her shoulder tighten, but the guy in the monkey mask nodded.

"Fine," he said, "but quickly."

Dikran leaned in over Shake's shoulder. Shake could feel him trembling.

Shake scribbled another note and held it next to the screen so Dikran could see it.

"Stay cool and DO NOT LOSE YOUR SHIT."

Dikran ignored the note. He stared at Lexy. *"Yes aystegh yem,"* he said quietly.

"Speak English," the second guy said, and then the barrel of a gun appeared in the frame. The second guy pressed it to Lexy's temple.

The guy in the monkey mask wasn't happy about the gun. Shake could tell. His pale lashes were blinking like crazy.

Lexy was ice. But then she remembered she was supposed to be Veronica—a woman who'd be scared by a gun to her head.

So she cringed. Her lower lip trembled.

Dikran, to Shake's surprise, stayed cool. "I am here," he said.

"The money. You know how to get it, yes?"

"I know."

"Good. Just—"

"We're done," the second guy said. "Let's go."

He yanked Lexy to her feet and out of the frame. Shake got a glimpse of the guy's forearm, his watch. The watch was just an old Timex with a leather strap, but something seemed familiar about it, about the muscular forearm.

There was something familiar about the guy's voice, too. Shake tried to place it.

"Four million dollars American," the guy in the monkey mask said. "I'll let you know if an exchange with—"

Without warning, the second guy shoved in front of his partner. A Cambodian-style devil mask filled the screen, and a pair of dark eyes studied Shake. The guy was thinking, Shake sensed, exactly what Shake was thinking.

I know you, don't I?

The pool player from the Friendly Fireplace. Shake realized that's who the guy in the devil mask was—Mr. Personality, the blank-faced ex-con at the bar.

What was the guy's name? Shake tried to remember. The bartender said it when she answered the phone. Romero? Rodriguez? Something like that.

"What are you doing?" Shake heard the guy in the monkey mask say to his partner. "Will you just—"

Shake didn't hear the rest of it. Dikran gave him a hard shove and knocked him out of the chair. Shake's head thumped against the wall.

"Hear me well, you asshole of a dirty camel," Dikran hissed into the camera. "If you harm one hair of her head, I will kill you. I will kill your family. I will kill the family of your family."

"Stop it!" Shake said.

"I will make sarma from your penis skin. This is Armenian delicacy, like egg roll. How will this feel to your penis, do you think?"

Shake tried to reach up and slap the iMac's power button. Or any button. Dikran kicked him away.

"Do you know who she is? This one you treat like a dog? This one you stick your gun in her face? I will tell you. The smallest flea does not jump unless she gives it her permission. The brightest star does not shine."

"Dikran! Stop! Fuck!"

Dikran had lifted the iMac's monitor off the desk. He brought it so close to his face that Shake thought he might try to ram his bald, bullet-shaped head through the glass.

"She is *pakhan* of all the Armenians in Los Angeles, you shit-eating rat," Dikran said. "She is *Alexandra Yeghisapet Ilandryan*! Remember this name, because I will carve it into the inside of your dead broken skull."

Chapter Twenty-Four

French ended the Zoom session.

"What is he talking about?" French asked Ramos. "Armenians in Los Angeles? She has a private venture-capital firm in San Francisco."

Ramos was frowning, thinking. "Shit," he said.

"What?" French turned to Veronica. "You have a private venture-capital firm in San Francisco."

"Shit, shit, shit."

Veronica said something too softly for him to hear. French stepped closer and she hammered her forehead into his face. He reeled backward, blinded by pain. When he could see again, Ramos was already on his ass, clutching his throat.

Ramos's gun had fallen to the floor beneath the table. Veronica lunged for it and Ramos lunged for her. They crashed against the table. Ramos pinned her arms above her head, but Veronica yanked a hand free, snared one of Ramos's wrists with the steel links between her cuffs, and twisted. French heard Ramos's wrist pop like a pencil snapped in two. Ramos tumbled off her. Veronica rolled away.

French was paralyzed. Everything was happening too fast, and nothing made sense. Veronica crawled toward Ramos's gun. She was forced to crawl because Ramos had insisted on cuffing her ankles when he brought her down for the Skype chat. Absurd, French had thought at the time.

Ramos managed to kick the gun away. Veronica yanked a drawer from the cabinet above her. Cutlery spilled from the drawer and clattered across the tile. She grabbed a large serving fork.

The gun had spun to a stop a few feet away. Veronica started crawling toward it. No, she started crawling toward *French,* the serving fork gripped tightly in her hand.

He realized Ramos was yelling at him. "Gun!"

French roused himself and picked the gun up. He couldn't bring himself to aim it directly at Veronica, so he pointed it in her general direction.

"Stop!" he said.

She paused for a moment but continued toward him.

"Stop!"

She was five feet away. She lifted the serving fork. French saw it had three sharp tines. And then . . .

Ramos was on top of her. He jammed his knee between her shoulder blades and locked her neck in the crook of his thick arm. She stabbed blindly up at him. He smacked her head against the floor.

"Drop it," he said.

She stabbed at him again. The cords of muscle in his forearm tightened as he increased the pressure on her windpipe.

"You can die now," he said, "or you can die later."

FRENCH WRAPPED A handful of ice cubes in the dish towel and placed the pack gently against his nose. His whole skull still throbbed, but he didn't think the nose was broken. His Hanuman mask had absorbed a lot of the blow.

"Calm down," he said.

Ramos wouldn't stop pacing. He swirled around the kitchen—to the window, to the counter, to the table, back to the window, the counter, the table—like wine around the bottom of a glass. It was making French dizzy.

"You understand who these people are?" Ramos said.

The Armenian mafia in Los Angeles. French had never heard of them, but Ramos was from L.A. and had served time in the California prison system. He said that even the Russians in L.A. were scared of the Armenians. French didn't know what this meant, exactly, except that it seemed to scare Ramos.

"You say they're dangerous," French said. "And I believe you."

"You don't understand who these people are."

French offered him the Buddha he'd fired up. Ramos ignored it. He stopped pacing only long enough to glance out the window and try to flex the wrist Veronica had snapped. The swollen wrist was a jaundiced yellow, marbled with blue and black streaks.

Alexandra, French reminded himself, not Veronica.

He was still trying to process that. This elegant, charming, beautiful woman was the leader of a murderous criminal organization? French's mind was blowing in super slow motion, like an explosion in a bad Hollywood movie.

She'd finally stopped resisting and dropped the serving fork. Ramos had held the gun on her while French unlocked her handcuffs and then refastened them behind her. Ramos made him do it again, tighter, and then he'd taken her back up to the attic.

Ramos left the window and resumed pacing.

"Sit down for a minute," French said. "We need to discuss the situation calmly."

"And they're here! Fuck. That guy, I told you. He's the one I talked to in the bar."

"Are you absolutely sure?"

"That's him. It took me a minute." Ramos stopped at the window again and glanced out. "They're on us."

Even if the Armenians were as dangerous as Ramos said they were, *especially* if, French and Ramos needed to keep their wits about them.

"They're not on us, Mason. It was only a chance encounter. They're just in town looking for her. Think about it. Otherwise they'd be here already, wouldn't they?"

French offered Ramos the Buddha again. Ramos hesitated, then accepted it. Ramos took a long, deep drag.

"Maybe," he said.

"Not maybe. They would have been here two days ago."

"We'd be dead already."

"Calm down. And he won't make the connection between the bar and tonight," he said. "You were wearing your mask, remember."

"He heard my voice."

"You barely said three words. We're fine."

It had taken Ramos only a couple of drags to burn the Buddha down to his fingertips.

"You know who these people are?" he said again.

For God's sake. Maybe French *was* dead already and this was the circle of hell where he'd landed.

"Yes. I know who they are. But Los Angeles is a long way from Cambodia."

"I told you. They're here."

"Two of them."

"At least two."

"What I'm saying, I'm saying that they're on foreign soil. Literally. Our partnership with Bjorn gives us the upper hand. And those threats the other one made, the bald one, that was gamesmanship, Mason. Good cop, bad cop. It's the oldest trick in the book."

"They're not cops."

"I didn't mean . . ." A thought occurred to French. "Wait. Wait a minute."

"If they *were* cops, we'd be better off."

"I think there might be a silver lining here."

Ramos looked over at him. "You think what?"

"If what you're saying about the Armenian mafia is true . . ."

"It's true."

". . . then she's even more valuable than we thought. Don't you see?"

Judging from the blankness of Ramos's expression, French might have been speaking Aramaic.

He went to the fridge and returned with two cold cans of Angkor Extra Stout. He popped the tops and set one of the cans in front of Ramos.

"We'll double the price," French said. "We'll ask for eight million dollars instead of four."

"What?" Ramos said.

"They want her back, right? You heard what the bald one said. She's the . . . what did he call her? She's the supreme leader, whatever."

"You're crazy."

"What's an extra four million to the Armenian mafia? They're powerful, yes?"

"You don't know who these people are."

"So they'll pay eight million dollars to get her back. They won't think twice. They . . ." Wait. Wait, wait, wait. French had spotted another, even more lucrative opportunity. "And listen to this, Mason."

Ramos drew the gun from his waistband. He checked the magazine and slapped it back in.

"No," he said, "I'm gonna take care of this."

French didn't understand. "The guy from the bar?"

"No."

"Then what are you . . . ?" French realized with a stab of alarm who Ramos was talking about. "Mason! No!"

"Don't call me that. Nobody calls me that. Like I'm your student."

"Like you're my . . . what?"

"We need to pull the plug. Put her down and get the hell out of the country."

Ramos headed for the stairs. French sat stunned for a moment, then leaped from his chair. The sudden movement made it feel like he was getting stabbed in the nose with an ice pick.

"You can't kill her! Please, Mason." He stepped between Ramos and the stairs. "Just stop for a second and listen to me."

"What did I tell you? Everybody just calls me Ramos."

French took a deep breath. *Stay calm.*

"Ramos," he said. "We're so close."

"You want to do her, I'm all right with that. But we have to put her down."

"This is the opportunity of a lifetime."

"I'm not taking on the Armenians for a million bucks."

"That's what I'm trying to tell you. We'll split the extra four million fifty-fifty. Which means we end up with three million dollars each."

"Nobody would take on the Armenians for a million." But then French's point seemed to land. Ramos walked over to the table and picked up a can of beer. He took a swallow. "We split the extra four million?"

"We do," French said. "Because, like you said, *we're* taking all the risks here, not Bjorn."

It was almost midnight, but the house was still oppressively hot. French could feel the sweat gathering in the small of his back. He had no idea what he'd do if Ramos started toward the stairs again.

Three million dollars each. They were so close. Why couldn't Ramos, even as dense as he was, understand that?

The can of beer dangled from the fingers of Ramos's left hand, the gun from his right. He was gazing at the kitchen wall again. French bit his tongue, fighting the impulse to add bricks to his argument. *Don't sell past the close,* his father used to say.

A minute passed. Ramos closed his eyes.

"We pull the plug now," he said, "we're still in deep shit."

"That's right," French said carefully. "With three million each or without."

Ramos lifted his beer and drained it. "Yeah."

French, relieved, lit another Buddha. The smoke filled his lungs the way a breeze fills a sail.

"We'll get some sleep and call them back tomorrow. We'll tell them our new terms."

"And the goof? He'll agree to it?"

"Bjorn? He only needs to know what he needs to know," French said. The Armenians were insisting on a cash exchange, in person. Well, that was perfect. "Do you understand?"

"We make the pickup. Cut the goof out of the extra four."

"He never knows about it. He only knows what he needs to know."

Ramos nodded. "Okay. But you had a good idea."

"A good idea?"

"The one guy. From the bar, who saw me."

"What about him?"

Ramos took out his gun and checked the clip again.

"Tomorrow I'm gonna find him," he said. "I'm gonna take care of him."

Chapter Twenty-Five

About three seconds after the iMac's screen went dark, Dikran began to realize how badly he'd fucked up. Shake watched the blood drain from his face. He watched the horror flood in.

"No . . ." Dikran said.

Shake didn't turn the knife. "Let's go upstairs."

They went back to Shake's room. Shake grabbed a couple of tiny bottles of Jack Daniel's from the minibar. He tossed one of them to Dikran. For a few minutes, they just sat there in silence, Shake on one bed and Dikran, clutching Lexy's cross in his fist, on the other.

"They will kill her now," Dikran said.

"We don't know that for sure."

"*I* will kill her now. If they are me."

"If you were them."

"What?"

"Nothing."

They sat in silence for another few minutes. Shake was thinking about what Dikran had said. *If they are me.* The kidnappers, though, *weren't* Dikran. Shake was absolutely sure of that now.

"If you were them, you'd kill her," Shake said. "But you're a professional."

Dikran glanced up, wary. There had to be an insult in there somewhere.

"Heh?"

"These guys aren't professionals," Shake said. "They're amateurs. So we don't know what they'll do."

"This is good? That they are amateur?"

"Maybe."

Maybe. The best he could do at the moment. But it was better than nothing. Shake had lived a life filled with tight spots and hairy fixes. If he'd learned anything from that, he'd learned you never dumped a hand until you knew for sure it was dead. You kept scrambling until you had nowhere else to go.

"Go get some sleep," Shake said. He was exhausted. He wasn't sure he'd ever been this tired in his life.

Dikran, to Shake's surprise, nodded and stood.

"If you say maybe she lives," he said, "I will believe you."

The next morning Shake woke early, to the wet-leather squeak of bats returning home after a long night out. He walked down to Dikran's room and knocked on the door. No answer. Shake checked the lobby, the restaurant, the pool. He finally found Dikran sitting in the atrium behind the lobby. The atrium was open to the sky, built around a long, narrow pool.

A sign next to the pool said NO SWIMMING! Shake understood why when he saw what he'd thought was a rock flick its tail and slide beneath the surface of the water. A small crocodile.

"Do they call?" Dikran said, without looking up.

"No." Shake had Dikran's phone. He'd slept with it on the pillow next to his head. "Not yet."

"How long do we wait? Before we know?"

Dikran meant how long did they have to wait before they had to admit Lexy was dead. Shake didn't have an answer for that. Every minute that passed was a bad—

The Bee Gees started singing "To Love Somebody." Dikran's ringtone. Dikran jerked around, and two more rocks dipped beneath the water. Shake put a hand in Dikran's face: *Stay cool.*

He checked caller ID—blocked—and hit the talk button.

"Yeah," Shake said.

"We'll do the cash exchange." It was the first guy, the one in the monkey mask.

Shake gave Dikran a thumbs-up. He caught a glimpse of what maybe Lexy still saw when she looked at Dikran, the ungainly seven-year-old boy with wide, hopeful eyes.

"That's good," Shake said into the phone. "We all want the same thing here."

"But the price for her return is now eight million dollars, not four."

"Eight?"

"Yes or no. If you answer no, this will be the last time you hear from us."

Shake didn't think the guy was bluffing this time. "All right."

"Have the money in twenty-four hours. American cash. One moment."

Shake heard the rustle of movement. And then, "Hello, Shake." Lexy's voice.

"You're okay?"

"Yes."

Another rustle. "Are you satisfied?" The guy in the monkey mask again.

"Just let me—"

"We'll be in touch with further instructions."

The call went dead before Shake could respond. He worried that Dikran was about to pass out and topple into the crocodile pool.

"She's alive," Shake said. "They'll do the deal."

Dikran went slack with relief. Shake was right there with him.

"Can you get eight million?" he said. "They doubled down on us."

"Yes. It is not a problem."

"She has a rainy-day account or something, right? That you have access to?"

"It is not a problem. I tell you this already, stupid cockjob." Dikran was getting some of his swagger back. Shake, despite himself, was glad to see it. "For her, eight million is like wiping my ass."

What was going to be tricky, Shake realized, was transferring the funds to a local bank and then turning that into cash. Maybe Quinn's buddy Ouch would be able to grease the wheels.

Dikran kissed Lexy's cross and muttered something in Armenian that sounded like a prayer.

"*Shnorhakalut'yun,*" he said. "*Shnorhakalut'yun.*"

That was an Armenian phrase Shake understood. *Thank you.*

It wasn't time to celebrate yet, though. Lexy was alive, but that didn't mean she'd stay that way. Shake had heard about plenty of grabs that had gone sideways—the ransom paid, the hostage killed anyhow. In a situation like this, you needed a Plan B.

Lexy was a twenty-minute drive, in some direction, from the place where she'd been grabbed. That was all Shake knew, and not enough. He needed more to go on. He found Ouch's business card and dialed his number.

"Shay?" Ouch said.

"There's been some movement," Shake said, "that thing we discussed. Anything on your end?"

"Yes, Shay, I've made some inquiries and been quite sexy food."

Shake was always wary when his lucked turned, because it had the habit of whipping back at him twice as hard. Right now, though, he was happy to ride a hot streak.

"That's good news," he said.

"I would like to show you a place, Shay. It is not far from here. I will send Tom Gone to pick you up in one hour."

"Great. Thanks."

Shake hung up.

"I'm gonna go meet with Ouch," he told Dikran, "find out what he knows. You stay here until I get back."

"I come with you."

"No. You're staying here."

Shake waited for Dikran to blow. But it seemed as if Dikran, even with his swagger back, remembered how close he'd come to getting Lexy killed.

"Yes," he said.

"I'll keep your phone, in case they call about Lexy. You can have mine, but don't call or text me unless it's an emergency. A *real* emergency. After I talk to Ouch, I'm gonna stop by that bar from yesterday."

"The bar?"

"The second guy from Zoom, the one in the devil mask. I think I talked to him yesterday. I'm gonna see if I can get a line on him."

"I go with you."

"What did I just say?"

"For protection of you."

"I'll be fine," Shake said.

AN HOUR LATER a Honda Hornet came buzzing up the hotel drive. Ouch's dead-eyed kid bodyguard, Tom Gone, tossed Shake a helmet. There was a crack in the helmet that ran all the way from the crown to the chin vent. Shake could fit the tip of his pinkie finger inside.

Tom Gone barked something in Khmer at Shake. Shake put on the helmet and climbed up behind him. They buzzed off, away from the center of town, and caught a two-lane highway that headed north. Forty-five minutes later, they turned onto a dirt road that led into the jungle. When they reached a clearing where two vehicles were parked, a *tuk-tuk* and a Land Rover, Tom Gone pulled the motorcycle over.

Shake got off the bike. Ouch hopped down from the Land Rover. Shake wondered where the other driver was. And then he noticed the spray of dried blood on the flank of the *tuk-tuk*.

"Hello, Shay," Ouch said. He was sweating, his pitted cheeks flushed. He flicked a hand at the blood-spattered *tuk-tuk*. "I badger Congress."

"What's that?"

"I badger Congress what happened here."

I bet you can guess what happened here.

Yeah, Shake was pretty sure he could. The kidnappers had paid off Lexy's original driver so she'd be stranded, then had an accomplice with a *tuk-tuk* swoop in to "rescue" her. The accomplice, once he'd brought Lexy here, had been disposable.

The kidnappers might not be professionals, but a lot of bad people weren't.

"He is just over there, the driver." Ouch flicked his hand at the trees. "Do you want to see his body, Shay?"

"I don't," Shake said. So this was where Lexy had been grabbed, not at the temple.

Ouch said something in Khmer, and Tom Gone went over to the Land Rover. He opened the tailgate of the truck, and a skinny Cambodian guy spilled out. Shake recognized him—Lexy's *tuk-tuk* driver, the one Shake had talked to outside her hotel.

The driver began talking fast in Khmer, pleading with Tom Gone. His hands were zip-tied behind his back, and his face was bruised, bloody.

"What are you doing with him?" Shake said.

"He told us what he told you, Shay," Ouch said. "The *barang* paid him so he would leave. And so on. But perhaps he knows more than he is saying. We will find out."

Ouch flicked a hand at Tom Gone. Tom Gone pulled a rope from the back of the Land Rover. He tied one end around the driver's right ankle and the other end around the Land Rover's ball hitch.

"Stop," Shake said. "Don't do this. He doesn't know anything else. We know what happened here."

Tom Gone pulled another rope from the Land Rover. He tied one end of this rope around the driver's left ankle and the other end to his motorcycle.

"I am a careful man, Shay," Ouch said. "I like to make sure."

"Let him go," Shake said. "I've got information, but I'm not giving it to you until you let him go."

Ouch regarded Shake pleasantly. Shake felt his balls tighten.

"Please," he said.

Ouch said something in Khmer. Tom Gone, dead-eyed and impassive, untied the ropes. He took out a knife and cut the zip tie. The driver started running. He ran straight into the jungle and never looked back.

"Okay, Shay," Ouch said. "What information do you have for me?"

"I know where they've got her," Shake said, "more or less."

He told Ouch about the Zoom call with Lexy, the twenty-minute drive, how she let Shake know that the kidnappers had her somewhere quiet and secluded.

"Does that help us any?" Shake said after he finished.

Ouch popped a stick of Juicy Fruit in his mouth and chewed pensively.

"I don't know, Shay," he said. "Twenty minutes which way? There are so many places to look. I will investigate. I will investigate very carefully."

Tom Gone dropped Shake across from the Friendly Fireplace. The place was just as dead and depressing as the first time Shake experienced it. There were a few couples in the booths, middle-aged *barangs* with much younger Cambodian women, and a few solo drinkers at the bar. Shake spotted, near the back of the room, the German who'd been asleep the first time. He was awake now, eating noodles out of a Styrofoam container. The noodles must have been spicy, because they were making him sweat. After every bite the young Cambodian woman sitting next to him reached up and dabbed the German's forehead with a cocktail napkin.

There was no sign of the ex-con, Mr. Personality. Shake wasn't surprised. The guy had made Shake—he'd have to assume that Shake had made *him.*

The same bartender was working, the older woman with the steel-gray buzz cut.

"Remember me?" Shake said.

"Beer and a shot."

"Bring it on."

She poured the beer. Shake considered the painting behind the bar. He hadn't noticed, last time, how crowded hell was. There were dozens of faint, almost invisible faces worked into the flames— lost souls lurking in the background, watching Natalie Wood get pitchforked by Rock Hudson.

Gina would either love the painting or hate it. Shake wasn't sure which. He hated that she wasn't here, so he could ask. That was the curse of real love. When you were alone, you never felt more so.

"You remember that guy from yesterday?" Shake said after the bartender poured his drink. He still couldn't remember the guy's name. "Big arms, looked kind of Latino. He got a phone call. Rosales, maybe?"

"Ramos."

Ramos. That was it. "Right."

"Nope."

"I'm not a cop or anything like that."

The bartender laughed. "You don't say."

"Is it that obvious?" Shake laid a twenty on the bar. "You have any idea where I might be able to find him? Ramos?"

She took the twenty and tucked it into her bra. "I don't want your money."

Shake smiled. He liked her. "What do you want, then?"

"I wouldn't mind being twenty-five again."

"But a little smarter this time around, right? Get in line."

"Yeah."

He laid another twenty on the bar. She tucked it into her bra.

"He's been in here a few times," the bartender said. "Maybe five or six times, the last few months. Drinks Carlsberg from the tap, never says much. Tips okay. I don't know where he lives, anything like that. But . . . he drives an old Benz. If that helps. Yellow."

"You know cars?"

"Like a '72 or '73, my best guess. Sedan, not the coupe."

"You know cars. Anybody else here might have a line on him?"

"Doubt it."

But she came out from behind the bar and walked over to the German. The German glanced up from his noodles and listened to what the bartender had to say. He shook his sweaty head.

"Let me guess," Shake said when the bartender returned.

"Sorry."

"Don't be. The Mercedes might help."

"Hope so."

Shake was about to leave when he stopped and looked back at the painting. There was just no way, he told himself, that the hippie chick could have real psychic powers, that Mitch's dream had led him straight to one of the kidnappers.

She'd been here. Shake knew it. But that meant she might know something about Ramos.

He decided to try Gina again, before he headed to the Golden Moon. He figured she'd have to pick up at some point if he kept calling every two minutes. Then he remembered that he had Dikran's phone. She wouldn't recognize the number. She wouldn't answer.

Shit. Shake stepped outside. He noticed, parked across the street and down the block, an old Mercedes. Yellow, a '73 280SE with the big front grille.

"I'll be damned," Shake said.

And then he heard, behind him, the unmistakable click of a gun hammer cocked back. He started to turn and felt the soft, cool kiss of metal against his ear.

Chapter Twenty-Six

First time Ramos heard about the Armenians, he was up at Folsom on a bullshit accessory beef. Seven, eight years ago now. One of the guys he jailed with, a skinny Barrio 18 *chacho* just out of the ding wing, was missing his fingers. All ten of them, like he had hooves. The *chacho* told Ramos that his *cabrón* back in Rampart wasn't as lucky. The Armenians left only his fingers, nothing else.

Yeah? Ramos had seen worse. He'd done a few runs for the Tijuana Cartel back when they were on top of things. They were crazy, those boys. But then, right after he got out of Folsom, Ramos heard about what happened to a stickup crew who knocked down the wrong bank in Glendale, where all the Armenians lived. He heard about the big slice of the action the Armenians took from La Eme, and the Mexicans rolling right over. He heard about the big slice of the action the Armenians took from the Russians. He saw one Russian one time, a stone-cold killer, just about piss his pants when an Armenian walked into the bar.

French didn't get it. He didn't get any of that. But he was right about one thing: There was no going back. He and Ramos were already in the shit. Three million cash might be able to pull Ramos out of the shit.

He had relatives in El Salvador. His mother's cousins. Maybe he could go down there and try to disappear.

First, though, Ramos needed to sweep the porch. That's what his brother had called it. Sweep the porch so you don't stumble. *Barrer el porche para que no viaje.*

Maybe the guy hadn't recognized Ramos behind his mask. Like French said. Maybe it was a coincidence, running into him at the bar. Maybe Ramos's porch was clean. But maybe not.

Ramos parked down the block from the Friendly Fireplace. This end of the street was empty. He shut off his engine and settled in. If the guy didn't show up today, Ramos would come back tomorrow and settle back in. He didn't mind waiting. Waiting was the part of life he liked.

He was pretty sure the guy would be back at some point. Ramos had a feeling.

Next door to the bar, there was a place that had gone bust. Out front was a big glass tank. Several places in Siem Reap, over on Pub Street mostly, had big glass tanks like that, filled with water and hundreds of tiny fish. Thousands of fish. Tourists paid a couple of dollars each to roll up their pants and stick their feet in the water. Fish pedicure, it was called.

This tank was empty, the glass smoky and cracked. But you could still read the letters on the tank.

Please feed our fish
You're dead
Feet skin!

Ramos wondered what had happened to all those little fish when the place went bust. The last girl out the door—did she put the fish in a garbage bag with some water in it and haul them down to the river? Ramos wasn't sure how reincarnation worked.

Did the fish come back as other fish? Did people come back as other people? What happened to you while you were waiting to come back as somebody else?

He glanced in the mirror, at the empty alley behind him. There were ghosts everywhere in Cambodia. Ramos didn't know why anyone would want to live in a place like this. Though maybe there were ghosts everywhere else, too, and you just didn't realize it.

Five minutes later, not even that, a motorcycle pulled up in front of the bar, and there he was, the guy Ramos was waiting for. Ramos wasn't surprised it was so easy, and he wasn't not surprised. He took his gun out and set it on the seat next to him.

The guy went inside the bar. Ramos waited some more. The letters on the empty fish tank were white, floating in the shadows.

Please feed our fish

You're dead

Feet skin!

When the guy came out of the bar, he'd have to walk down to the main street to catch a *tuk-tuk*. Ramos would get out of the car and come up from behind. Bang. After that, Ramos would go get a massage. Maybe the girl he liked could do something about his hurt wrist. When he tried to make a fist, the pain was so bad he had to close his eyes for a second. But it wasn't the end of the world. His left hand wasn't his gun hand.

Fifteen, twenty minutes later, the door to the bar opened. The guy came out, on his phone. Ramos picked up his gun. He made sure again that there was a round in the chamber.

And then he saw the other guy. A skinny guy in a dark suit, glasses. Ramos didn't know where he'd come from. He moved up fast behind the first guy. Quiet. The first guy was on his phone, not paying attention. The guy in the suit pulled a piece and put it to the other guy's head.

Ramos waited. A car barreled around the corner, a big shiny SUV.

It jumped the curb and slammed to a stop a few feet from the two guys. The guy with the gun shoved the other guy into the backseat of the SUV, then climbed in after him. The SUV went barreling off.

Huh, Ramos thought.

BJORN CALLED TO find out how the Zoom had gone. French gave him a less-than-full account. He didn't mention the Armenians. He didn't mention Alexandra attacking them. He didn't mention, of course, the $8 million.

"They're still insisting that we make the exchange in person," French said. He knew he couldn't seem too eager. "I don't know about that."

"If they can come up with the cash, it's coolio with me," Bjorn said.

"You're sure? I suppose . . ."

"But no way we're handing the chick over right there. They bring the money, then we drop her off in town a couple of hours later."

French frowned. "I don't know if they'll go for that."

"We'll see what they say. We don't want to worry about dye packs, GPS trackers, all that shit."

"Where should they bring the cash?"

"Let me put my head on it, and I'll bounce by later. Then you can hit them up with all the deets."

"Okay. Good."

Very good. French hung up and mixed himself a Bloody Mary. Now, if only Ramos didn't find a way to screw up this new plan. He'd left the house right after breakfast. French had tried to explain why killing the man was a terrible idea. The Good Cop, that's how French had started to think of him. He was their best chance at getting the money. French sensed that the Good Cop was genuinely reasonable, genuinely eager to cut a deal that benefited everyone. He didn't seem to be just playing a role.

Unfortunately, French thought uneasily, the other man didn't seem to be playing a role either. The Bad Cop. French, after getting a taste of the Bad Cop, didn't find the horror stories Ramos told him about the Armenians that much of a stretch.

So why did Ramos want to deal with *that* dude instead of the Good Cop?

Once again, though, Ramos had refused to listen. French wasn't *too* worried. He doubted that Ramos would be able to find the Good Cop. French considered the possibility that the Good Cop or the Bad Cop might manage to kill Ramos. It wouldn't be the end of the world, necessarily. Ramos was useful, but was he $3 million worth of useful?

French moved into the parlor and took a seat in the leather chair. Ramos had told him to stay away from the attic. French didn't need the warning. He *wanted* to stay away from the attic, for God's sake. He'd experienced, intimately and painfully, what the woman was capable of. She'd almost overpowered two men who outweighed her, each of them, by sixty or seventy pounds. One of whom was armed! If her wrists and ankles hadn't been cuffed, she *would* have overpowered them. Or worse.

Her expression as she'd crawled toward him, the serving fork gripped in her hand, had been terrifyingly calm.

He tried to nap. Every time he started to drift off, though, Alexandra's face was there, her eyes filled with gray smoke and an amused smile playing across her red, red mouth.

He got up and moved back into the kitchen. He glanced at the stairs up to the attic. Her hands were cuffed behind her back now, and Ramos had used a second chain to shackle her even more securely to the iron bed frame. What did French have to fear?

He climbed the stairs, put on his mask, and unlocked the double dead bolts. He stepped into the attic. Alexandra saw him and smiled.

"Ah," she said. "I thought perhaps you have forgotten me."

French pulled the chair over but kept his distance. The attic was even more stifling than normal. After she attacked them, Ramos had nailed a sheet of plywood over the attic window, leaving only a slim gap for ventilation.

"So," French said. "Alexandra."

"Yes. Now we can be truly introduced."

"I think I've already been truly introduced to you."

Her smile was amused, wary, apologetic, inscrutable. Had it always been so . . . complex? Or had French just failed to notice? He wondered.

"I hope you will forgive me," she said. "Is it broken, your nose?"

"I don't think so."

"I am glad."

"Are you?"

"Of course. But tell me, now that we are old friends. What is your name?"

French snorted. "You think I'm going to tell you my name?"

"Your given name. Does it matter so much, if I know this? What will this change?"

She was probably right about that.

"Jeremy," he lied. "That's my first name. And your definition of 'friends' is an odd one."

"Is it? Please, Jeremy. Will you do me one favor? My shoulders are stiff. Will you free me for one moment only, so that I may stretch?"

He stared at her. Then she laughed, and he realized what was happening.

"You're fucking with me," he said.

"As friends will, yes?"

"I don't understand you at all," French said.

He didn't understand himself either. Why was he up here? To chat!

"You would have tried to kill me that day," he said. "When you gave me the number to call. If I'd unlocked your handcuffs, you would have tried to kill me with my own ballpoint pen."

"The past does not interest me, Jeremy."

"You would have killed me yesterday, in the kitchen. I'm certain of that."

"And still, though, you chose to save my life."

He was taken aback. "How do you know that?"

"Because I am alive, Jeremy. Your . . . associate. I know men such as this. He wished to make an end of me, yes? But I think you are smarter than that."

Naked flattery. Still, though, French was pleased she understood to whom she owed her life.

"So you're saying it's not the smart decision?" he said. "To . . . make an end of you?"

"It is, perhaps. Certainly it is the cautious decision."

"My associate says you're something of a monster."

French expected her to feign shock or dismay. Instead she calmly contemplated the statement.

"No, I think," she said. "I am not a monster."

"He's told me a lot of stories about your organization."

"In my business, Jeremy, there must be stories. Do you see? Stories must have power. Or my business will be taken from me."

"But some of the stories are true."

"Perhaps. But let me ask you."

"Ask me what?"

"Are you a monster?"

"What? No! Of course not."

"But you will do what is necessary to achieve your goal, yes?"

"Within reason, but I would never . . ."

French remembered Chan. He remembered how he'd forced himself to stop remembering Chan.

"Do you see, Jeremy?" she said. "This is why the past provides us no benefit. It tells us who we were yesterday, not today. Who are we today? Each new day we must choose."

A faint breeze found its way through the gap between the plywood and the window. After a moment French stood.

"Well," he said.

"You will come to visit me again?" Alexandra said.

"Maybe."

She smiled. "I think we have much to discuss."

Chapter Twenty-Seven

Hi there, asshole." Babikian gave Shake a tap on the crown of his head with the gun barrel. A hard tap. "Get in the car."

Shake got in the car. Babikian's flunky, behind the wheel, turned around in his seat to give Shake a grin. He couldn't compete with the boss, though. He didn't have half as many teeth, or half as gleaming.

"Seat belt," Babikian said.

They put on their seat belts. The driver floored it. Babikian stuck the gun under his seat.

"Don't worry, asshole. I'm not gonna shoot you. I'm a knife guy. Ever since I was a kid, couldn't get enough of them. Isn't that right, Jeff?"

The driver grinned into the rearview mirror and nodded.

"On *Top Chef* they call it knife skills," Babikian said. "That cooking show. I love that, 'knife skills.' I get some great ideas from that show. You ever watch it?"

"Every now and then," Shake said. He watched *Top Chef* religiously. The contestants could cook, but a lot of the food they turned out was silly and pretentious. Why would you ever want to deconstruct fried chicken, for example? Or stick foam on it?

"You're not running your mouth now, are you?" Babikian said.

"When did I run my mouth?"

"At that Christmas party. When you sucker-punched me."

"All I said, I said leave the girl alone. And it wasn't a sucker punch."

Babikian reached into the inside pocket of his suit jacket and took out a butterfly knife. He flicked it open.

"You know what a julienne cut is?"

"I used to be a chef."

"No shit? Were you a better chef than you were a driver?"

"If I was a bad driver, why'd you want to use me that time? Behind Lexy's back?"

"What's your favorite part of the show? I like when they do restaurant wars. And that one girl judge. Not the one from India, the other one. The one has some meat on her bones. I dig her. Oh, baby. She gets my motor running."

"Where are we going?" Shake said. He wanted to know how long he was gonna have to listen to this.

"We're there."

The driver turned down a narrow lane. Shake recognized the stone wall, the wrought-iron gate. It was the villa where he and Dikran had first looked for Lexy. Apparently Babikian had taken advantage of the vacancy.

The gate slid open. The SUV edged up the driveway to the main house.

"Let's go, asshole," Babikian said.

They went inside. Dikran was waiting for them in a living room with lacquered walls and Oriental rugs. Anything that could be gold-plated was gold-plated. It looked like a Chinese restaurant in Dubai.

Dikran, sitting glumly on a massive red velvet couch.

"They come right after you go," Dikran told Shake. "They ask me where you are."

"And you told them?"

"It was accident."

"Sit," Babikian told Shake. "You want a drink? Well, fuck you. You're not getting a drink."

His flunky thought that was hilarious. Shake took a seat in a gold chair shaped like a crouching panther.

"What do you want from me?" he said.

"Tell me where Alexandra is. Tell me what's going on."

"We tell you nothing," Dikran said.

"Then I'll kill your asshole pal here," Babikian told him. "I have—let me explain this to you, Ghazarian, and you, too, asshole pal—exactly no problem doing that. I'm gonna yawn while I do it. Watch me."

Babikian yawned. Holy shit, he had an enormous mouth and a lot of teeth. Even his flunky had to stop himself from staring.

"Like that."

"We tell you nothing," Dikran said.

"She's been kidnapped," Shake said. He had no problem believing that Babikian had no problem with killing him. Probably Babikian would give deeper thought to brushing the dandruff off the shoulders of his skinny suit.

Babikian's giant smiling mouth snapped shut. "She's been . . . *what*?"

Dikran glared at Shake, but without too much heat. He knew that Shake didn't have a choice. And probably felt guilty about telling Babikian where to find him.

"Seven days ago," Shake said. "Eight now, maybe, I've lost track. We didn't know for sure, though, till day before yesterday."

Babikian stared at Dikran. Then he took off his futuristic glasses and stared some more at Dikran without them.

"Why didn't you tell me?" he said.

"Because you are a snake," Dikran said.

Babikian put his glasses back on. He walked over to the bar. It was a life-size gold-plated Buddha, holding a tray and an ice bucket. Babikian brought the ice, a bottle of vodka, and three glasses back to the coffee table.

"Is she all right?" Babikian said.

"She's all right," Shake said. "For now."

Babikian poured a drink for himself, then one for Dikran and one for Shake.

"I want to know everything. You understand? Start talking."

Shake didn't see a way around it. He took the glass of vodka and gave Babikian the broad strokes. Why Dikran had been so worried about Lexy in the first place and come to Indiana. What the *tuk-tuk* driver outside Lexy's hotel had said about ditching her at the temple. Shake went through the first call from the kidnappers, the Zoom chat, the follow-up call. He left out only one detail.

"So they jacked the price when they realized who she was," Babikian said.

"Yeah," Shake said.

"But wait." Babikian had sniffed it out right away. "I don't get it. How did they find out? That she's the *pakhan*?"

Shake glanced over at Dikran. Dikran was staring down at his loafers.

"They must have just figured it out," Shake said. "I don't know."

"She wouldn't tell them, that's for sure," Babikian said. "Okay. Whatever. I can't believe they didn't just kill her and run, once they found out. Isn't that what you'd do, Jeff?"

Jeff didn't want to field that question. He shrugged noncommittally.

"Thank God they didn't kill her," Babikian said. "But the question now, how do we get her back?"

Dikran lurched up and loomed over Babikian. Shake saw Jeff tense.

"If you betray her, snake . . ." Dikran said.

"Sit down and shut up, Ghazarian," Babikian said, more weary than pissed. "Holy mother of God, man. You think I don't want her back as much as you?"

"No. I do not think this. It is the farthest place from where I think."

"So . . . what? With her out of the way, I slide on up the ladder and take over? That's your theory, Ghazarian?" Babikian laughed. "You've been taking advice from this cantaloupe, Shake?"

Shake still didn't think Babikian had anything to do with the kidnapping—especially after the Zoom call—but Babikian getting Lexy killed and then sliding up the ladder wasn't a stretch at all.

"Doesn't sound that crazy to me," Shake said.

"A pair of cantaloupes, Jeff. Wonderful."

"Wonderful," Jeff said.

"Ghazarian, don't you understand? If Alexandra's out of the picture, *I'm* out of the picture."

Dikran looked confused. "But you are her *aj dzerrk'y*. Her right hand."

"Yeah, dipshit, that's correct. I'm *her* right hand. I'm where I am because *she* put me there. When she got rid of Narek, she had to fight those old farts on the Board to get me in. She goes, I go."

Babikian's argument was plausible. Shake had always been amazed by the amount of palace intrigue that Lexy had to deal with. She negotiated a constantly shifting web of alliances, some of them essential and others disposable, some secret and others just for show, some real and others phony, others both real *and* phony depending on the day of the week and which way a certain old guy on the Board had parted his hair that morning.

Still, though . . . Shake didn't buy it.

"So explain it to me," Shake said. "With Narek, why did she—"

"Shut up now, asshole," Babikian said, "or Jeff's gonna shoot you. Okay? This is family business. This is *our* family business. It doesn't concern you. You can stay if you want to stay, but it's up to you if Jeff shoots you or not. Jeff?"

"Up to you," the flunky told Shake.

"You are a snake," Dikran told Babikian again, but this time without quite as much conviction.

Babikian sighed. "Whatever I am, it's why she picked me to be her *aj dzerrk'y*. Dikran, open your eyes. My purpose in life, right now, is to get Alexandra back in one piece, whatever it takes. I'm your best friend in the world right now, you dipshit, whether I like it or not."

Again, it was plausible. Babikian was a guy who spent his whole life in orbit around the hot little sun of his own self-interests. He wasn't lying about that. Shake was just pretty sure he was lying about what, in this case, those specific self-interests were.

"So what were you planning to do about the eight million?" Babikian said.

"Ha!" Dikran said, before Shake could shoot him a warning look. "You think I don't have her money?"

"Access to some account? That's what you're talking about?" Babikian shook his head. "That's no good. Best case, and I mean *best* case, the transfer goes through without any problem, and it's still three or four days before we can turn that into hard currency. No."

"We're not gonna pay them off, are we?" Jeff said, frowning.

"Are you a cantaloupe, too?" Babikian said. "*Yes,* we're gonna pay them off if that's what it takes to get her back. We are gonna do—say it with me now—*whatever it takes*."

"You are wrong about this transfer," Dikran said. "We can grease a wheel. Yes?"

Babikian shook his head again. "You don't understand. It's three or four days *if* we grease the wheels. If we grease the *shit* out of the wheels. There's not eight million in U.S. cash *in* Siem Reap."

"Says who?" Shake said.

"Says anyone," Babikian said. "Go to a bank tomorrow. Any bank, ask them. But here's what we can do. The organization has diamonds in Hong Kong. Worth eight million easy. I'll call the old farts back home, bring them up to speed. They can have the diamonds on a plane first thing tomorrow morning."

"I'm telling you," Jeff said. "We can't put all our eggs in that basket. We'll pay them off, and they'll pop her anyway."

"Did I say we're gonna put all our eggs in that basket?" Babikian said. "Jeff? No. We're gonna have different baskets."

Dikran was staring a hole through Babikian's big head. "What do you mean, baskets?"

"I mean I'm gonna put every resource we have on this. If they fuck with us, these people who took her, if I smell any stink at all, I'm gonna light the sky up with the almighty wrath of a vengeful Armenian God like you've never seen before."

Jeff nodded. "So you're bringing in the twins."

"And Danny Palmer, too. Everyone." Babikian turned to Shake. "Now give it to me."

"What?"

Dikran's phone. Shake knew if he handed it over to Babikian, he was handing over the only link to the kidnappers. He was handing over all the power.

"Give me the phone," Babikian said, "or . . . you remember, right?"

"Jeff shoots me."

"That's right."

Shake tossed Babikian the phone.

"Now get out of here, Dikran," Babikian said. "And take your asshole pal with you. Make sure he stays out of the way and doesn't screw this up. I'll call you in the morning, when I know more."

"I go nowhere," Dikran said.

The flunky unbuttoned his suit jacket and showed them his gun.

Babikian sighed. He put a hand on Dikran's shoulder.

"We're gonna get her back," he said. "You have my word as a man. Give me some space, and let me do what I do."

Chapter Twenty-Eight

Babikian's flunky just laughed when Shake asked if they could get a ride back to the hotel, so he and Dikran had to walk down the lane and wait for a *tuk-tuk* on the corner. They stood next to a couple of monks who kept glancing at Dikran and giggling at the size of him. The monks looked like they were about eighteen, nineteen years old. Shake wondered if they were in for life. He didn't know how that part of the religion worked over here.

"*Shit*," Shake said. "All right. We need to come up with a plan here. A way around him."

If Shake had to guess how Babikian would play this, he'd guess that the shipment of diamonds would be mysteriously delayed in Hong Kong. Something like that. The ransom would never show up in Siem Reap, and the kidnappers would kill Lexy.

Shake had one hole card left: Quinn's buddy, Ouch. Who, Shake knew, was just as motivated by self-interest as Babikian, and probably even more dangerous. Would Ouch see any advantage in helping Shake? He hadn't called Shake back yet. At least Ouch would—*shit*. Shake remembered he'd given Ouch the number for Dikran's phone. He needed to call and leave a new message.

"Let me have my phone back," Shake said.

"No," Dikran said. He'd been quiet ever since they left the villa. Working up a righteous rage at Babikian, Shake had assumed.

"I can't have my phone back?"

"Here. Take your phone."

Shake saw that Gina had called three times.

"Did you answer? When my wife called?"

"Why do I answer? Do I care what your wife says?"

Great. Gina probably thought Shake was blowing her off.

"Then why did you say no?" Shake said. "When I asked for my phone back?"

"I say no because we need no plan. We do as Babikian says."

A *tuk-tuk* pulled up. Shake held Dikran back and let the two monks have it.

"The snake?" Shake said. "You trust him now?"

For the first time, Shake realized how tired Dikran looked, how burned down and wrung out. He seemed to be struggling to stand erect beneath the weight of his own bulk.

"I don't know," Dikran said. "He does not lie about Narek."

"Lexy pushed Narek out, you mean? But that doesn't—"

"Do you hear him? Babikian will send for these diamonds, to Hong Kong."

"There aren't any diamonds. He just wants to stall you on the wire transfer, take that off the table."

"He will bring the twins. Do you know the Mooshagian twins? They are like bloodhound. And Palmer. Sniper from Australia. He will shoot you from one mile away. I see this with my own eye, two times."

"Dikran. Listen to me."

The old Colonial house behind them was being renovated. Dikran walked over to a pile of broken bricks and sat down.

"Everybody says this to me," he said. "Dikran, listen to me. Like I am a child."

Another *tuk-tuk* pulled up. Shake waved it on. The heat and the exhaust fumes and the overpowering smell of sweet, exotic rotting fruit was giving him a headache. Cambodia was giving him a headache.

He went over and sat down next to Dikran.

"I'm sorry, but you need to listen to me. If Babikian's as tight with Lexy as he says he is, why didn't she have the kidnappers call him? She had them call *you*, because she doesn't trust him."

"You know this. You have no doubt."

"Yes, I have doubt. There's always doubt. Nothing in life is a hundred percent certain. But . . ."

"Ah."

"Dikran. Babikian was telling you what you wanted to hear. What he knew you wanted to hear. You've got to trust me. I want to make sure she's safe as much as you do."

"No."

No. Dikran was right. Shake was concerned for Lexy, seriously concerned, but she was his friend, not his life. Gina was his life. Lexy was Dikran's life. If she didn't survive this, neither would Dikran.

"No," Shake said. "Okay. But you've got to trust me on this."

"I ask you a question now. An important question."

"Ask it."

"Who are you?"

"Who am I?"

"You are driver only. You tell me this yourself, yes? In Indiana you tell me. 'I am retire driver only, Dikran. How will I ever help you?' Okay, then. Do you have better resource than Babikian? Do you have diamonds and Palmer and Mooshagian twins? Do you have better plan? No. No, no. No."

Shake couldn't really argue with that.

Black clouds were beginning to stack up overhead. The light slid away, and *tuk-tuk* headlights popped on.

"Maybe I don't have a plan yet," Shake said, "but at least you can trust me. You can't trust him."

"You are worthless," Dikran said, but with a sigh, without malice. He stood. "I am worthless, too. She has maybe chance if I follow Babikian. Best chance, I think. So I will put Babikian in my bed."

A few fat drops of rain smacked against the pavement. The day got even darker. People scurried down the street and ducked into doorways.

"Dikran, listen."

"You are loyal to her. You prove this to me." Dikran put his hand on Shake's shoulder. "But understand me now. You will do nothing, you will keep from our way, or I will kill you."

A *tuk-tuk* pulled up. Dikran climbed in and ordered the driver to go. He didn't glance back at Shake.

Shake sat on the pile of broken bricks for a few minutes. The street emptied, and no more *tuk-tuks* passed by. Finally the sky opened up and the rain pounded down, making the power lines overhead bounce and sway.

The building's overhang kept Shake dry. He called Gina. Straight to voice mail.

"I know you're pissed off at me. You have every right to be pissed off at me." He thought about how she might take that. "I'm not saying you need my permission to be pissed off at me. I'm just saying I'm aware of the . . . I understand you're in the right here."

He thought about how she might take *that*.

"Which probably makes you even more pissed off at me than you would be otherwise. That I know you're right and I'm still doing what I'm doing. I understand you're in the right there, too."

Gina wanted Shake out of Cambodia. Dikran wanted Shake out of Cambodia. *Everyone* wanted him out. So what was keeping him in? The same thing, Shake supposed, that had brought him here in the first place.

The rain had started to let up, but it was still dark, a gray, wet twilight. A monk in orange robes drifted past on a bicycle, like a spark floating away from a campfire. A second later the monk came drifting back and braked to a stop in front of Shake.

"Hi," he said. He was a young guy, early twenties or so. When you grew up Catholic, like Shake had, you always pictured monks as old guys, wizened and wrinkled.

Shake lowered the phone. "Hey."

"Everything is okay? You need some help?"

Was it that obvious? Shake had to smile a little.

"Yeah," he said. "No. I'm good, but thanks."

"Okay. Bye-bye."

The monk floated off. Shake put the phone back to his ear.

"You hear that?" he said to Gina's voice mail. "That was a monk. They're young guys here. A lot of them are. They shave their eyebrows. I guess they shave everything."

He could guess what Gina would say to that, but guessing wasn't nearly as good as actually hearing her say it. Not even close.

"Look, I know why you're not answering. You're upset. You don't want me to hear you crying because you miss me so much."

If that provocation didn't get her to call him back, nothing would.

"So if you want—"

The phone beeped and cut off his message. Shake had run out of time.

Chapter Twenty-Nine

When she got back to Bloomington, Gina called Yvette and told her to meet her at the Starbucks by campus. She gave Yvette the three hundred dollars she'd collected from Dominic, the casino boss. Yvette's eyes went wide.

"Yo, Ms. C! How'd you make that shit happen?"

"Tomorrow morning. Sign up for the GED prep courses. Understand?"

"Yeah!" Yvette said, and hugged her within an inch of her life.

After that, Gina took a long nap, made dinner for herself, and picked up a book she'd been meaning to read for months. At a quarter past nine, she put the book down and stepped out onto the porch. Stars sparkled overhead, but there was still a little light left in the sky, a band along the horizon like faded denim.

A beautiful evening for a stroll, wasn't it? Gina decided it was. And she wouldn't have to worry about running into Dominic. He'd asked her to meet him at nine. He would be long gone by now. She was safe.

She strolled downtown, pausing to pat the occasional Labradoodle. As she approached Courthouse Square, she saw Dominic on the corner, leaning against a lamppost. He'd changed out of the suit and was wearing jeans, a T-shirt, and a leather jacket. Gina came up behind him. He jumped a bit when she poked him in the ribs.

"Ticklish?" she said. "Or do you have a guilty conscience?"

Her turned to her with a loose, easy smile. "Some of both, probably."

"I'll keep that in mind."

He tried to think of something to say but stalled out. Gina could tell that behind the smile he was a little nervous. She found it endearing.

"You're like the dog in that old joke," she said.

"What joke?"

"There's a dog who chases the same car every day. He chases it and he chases it. Then one day, what do you know? He catches the car. And . . ."

It took him a second. "And he doesn't know what to do with it."

"That's right."

He shifted his position against the lamppost so that his shoulder almost touched hers. Gina decided that maybe he wasn't nervous after all.

"So does that mean I've caught you?" he said.

He smelled like heat and leather and unfiltered Camels.

"Not even close," Gina said.

You better turn around and walk away, the annoying voice in her head said again.

Why? Gina argued back. So what if this guy wanted to get into her pants? So what if she got a charge from that? She wasn't going to *let* him in her pants. This was just a harmless, enjoyable diversion, a distraction to take Gina's mind off the fact that her husband was thousands of miles away and not answering her calls.

"So how about some dinner?" he said.

"I'm fine right here for now."

"For now."

She ignored that. "It's almost nine-thirty, Dominic. How long were you going to wait for me? Some people might find that level of commitment a tad embarrassing."

"Is this another test?"

"Why not?"

"I didn't have anything better to do." His shoulder was touching hers now. "Not even close."

Gina craved a cigarette. Kicking the habit three years ago had been easy. Keeping it kicked was the tough part.

"So you said you have a plan. You're not going to spend the rest of your life at the Terra Splendida Casino."

"Six more months and then I'm gone. I know the business now. I know what I need to know."

"Vegas next?"

"Maybe. I know a guy there. I know some people in L.A., too. But the real action is in Macau."

"Is it."

Gina remembered what it was like to be young and unencumbered, the future a buffet of enticing choices.

"A buddy of mine has a place over by campus," Dominic said. "He's letting me use it tonight."

"What kind of action in Macau?"

"It's the Wild West over there. So much money pumping in from the casinos you wouldn't believe it." He took out a crumpled pack of Camels and stuck a cigarette in the corner of his mouth, with a casual flick that reminded Gina of the way Robert Mitchum did it in old movies. "You want one?"

"No, thank you."

He lit up and blew the smoke away from her, up toward the corona of light trembling at the top of the lamppost.

"A year or two in Macau," he said, "and then I can come back home and call my own shots."

Gina reached for his cigarette and took a drag. Pleasure spread through her like a string of firecrackers popping off.

A frat boy and his girlfriend walked past. They kept to the far edge of the sidewalk, giving Gina and Dominic a wide berth. That shouldn't have made her smile, but it did.

"I remember one time when I was nineteen or twenty," she said.

"What?"

She shook her head and took another drag. "Nothing."

"Let's go to my buddy's place," he said.

"Okay."

His buddy's apartment was on the ground floor of a dumpy fourplex next to a liquor store. Dominic shut the door behind them and pressed Gina up against the wall. He kissed her. She kissed back. It felt good, the pressing and the kissing. It felt good, for a moment, to feel reckless and stupid and wild again.

But then the moment passed. Gina knew it would. As Dominic started to undo the buttons of her blouse, she thought about her conversation earlier that morning with Yvette. *It's hard,* Yvette had reminded her, *but it's not complicated.*

Words of wisdom from the girl wearing a FOUR FINGERS IN THE PINK T-shirt. But Yvette didn't have it right, not exactly. Because really the decision Gina faced right now was neither complicated nor hard. Shake was her guy, and she didn't want to be with anyone but him, not even for a minute. That made this the easiest call in the world.

"No." She pushed Dominic gently away. "Thanks, but no thanks."

He smiled down at her, like he was waiting for the punch line. Gina started buttoning herself back up.

"What's going on?" he said.

"I'm going home. I wish you all the best with your future endeavors."

"What? But before, I thought . . ."

She wanted to sigh. Had he been this dense all along and she just hadn't noticed?

"Whatever you thought before doesn't matter now," she explained as politely as she could. "Because it's now and not before."

She turned to the door. He grabbed her wrist and jerked her back around. His smile was gone.

"What the fuck?" he said.

"Let me go," she said quietly. "Right now."

She saw the slap coming, felt the rush of air, but wasn't able to twist away in time. The bright flare of pain dazzled her for a second.

"No," he said.

He tightened his grip on her wrist. Gina lifted her foot, aimed for his instep, and stomped hard with the fat heel of her Jimmy Choo pump. Dominic dropped her wrist, and she kicked the side of his knee. It jumped sideways, leaving the rest of his leg behind. Dominic howled and hit the floor.

Gina was on her way out when she noticed an open laptop on the coffee table. She stepped over Dominic—he was still howling—and hit a key to wake the laptop. His Web browser was open on the screen. She scrolled through his search history. Porn, fantasy sports, more porn. Finally she hit pay dirt: the Bank of America log-in page.

"You *bitch*," Dominic managed to say between howls. "My *knee*."

"What's your bank password?" Gina said. "Never mind. Just kidding."

He didn't need to tell her his password. Gina knew her way around a computer, and her tech guy at the venture-capital firm back in San Francisco had taught her a few party tricks. She downloaded a simple keystroke-search script from the Web and ran it. Fifteen seconds later she was clicking open an unencrypted Word file where Dominic kept all his log-in info and passwords.

"What the fuck are you doing?" Dominic said. He tried to stand, which was his second-worst idea of the night. Down he went again.

There was close to a hundred grand in the Bank of America account. Wow. Gina wondered how he'd ended up with that kind of money, then decided she didn't care. She transferred out twenty thousand. That was enough to teach him a lesson, and she wasn't the vindictive sort.

"Thank you for your generous contribution," she said, "to Heads Held High."

"Where the fuck do you think you're going?" he said.

He lunged for her ankle as she stepped back around him, but she danced away.

"Home," she said.

Chapter Thirty

The rain cleared, the sun beat down again, and the wet streets began to smoke. Shake managed to flag down a *tuk-tuk*. When he got back to the hotel, he cranked the air conditioner and fell asleep. He set his alarm for an hour but slept through it and didn't wake until long after dark.

He rolled over and checked his phone. Gina hadn't called him back. Neither had Ouch.

What now? Shake thought he should probably get that tattooed on his arm.

He took a quick shower and went downstairs. He didn't see Dikran in the lobby or the restaurant. The bellhop stationed out front of the hotel knew Shake by now.

"Where is your friend, monsieur?"

"Just me," Shake said. He asked the guy to get him a *tuk-tuk*.

The lobby of the Golden Moon Hotel was empty, the same as it'd been on Shake's first visit. He wondered if the Cambodian hippie chick had the night off. He hadn't considered that possibility.

Shake went back outside. He counted four, five, six individual bungalows. The bungalow closest to the main house was the smallest one, with a neat little garden out front. Cabbage and some kind of dwarf melon. Shake figured that was his best bet.

He knocked. Waited. Knocked again. This time the door opened.

"Hiya!" the hippie chick, Mitch, said. She was wearing a towel and nothing else. And even the towel, knotted below her sternum, didn't seem big enough to meet the minimum requirements for a towel. "Sorry, I was just about to have a shower."

"I see that. You want me to come back in a minute?"

"Why?" She seemed genuinely puzzled. "Come on in. Want a beer? I've got some ganj, too, if you smoke."

"A beer's good."

She headed to the kitchen. Shake stepped inside. Her place looked less like a Grateful Dead album cover than Shake had expected. Lots of bookcases, lots of books. On the walls were dozens of vintage postcards, individually framed. The only real splash of psychedelia was the sofa, which looked like a Grateful Dead album cover.

Queenie, the rottweiler from hell, was asleep in the corner, 150 pounds of dog piled up like a rockslide.

Shake gave her a wide berth and took a seat on the couch.

"Angkor or Heineken?" Mitch called from the kitchen.

"You don't know?"

She stuck her head out of the kitchen and smiled. "Very funny."

"I'll try the Angkor."

She brought a couple of bottles back into the living room. When she handed Shake his beer, her towel started to slip. She tugged it back up into place, but not before Shake saw the swell of breast.

He looked away and saw that Queenie was awake now, eyes open and watching him.

"So what about your friend?" Mitch said. "Veronica? Is she okay?"

"Yes and no. And her real name's Alexandra. Lexy."

"Oh. You should have told me. A name makes a difference. I

know it sounds daft, but . . . Lexy. *Alexandra.* Okay. That makes more sense, when you think about her energy."

Her towel slipped again. Shake concentrated on the framed postcards next to the chair. There was one of Paris in what looked like the thirties. Another one of Palm Springs in the Swinging Sixties.

"Why all the old postcards?"

"They help me get a feel for the past. They're not just pictures, you know. Each one is a part of a *life.*"

She took one of the postcards off the wall and handed it to Shake. A cartoon drawing of three dachshunds eyeing a beer stein and a platter of sausages.

The back of the frame was clear plastic, so he could see the neat, tiny handwriting on the flip side of the postcard. The writing was in German, ink faded away to almost nothing.

"What's it say?"

"I don't know what it *says.* I just know how it *feels.*"

She studied the spot above his head and pursed her lips. Shake didn't need to ask what she thought about his aura.

Queenie heaved herself up, padded over, and collapsed again at Shake's feet. He gave the giant head a tentative pat. Queenie smacked her lips and went back to sleep.

"So how did you end up . . . ?" Shake wanted to ask her how a Cambodian girl in Siem Reap belonged on the Venice Beach boardwalk, selling crystals and flipping tarot cards.

She smiled. "End up like me?"

"Okay."

"Lots of reasons, I suppose. If you want me to explain it properly, we'll need another beer."

Shake almost said yes, then remembered why he was here.

"She was definitely kidnapped," he said. "Lexy was, like I thought."

"Oh. Wow."

"She's all right. They haven't hurt her."

"Wow. Are you *sure* you shouldn't call the police to sort it out? Or . . . I don't know."

Shake knew that bringing in cops, at this point, even if they *could* be trusted, would just make a dangerously mucked-up situation even more mucked up than it already was. It would be like trying to stop a bar brawl by lobbing a hand grenade at it.

"I'm sure," he said. "But I'm hoping you can help me."

"Anything, absolutely."

She sat down next to him and put a hand on his knee. It was innocent, just a small act of human compassion and nothing sexual about it. Shake knew, though, that this was a case he didn't want to ever have to bring before the grand jury of Gina. He cleared his throat.

"Do you . . . If you want to get out of that towel and get dressed . . ."

"Oh. Right!"

She bounced up and disappeared into the bedroom. A second later she popped back out—completely naked now except for silver rings on her toes and an elaborate black-ink flower tattoo that curled across her ribs.

"I was thinking about the dream I had," she said, completely unself-conscious. "After you left? And I really think it might be important. I really wish I had more formal training in dreams. I'm just mostly a—"

"I really wish you'd put some clothes on," Shake said.

"Oh. Right, sorry."

She went back into the bedroom. She came out in a tank top and denim cutoffs.

"It's that dream I wanted to talk to you about," Shake said. "You were dreaming about a place you'd been before. That bar downtown, the Friendly Fireplace."

He waited for realization to dawn, for her to say, *Oh, of course!* Instead she pursed her lips.

"Hmm," she said.

"I'm looking for a guy I ran into there, and I thought maybe you've crossed paths with him. His name's Ramos. Mid-thirties, I'd say, and . . ."

Her lips stayed pursed. "Where?" she said. "The Friendly what?"

"The Friendly Fireplace," Shake said. "On Kingdom Street. Maybe it used to be called something else."

"I never go down to Kingdom Street. If you're a Cambodian girl, the *barangs* just assume you're a prostitute."

"You've been to this place, at least once. There's this huge crazy painting behind the bar. Old Hollywood actresses in hell?"

"Sounds far out."

"No. Don't you see? It's your dream. It's your dream exactly."

She shrugged. "Okay."

Shake refused to believe that Mitch's psychic powers had led him directly to one of the kidnappers. It had been a crazy coincidence, that was all.

He stood. "I'll get out of your hair."

"Maybe I can help some other way. Your friend was at Banteay Srei, right? If we go out there, maybe I can get a vibe on where she is now. I can't promise anything, but you never know. Now that I know her real name."

"That's all right," Shake said. "Thanks anyway, and thanks for the beer."

He started to move past her, but she stepped over and laid her palm flat against his chest.

"What are you doing?"

"Shhh. Let me have a go at your past lives. Close your eyes. Empty your mind."

Shake sighed and closed his eyes. "All right."

She pressed her palm gently against his chest. "I see a wall."

"That narrows it down."

"It's painted light blue. Pale blue with . . . a bit of purple mixed in? And I feel . . . sticky. Sweaty. We're somewhere tropical, I think. *Shhh.* I know what you're thinking."

"So you really *can* read my mind."

She ignored that. "This is a long, long time ago. A small, hot room with pale purplish blue walls. I feel an energy like . . . like a guitar playing. A steel guitar, but a duff one, just one string. The E string, maybe? Really harsh and monotonous. *Da . . . da . . . da.* Tell me what you feel. Where are we?"

"Where are we? I thought *you* were supposed to tell *me* that."

"I'm just a guide to your past lives. I can't do this alone."

Shake didn't want her to do it at all. "I don't know where we are. Sorry."

"I keep seeing that wall. It's made out of concrete blocks. In the groove between two of the blocks, there's a bolt. Two bolts, actually, holding a chain. It's bloody humid. I can smell sweat. Sweat and . . . butterscotch, I think."

Shake opened his eyes, startled. "What?"

She'd just described, in perfect detail, the infirmary at Angola, the prison in Louisiana where Shake had done his first stretch for grand theft auto, almost twenty-five years before. A month in, his appendix had burst and he'd spent almost a week in the infirmary. Next to every hospital bed was a chain bolted into the wall, so, if necessary, a CO could cuff you to it. A pale blue wall, with a little purple in it. The air-conditioning never worked. Dessert, most meals, had been the worst butterscotch pudding Shake had ever eaten. He could still taste it.

"You feel something?" Mitch said.

"No. Maybe. Nothing, really."

"Sometimes a past life is buried so deeply you can hardly sense it. But it's always there. It's always closer than you think."

The memory of the infirmary at Angola was just another coincidence—Mitch had started him thinking about the past, and Shake's mind had made the jump. But . . .

"I've got to go," he said. "Thanks again."

Shake made his way back to the street, through the banana trees, thinking about Mitch, thinking about past lives. What if he had the power to do it all differently? What if he could go back in time and not join his uncle's crew, not steal the car that had landed him in Angola?

But then what? His life would be better, maybe, but it wouldn't be his. Some other guy, some other version of Shake, would be living it. And he never would have met Gina.

He heard Mitch following him and turned.

It wasn't Mitch. It was Ramos, with his gun up and aimed at the center of Shake's chest.

Not again, Shake thought.

"Hey," he said. "Why don't we talk about this?"

Chapter Thirty-One

O kay," Ramos said.

Shake had braced himself for the gunshot.

"Okay?" he said. "Okay we can talk about this?"

"You remembered who I was. Yesterday on the computer."

Shake didn't know if that was a question or not.

"Yeah." Shake guessed that a lie, at this point, was more likely to get him shot than the truth. "Took me a minute."

The guy used the palm of his free hand to wipe sweat from his forehead. He did it without moving the gun an inch off the center of Shake's chest.

"Hot," he said.

Shake needed to get the guy away from here in case Mitch *did* come out of her cottage. If she came out and surprised him, Ramos was likely to shoot her without even thinking about it.

"Let's go somewhere and cool off," Shake said. "I'll buy you a beer."

"I don't want a beer."

The sounds of the street, just thirty feet away or so, drifted over. People chattering away in Khmer. Motorcycle engines spitting and popping.

"How long you been tailing me?" Shake said.

"Since this morning. Outside the bar."

"You want to put that gun down?"

"No."

"Let's go find some air-conditioning. I'm from New Orleans, but it's even stickier here."

"I didn't know who she was. When we grabbed her."

"But you understand now."

"Yeah."

Ramos wiped the sweat off his forehead again. When he did that a third time, Shake knew he'd have to make his move for the gun and hope for the best.

"New Orleans?" Ramos said.

"That's right. You ever been there?"

"I thought the Armenians were all Armenians."

"I used to freelance for them. Driver. They use a few freelancers they trust. But they keep most of it in-house."

"I heard all about the Armenians. Stories."

Again, Shake couldn't tell if that was a question or not.

"A lot of the stories are true," Shake said, "you want me to be honest with you."

Ramos nodded.

"There's a way out of this for you."

"I know a way," Ramos said. "Wrap it up. Wrap it up fast."

Shake knew what that meant. Kill Shake, kill Lexy, start running. But Shake had to think Ramos was keeping an open mind about it. He couldn't see another reason Ramos hadn't killed him yet.

"There's a better way," Shake said. "You want to hear it?"

"Let her go."

"Let her go. I'll talk to her people. I'll explain the situation. I'll talk to her. We go way back."

"And she'll be good with that."

"I didn't say it would be easy. But it's your best shot."

Shake thought he heard footsteps approaching. He tensed. The steps faded away.

"Three million dollars," Ramos said. "Maybe that's my best shot."

"Is that what your partner says?"

"Yeah."

"You trust him?"

For the first time, the barrel of Ramos's gun moved. Just a fraction of an inch, but Shake could see he'd hit a nerve.

"Think it over," Shake said. "I'm staying at the Victoria Angkor. Charles Bouchon. You can get hold of me that way."

"Why don't I pop you and then cut a deal with them after," Ramos said. "The real Armenians. You're the only one saw my face. It's safer that way."

"Cut a deal with the bald guy? All those stories you heard about the Armenians, he's probably responsible for most of them."

Ramos looked like he might be about to wipe his forehead again. Shake prepared himself. But then Ramos lowered his hand. He clenched his fist.

"I'm the one you want on your side," Shake said. "But we need to cut a deal soon. You know?"

"You're not on my side."

Fair point. "But we can cut a deal. That's what I'm saying."

"I know you?"

"What?"

"You ever do time in California?"

"Three years at Mule Creek. Before it was all ad seg."

"I was there after you."

"Listen to me," Shake said. "Let me go tell my friend to stay where she is. I'll come back. You have my word."

"Turn around. Do it."

Shake needed Ramos to wipe his forehead again, that split-second blind spot, or he'd never get to the gun before Ramos shot him. Even with the split-second blind spot, Shake's odds weren't good.

Ramos looked like he might be about to wipe his forehead again. But he was just lifting his hand to point.

"I said turn around," he said.

"You gonna pop me?"

"I haven't decided."

Shake didn't have a choice. He'd done his best. He turned around. Through the banana trees, he could see the wall of the building next door. The wall was an old one, the stucco peeling off in layers. At one point in the past, the wall had been painted yellow. At some other point in the past, the wall had been painted maroon.

"You believe in past lives?" Shake said.

"No. That reincarnation shit all the Cambodians believe?"

"Yeah. No. More like there's different parts to one life. Like you stop living the one kind of life and you leave it behind."

"You can't leave your own life behind."

"I guess. Yeah."

"I don't trust anybody," Ramos said.

"What?"

"You asked did I trust him."

The partner.

"There's a way out of this," Shake said, "where you don't have to spend the rest of your life checking your shadow."

Shake waited. He told himself that Ramos would have shot him by now, if he was going to shoot him. He told himself that over and over, like he was working his way down the beads of a rosary.

"Hiya!" Mitch said.

Shake turned back around. Ramos was gone.

"What are you doing?" Mitch said.

Shake turned and sprinted after Ramos, but when he got to the street, Ramos had disappeared. Shake didn't see any sign of the old yellow Mercedes. He didn't even know which direction Ramos had headed.

He walked back to Mitch. "Nothing. Just leaving."

She wasn't paying attention to him. She was looking around as if the banana trees were closing in on her.

"Can you feel that?" she said. "This really ominous, squiffy energy? A sort of *squeeee, squeeeeee.*"

"No. Sorry."

"Like when you're blowing up a balloon and it's about to pop."

"I'm gonna get out of here now," Shake said. "Take it easy."

Chapter Thirty-Two

French decided to risk another trip upstairs. It was almost one in the morning, and chances were Ramos would be back soon. But the muffler of the stolen Mercedes was more rust than metal. If he kept close to the attic window, he'd hear Ramos coming from a mile away.

He sliced up a pair of mangoes, arranged them on a plate, and climbed the stairs. Alexandra was still awake.

"You have come to save my life again," she said.

French smiled uncertainly. "What?"

"From boredom, Jeremy. I will tell you a secret. For me, the boredom will kill me before a gun."

"My father used to tell me," French said, "or lecture me, I should say, that only boring people get bored. Of course, he was drunk off his ass at the time. All the time."

"My father, too, in Armenia."

"The drinking?"

"And the lectures."

French pulled the chair closer to the bed and sat. "I brought you some fresh mango."

"Ah. Mango is my favorite. Of all the fruit."

He realized he hadn't considered the logistics of the situation. Alexandra's hands were cuffed behind her back.

"I'm afraid we have a dilemma," he said.

"Who is the poor man, do you remember? In the Greek stories?"

"Tantalus. Of course. His eternal punishment was to stand in a pool of cool water, beneath a tree loaded with fruit. When he reached for the fruit, the branches of the tree would lift away from him. When he bent to drink, the water would recede."

She smiled. "Do I deserve such a punishment, Jeremy?"

What the hell is wrong with me? French wondered. As screwy as it seemed, he found Alexandra *more* attractive now that he knew how dangerous she was, not less.

He hesitated, then picked up a slice of mango. She caught his hesitation.

"I will not bite, Jeremy. You have my word."

"I'm not sure I believe you."

Even so, he lifted the slice to her mouth. She leaned forward, and French tried not to flinch. She bit into the ripe, rosy flesh of the mango.

"Good?" he said.

She sighed with pleasure. "Oh, Jeremy. You do not know."

She took another bite. This time her lips grazed his fingertips. French watched her chew and swallow.

"Take off your mask," she said.

He laughed. "And why would I do that?"

"Are you not curious?"

"About what?"

"If I will find you handsome."

He laughed again, and then—*fuck it*—he took his mask off. He ran a hand through his hair and enjoyed the surprise on her face, the soft O of her mouth. French doubted that many things, or many men, managed to surprise her.

"It doesn't really matter, does it?" he said. "You're going to find out who I am. Your people will. I'm not stupid. This mask won't protect me, will it?"

She looked at him in a new way now, her otherworldly eyes reaching deeper and deeper into his.

"No," she said. "The mask will not protect you."

"But *you* can. That's what you were implying this morning, weren't you? When you were talking about the past, the future. When you were talking about my associate."

Her shrug was just as expressive as her smile, and equally inscrutable.

"Sometimes what is in one's best interests, these interests shift. Yes? One must always watch for such a shift. In himself and his associates."

"What are you saying?" French knew what she was saying. He stood and moved to the window. He put his ear to the gap between the plywood and the window. Listened. The night was quiet. "I trust him. My associate."

"You do not. You are no fool. And my answer is yes."

He returned to the chair. "Your answer?"

"Yes, you are handsome. But many men are handsome. I find you . . . intriguing."

Again, French knew what she was doing. He really wasn't a fool. But the way her otherworldly gray eyes reached deeper and deeper into his . . .

"You want me to let you go," he said.

"Of course."

"Betray my associate."

"This is your most important concern?"

No, French had to admit, it was not his most important concern at all.

"I'd be walking away from millions of dollars," he said.

"But you will have your life, Jeremy. You will not be held responsible for taking me. I give you my word."

He stood and went to the window again, to listen for the Mercedes.

"Isn't this where you offer me the carrot?" he said.

She cocked her head, puzzled. "A carrot?"

"The stick first, the threat. And then the carrot, to sweeten the deal."

"Ah. I see. Of course. You think I will offer you money. A million dollars. Two."

"No?"

"No," she said. "The carrot I offer you is more appealing than money, I think."

"And what's that, exactly?"

"I will grant you three wishes."

He laughed and returned to the chair. "Three wishes?"

"Like the genie."

"If I remember my fairy tales correctly, that usually goes rather poorly for the wisher."

"I have many friends, Jeremy. People of importance. What do you desire most in the world? Not money. Money is only . . . how would you say it? The middleman."

"A means to the end."

"You told me you are a writer, yes? Perhaps, for example, you desire to direct a film as well. In the film business, I have more friends than I can count. Does two million dollars buy you friends such as these?"

A vision of his future Hollywood life flashed before French's eyes. It embarrassed him—every cliché in the book, straight out of an episode of *Entourage*. The truth was, though, French *did* have real talent. He'd always known it. The reviewers of his first novel had known it. He just needed the opportunity.

"And still you have two wishes left," Alexandra said. "For whatever you most desire."

The scent of ripe mango had filled the attic. French swallowed. He wanted her so badly. Another vision flashed past, the two of them together on an island, someplace like Santorini. In bed, the sheer white curtains billowing in the breeze, a view out over an impossibly turquoise sea.

French realized he'd never been involved with a woman he considered his intellectual equal. A woman who *challenged* him. Oh, sure, he'd dated smart women before, sharp, brittle academics who could read the *Iliad* in Homeric Greek or bore you senseless with their thoughts on narratives of displacement in Eastern European cinema.

Alexandra would never, ever bore him. She was most definitely a challenge. Was he, French wondered, up for it?

"You're sure you can guarantee my safety?"

For a fraction of a second, the glow of her gray eyes faded and revealed a glimpse of something darker, harder, like a cloud lifting off a granite peak. It happened so fast, the glow returned so quickly, that French wasn't sure if he'd imagined it or not.

Alexandra smiled. "Yes, Jeremy. I can do this."

There was something between them, something authentic. A spark. French knew he wasn't imagining it. But, oh, if only it were that simple.

In graduate school French had taken a creative-writing workshop with a famous, and famously curmudgeonly, Hungarian novelist. The novelist would sit slumped at the end of the table, the shoulders of his cheap suit bunched up around his ears, and listen sourly and silently to the discussions of student work.

"Eh," he would say occasionally.

Once, though—French couldn't remember the exact circumstances—the Hungarian novelist had been roused to proclaim that in every great work of literature the protagonist must be faced with a life-altering moral choice. Without it a story was not a story.

French heard, in the distance, the approaching clunk and fart of the stolen Mercedes.

"I have to go," he said.

"We do not have much time, Jeremy," Alexandra said. "You understand this? You must make your decision before your decision is taken from you."

He paused in the doorway. "I understand," he said.

THE NEXT MORNING French woke early. He was in the kitchen, making coffee, when Ramos shuffled in.

"So how did it go?" French said. He'd gone straight from the attic to his bedroom last night and had pretended to be asleep when Ramos entered the house. "Did you find the Good Cop?"

Ramos yawned. "The who?"

"The Armenian who recognized you during the Zoom."

"No."

"So where were you all evening?"

"Nowhere."

Nowhere. French didn't press the issue. Ramos, he'd learned by now, worked in mysterious ways.

Ramos yawned again and splashed Jameson into his mug. "You're strapped."

"I'm what?"

"You're strapped now."

He pointed his chin at the pocket of French's blazer. French was surprised that Ramos, who noticed nothing, had noticed the slight bulge.

"Just a precaution," French said. He hadn't touched his gun since the day they'd kidnapped Alexandra, but after talking to Alexandra, after watching Ramos check the magazine in his gun a couple of days ago, French had decided it couldn't hurt to be prepared.

Maybe, he decided, it was better that Ramos *had* noticed the gun.

"You ever fire one before?" Ramos said.

"Of course," French said. A lie, but how difficult could it be, really, to line up a sight and pull the trigger?

A sharp rap on the back door startled them. Ramos crept to the window and peeked out. He relaxed.

"It's the goof."

"Don't . . . please don't call him that when he's around."

"Okay."

French opened the door. Bjorn, this morning, was wearing what looked like yoga pants, a formal English waistcoat, and a tiny fedora. The tiny fedora was secured at a rakish angle by a pair of bobby pins.

He gave French and Ramos a shit-eating grin. "Sup-sup, soul brothers? Are you ready to bring this biznuts home? We're finna bring home the *cheddar*! I found a primo spot for the handoff."

"Where is it?" French said.

"An old charcoal pit outside of town. Nobody uses it anymore, nobody around. *Nobody.* Tell them to take the National Highway 6 east to 99, then north on 99 for eighteen klicks."

"National Highway 6 to 99," French repeated, to make sure he had it right, "then eighteen kilometers north on 99."

"At exactly eighteen klicks, there's a road on the right. Barely a road, so watch the odometer. Follow that two, three hundred meters, you're there. They'll see it."

"The charcoal pit."

"It's like a . . . I don't know. Like a mound, sort of. You take the wood inside, you set the wood on fire, the wood turns to charcoal. Like that. They'll see it."

"How'd you know about her?" Ramos said.

"Say what?" Bjorn said, still grinning.

"You put us on her," Ramos said. "The woman we grabbed. Who put you on her?"

"That's none of our business," French said.

Now that Ramos had raised the question, though, French was curious what Bjorn might say.

Bjorn shrugged. "The grapevine, dude. Na'mean? My boy French here told you, didn't he? That I have this town *wired*. A birdie here, a birdie there. It's all good."

"What birdie?" Ramos said, but Bjorn had already turned away and was helping himself to the Jameson.

"So when you hit them up, tell them it's on for tonight," Bjorn said. "Let's get bumpin'. Tell them eight o'clock. I'll be there early, at six or seven, and set up down the road on 99. Catch them if they try anything twisty."

"Wait," French said, but then stopped himself. If Bjorn went to pick up the ransom, that screwed up French's original plan—Bjorn would find out about the extra $4 million. On the other hand, though, if French was going to betray his partners and free Alexandra, this was an excellent development. He could find some way to send Ramos with Bjorn to the exchange and slip away with her while the two of them were gone.

"What?" Bjorn said.

But *was* French going to betray his partners and free Alexandra? That was the question. All night he'd tossed, turned, and been unable to make a decision. Or, more accurately, been unable to stick to a decision for more than a few minutes at a time. Back and forth, back and forth, the worst kind of intellectual vertigo.

"I'm going," Ramos said. "Not you."

Bjorn dropped the grin. "This is my party, *m'ijo*. Real talk."

French remembered the old Roman aphorism. *Deliberando saepe perit occasio.* In deliberation, opportunity is often lost.

"Gentlemen," French said, "I may have a solution."

Chapter Thirty-Three

The first morning they arrived in the USA was Dikran's favorite memory of all his life. He and Sandri (this is what he called her, before she became *pakhan*) had walked up the road to hitchhike away from the port. New Jersey. So hungry, both of them. So thirsty. Scared, too.

"Don't be scared, *jigyars*," Dikran had said to her. *Jigyars,* a term of affection in Armenia. Dikran did not know the English translation of it.

Finally a car stopped for them. The man rolled down his car window. He looked at Sandri the way a wolf looks at meat.

Neither Dikran nor Sandri had much English yet, but it was not hard for Dikran to suppose what the man was saying.

You, girl, come ride with me. You, boy, stay here.

"No," Dikran told the man. Dikran had only English words such as these: "yes" and "no," "please" and "thank you."

"No?" the man said. He opened his door. He moved out of his car. A large man, smiling like a wolf. He gave Dikran his middle finger and reached for Sandri's arm.

"No, thank you," Dikran said.

Later Dikran and Sandri sat at McDonald's restaurant, far from the port. They ate and drank. The wolf-man's wallet had been fat with money, his car tank filled with gas. Dikran had been surprised that Sandri could drive a car so well as she did. She had never driven a car before, not once, in Armenia.

Dikran ate two Big Mac sandwiches and french fries. He remembered the taste of the food like it was in his mouth now. The taste of USA! A new life for him and her!

He remembered how Sandri had put her hand on his shoulder.

"'Don't be scared,'" she'd said, "that's what you told me earlier. Yes?"

"Yes."

"But why would I ever be scared? I am with you, *jigyars*."

"Hello?" Babikian said. "Knock, knock."

Dikran looked up. He had not been listening to Babikian. He had been thinking of that first day in USA.

"What?" Dikran said.

"I asked do you want something to eat. A bagel? Some fruit?"

"I want nothing. Why do you bring me to this place?"

Dikran sat on the old tire of a tractor. This empty warehouse smelled of grease and spiders and Babikian. Babikian smelled of fancy cologne, expensive powder.

"We're using this as our new HQ. We're gonna need the space once everybody gets here."

"I ask why do you bring me."

"Because we need to discuss the situation. You're a part of this. All right? I'm gonna have a bagel. You want something, Jeff?"

The other one, the minor snake, shook his head. "Nah. Later maybe."

"What is English translation?" Dikran said. "For *jigyars*? Do you know this?"

"Is there one?" Babikian said. "I don't know it."

"The literal translation is 'my liver,'" the minor snake said.

Babikian frowned. "Really? You're saying all my life my *tatik*'s been calling me 'my liver'?"

Was Sandri scared now, with the men who had kidnapped her? Dikran wondered. Was she sad? Did she remember that first day in USA?

"Where are the Mooshagian twins?" he said. "Where is the sniper, Daniel Palmer?"

"I told you, they're on their way." Babikian made another big sigh. "You're gonna wear me out, Dikran. They'll be on the four-o'clock flight from Bangkok. The twins are. Palmer's coming in from—"

Dikran's phone sang the Bee Gees. The phone in Babikian's hand. Babikian looked at the calling number.

"Shit. Here we go, I bet." He set the phone on the table. "I'm gonna put this on speakerphone, all right? You're part of this, Dikran, like I promised. I want you to hear everything that goes on. No secrets between us, right?"

"Good," Dikran said. "Yes."

Babikian tapped one button of the phone. Another button.

"Hello," he said.

"Listen to me carefully," a man from the phone said. One of the men who had kidnapped her. Dikran recognized him, but his voice now was like metal and hollow. Maybe because of the speakerphone, maybe because of the mask he wore.

How are you always so stupid, Dikran? Dikran asked himself. Why would the man wear his mask when he is on the phone, when they cannot see him?

"I'm listening," Babikian said. "I want to cooperate in every way possible."

Quiet. Then, "Who is this?"

"What do you mean?"

"You're not . . . Where's the person with whom we've been dealing?"

"I'm the one you're dealing with now. My name's Ruben Babikian. I'm in charge. I'm the person with the eight million dollars."

Quiet. Then, "Fine. Here are your instructions."

"I'm ready. I'm writing down every word." Babikian snapped fingers at the minor snake, who had already taken paper and pen from his suit. "Go ahead."

"Eight o'clock tonight," the voice of the kidnap man said. "Take National Highway 6 to 99, then head north for eighteen kilometers."

The minor snake wrote quickly. He showed the paper to Babikian.

"Got it," Babikian said. "Then what?"

"There's a road on the right at exactly eighteen kilometers. Follow that road two or three hundred meters until you reach an abandoned charcoal pit. Park there. Get out of your car. Come alone, unarmed."

"Wait, what's a charcoal pit?" Babikian looked over at the minor snake, who shrugged. "Is that just like a regular pit?"

"No. It's like a mound, actually."

"But they call it a pit? All right. I just want to make sure I'm crystal clear."

"You'll know it when you see it. Bring the eight million dollars. If the bills are marked or in any way—"

"It's gonna be diamonds."

"What?"

"Diamonds. And the eight million is the conservative valuation. You'll probably get eight and a half for these. I wanted to err on the side of making this happen."

"No. No. That wasn't the agreement. The agreement was *cash*, U.S. dollars."

"Well," Babikian said. "Another way you could look at it, the agreement was four million and you doubled up on us. I don't want to start an argument, it's your prerogative to raise the price. But you have to be flexible. And I'm telling you, you want diamonds, not cash. Diamonds you'll be able to get out of the country no problem. Put them in a sock, put the sock in a shoe. Try that with cash. You know how much eight million in cash weighs? A couple of hundred pounds, I think."

"A hundred and sixty pounds," the minor snake said. "If it's all hundreds."

"You hear that? A hundred and sixty pounds."

Quiet. Quiet. Quiet. Babikian showed his palm to Dikran. *Wait, wait.*

"How will we know they're real?" the kidnap man said.

"The diamonds?" Babikian said. "You have someone check them out, that's how. We'll give you twenty-four hours to check them out. Satisfaction guaranteed."

"I don't understand."

Dikran did not understand either. "What—"

Babikian showed Dikran his palm again. *Wait, wait.*

"We'll bring the diamonds tonight," Babikian said. "Okay? And you take the diamonds. If they check out, *when* they check out, then you drop Ms. Ilandryan at a location of your choosing. You call, you let us know where she is, we'll come get her. Easy-peasy, lemon-squeezy."

Still Dikran did not understand. He was stupid, yes, but even he knew this much: You give the cookie to a dog *after* he brings you the rubber ball, not before.

Wait, wait.

"So you mean . . ." the man who had kidnapped her said. "Yes. Okay. That's acceptable."

"I think that's fair."

"Eight tonight. Come alone and unarmed. If you attempt to double-cross us in any way, she dies. She dies tonight."

Quiet. A different kind now. Empty.

Babikian picked up the phone. Tapped a button.

Dikran wished he had pills to calm his blood. He had been a fool to throw them away. What did Sandri say when Dikran needed to calm his blood?

You are a river, Dikran. Feel yourself, so cool and flowing.

He tried now, for the sake of her, to feel such a way.

"What the fuck do you do?" he said to Babikian. "If you give dog cookie first, he will not bring you the rubber ball. He will eat cookie and go to lick his asshole!"

"That's . . . well, okay," Babikian said. "That's a vivid point, buddy. But we have to play it safe. We have to make sure *nothing* goes wrong. You agree with that?"

"Yes. But—"

"We can't give them any reason to hurt her. Right?"

"If they hurt her, I will—"

"And you forget something, Dikran. I'm gonna have the twins on them tonight. Keeping an eye on them. Remember? Those little dudes can track *anybody*."

Dikran nodded slowly. "They are like bloodhound."

"Exactly. Now, do you want a bagel?"

"I could probably eat a bagel," the minor snake said.

Dikran could hear Shake still. *You can't trust Babikian.* Shake. The asswipe had made his home in Dikran's head, would not shut his smart mouth. *You can't trust him, Dikran. Why did she have them call* you, *not him?*

"Show me," Dikran said. "Do you say you have these diamonds? Show me now."

There won't be any diamonds, Dikran. Trust me.

"No problem," Babikian said. "The diamonds came in from Hong Kong an hour ago. Jeff."

The minor snake opened a case. He reached inside. He handed Babikian a small sack of black velvet. Babikian turned the sack upside down and poured diamonds onto the bed. Many, many diamonds.

Dikran picked up one diamond, a large one. He brought it close to his mouth and put his breath on it. Again. His breath made no mark.

"What are you doing?" Babikian said.

Sandri had taught Dikran long ago how to see if a diamond was fake.

"Bring me water," Dikran said. "Glass of water."

Babikian shrugged. The minor snake went into the bathroom and came out again with water in a glass. Dikran picked a different diamond, also large, and dropped it in the glass. The diamond sank like a stone. Like a diamond.

Babikian laughed. "Shit, Dikran. I didn't know you were some diamond expert. A man of hidden talents."

The diamonds were no fakes. Dikran was certain of this. And every question he asked of Babikian, Babikian had an answer for it.

So why, then, did Shake living in Dikran's head still talk, talk, talk?

Don't trust him, Dikran. You have to trust me.

"What's wrong, buddy?" Babikian said. "Talk to me. You got any ideas about how this plays out, I want to hear them."

"I don't know," Dikran said.

"I know what's wrong. It's that asshole, isn't it? That Shake asshole?"

Dikran looked up, surprised. It was as if Babikian could also hear Shake in Dikran's head.

"You're worried he's gonna fuck this up, aren't you?" Babikian said. "Yeah. That worries me, too."

"It's a worry," the minor snake said.

Dikran did not understand. "What worry?"

"I'm gonna tell you the truth, my friend," Babikian said to Dikran. "I'm worried, too, that this Shake asshole is maybe gonna stick himself into the middle of everything. Try to be the hero and fuck it all up."

"He will not," Dikran said. "I warn him. Stay away."

"That's good. Yeah. But . . . I don't know. You know the guy better than I do, Dikran. Is he the type, you think, he'll do the safe thing and stay out of this?"

Dikran frowned. No, he knew, Shake was not this type. Even Sandri, who loved Shake, said so. She did not say his name at times, *Shake,* without also a big sigh.

"You thinking what I'm thinking, Dikran?" Babikian said. "I bet you are."

"What?" Dikran said. "What do I think?"

Babikian scooped the diamonds back into the sack. He found the diamond at the bottom of the glass and put it, too, in the sack. He sat down on the bed close to Dikran. He gave Dikran a long look in his eye.

"You need to shut him down, Dikran," Babikian said. "You need to shut the asshole down."

"Kill him?"

"We can't risk her life. Trust me."

You can't trust him, Dikran. You have to trust me.

Dikran tried to think. But he had no talent for this. For thinking. He had known this since he was a child in Armenia. His mother, may she rest in peace, would say, "Dikran, God gave you muscles everywhere, even inside your head."

All his life Sandri had told him: Dikran, do this. Dikran, do that. But where was she now? When Dikran tried to make a list himself—this reason for that, that reason against this—he became too confused.

So confused. So weary. The worry for Sandri would destroy him. It was a miracle he was not already broken into one thousand pieces.

So. Dikran would *not* think. He decided. He would ask his heart the question. Babikian or Shake? The snake or the asswipe? Who in his heart did he trust?

"Dikran?" Babikian said.

"Yes," Dikran said. So weary. "I will kill him."

Babikian gave him a long, long look in the eye. He nodded his head. He showed Dikran his many teeth.

"Good man," Babikian said.

Dikran nodded, too. In one moment Babikian would stand. He would turn to the minor snake, to grin with his victory. Dikran would stand, too. From behind he would break Babikian's neck. One twist, *snap*.

Babikian held out his hand for shaking. "It's the right decision, my friend."

After Dikran broke Babikian's neck, the minor snake would want to shoot Dikran. But—ah! Before he could pull out his gun, Dikran would throw Babikian with his snapped neck at the minor snake. Once Dikran had thrown an oil drum at a stone wall, and the wall had fallen down.

Dikran shook Babikian's hand. Babikian pulled him close. He waved his other hand in Dikran's face. Why? Dikran felt the sting in his throat. He saw now, the knife in Babikian's other hand.

The blood came from Dikran in one warm rush, then another. Dikran was wet, his whole chest, his lap. He had never been so wet in his life. He tried to stand but fell to one knee. He felt like a child, weak.

"No," he tried to say. But the word leaked away with the blood, with his breath.

Babikian stood. "Nice try, Ghazarian. I give you an A for effort. But why didn't you go for it? I thought you were going for it. What happened?"

"No," Dikran tried to say again. Nothing. He lay now on the floor, on his side.

"What's that?" Babikian said. "Okay, then. Sleep well."

Dikran watched Babikian's black shoes move away.

"Let's get out of here," Babikian said. "We're clean?"

"All wiped down," the other one said.

"Good."

Dikran heard a door open. He heard a door close. He remembered that day, their first one in USA. The Big Mac sandwiches and Sandri's hand on his shoulder.

One day, Dikran decided, soon perhaps, he would go to a place like Bloomington, Indiana, and have a cat for his own.

Chapter Thirty-Four

Shake decided to take one more crack at it, Dikran's thick skull. Maybe, just maybe, he could convince Dikran that Babikian was bad news for Lexy. Maybe Dikran wouldn't kill him for trying. Shake had already narrowly dodged death a couple of times this trip. Why not go for the hat trick?

He walked down to Dikran's room. His door was propped open, a maid's cart in the hallway outside. Shake poked his head in. A maid was dusting the dresser, swaying to the music in her head. No Dikran.

"Hello?" Shake said. "The guy who's staying here—he's not around?"

The maid—still swaying, still dusting—smiled and shook her head. "No, monsieur."

Shake went back downstairs. Dikran wasn't in the restaurant, wasn't in the bar. That left the one place Shake had been hoping he wouldn't have to look.

He caught a *tuk-tuk* and rode it across town. Shake was pretty sure he'd spent more time in *tuk-tuks* than he had with his two feet actually on Cambodian soil—if Dikran didn't kill him, he thought, the grit and exhaust fumes might.

Near the river, traffic was snarled. Shake saw a crowd gathered by one of the bridges. His *tuk-tuk* driver finally had to stop because the street was blocked. Shake climbed out. The atmosphere was festive. A couple of vendors had rolled their carts over and were selling fried meatballs and some kind of curry to the crowd. Shake smelled lemongrass and Kaffir lime.

He had a couple of inches on most of the locals, so he could see over the crowd. Two patrol cars were parked at the top of the riverbank, an ambulance wedged up behind them. Cops and paramedics stood down by the water, chatting and smoking.

"What's going on?" he asked a woman next to him. She had a face as flat as a pan, with a checkered scarf wrapped around her head.

"Dead," she said. She looked up at him. "Dead same you."

"What?" Shake wasn't dead, at least not that he was aware of.

The woman pointed down to the river. *"Barang,"* she said. "Dead."

And then Shake saw that the cops and paramedics were standing around a body, half in the water and half out of it. They'd dropped a sheet over the body, but Shake could make out an arm covered by a purple velour tracksuit.

Shit, he thought. *Shit.*

The woman next to him offered him some of her curry wrapped in banana leaf.

He shook his head and pushed his way back through the crowd. He walked fast along the river a mile, maybe a mile and a half, until he'd rounded a bend and left everyone behind.

Shake found a stone bench down by the water, sat, and told himself to stay cool. He knew he couldn't go back to the hotel now. There was a good chance that Babikian and his flunky were waiting there for him. Babikian had taken out Dikran. Next, if he wanted to check all the boxes, he'd go after Shake.

Luckily, Shake had his passport on him, his wallet. There was nothing back in his room he couldn't live without, just a change of clothes and his Dopp kit.

The lawn by the river was as short and smooth as a putting green, the vines wrapped around the tree trunks neatly pruned. But there was just something you could feel about this place, Siem Reap, something you could *smell*—if the people ever left, if they turned their backs for a few minutes, the jungle would stretch out a sleepy paw and take everything back.

Dikran was dead. *Dikran.* Shake didn't know if Lexy was still alive or not. Ouch hadn't called. Babikian would kill Shake on sight. The one kidnapper, Ramos, might kill him on sight, too, the next time he saw him. And even if Ramos agreed to do some kind of deal, there was no guarantee that he could be trusted. Shake had worked jobs with guys like Ramos in the past. Quiet guys, blanks, who saw only the *now,* not the *later.* They operated on instinct, by impulse. The wind shifted suddenly, and they did, too.

At some point, Shake thought, Ramos's partner might have his hands full. He might . . . *fuck.* Shake remembered now, that he'd told Ramos to call him at the hotel if he wanted to talk.

Go to the airport, Shake told himself. *Get on a plane. Go home.* What other choice did he have? He'd done his best, but this was out of his hands now. Lexy's fate was out of his hands.

But there had to be an alley that ran behind the hotel, a rear entrance, service stairs. If Shake was careful, very careful, he might be able to pop into his room for two seconds and check his messages, find out if Ramos had called. One last Hail Mary into the back of the end zone before he headed to the airport.

Why not? he thought. Understanding, even as he thought it, that asking yourself, *Why not?* was usually the beginning of a bad decision, the first domino tipping over.

He rode a *tuk-tuk* back to the hotel. Instead of going in through the lobby, Shake looped around to the rear. He spotted a door propped open by a plastic milk crate. A few yards away stood a guy in a chef's toque, talking on his cell phone.

Shake slipped through the door. The cook either didn't notice him or didn't care. Shake followed a service corridor past the kitchen until he found the service stairs. He took them to the fourth floor. Slowly, quietly. The perfect scenario right now, he considered, would be both Ramos and Babikian waiting for him and accidentally shooting each other. That would make for a nice Hollywood ending.

When he reached the fourth floor, he peeked around the corner and down the hall. Nothing.

His room was halfway down the hall. He put his ear to the door and listened. Nothing.

Feeling as good about this as he was ever going to feel, or as bad, Shake swiped his key card and eased the door open. The part of the room he could see was empty. The rest of the room, reflected in the TV screen, was empty, too.

He stepped inside, locked the door behind him, and checked the bathroom, the closet. Also empty.

He relaxed, a little, and hurried to the desk. The red light on the phone was blinking. Shake picked it up and hit the message button.

"You have . . . one . . . message. Press one for—"

He pressed the button. Before the message could begin to play, though, Shake heard a creak, a scrape, and the soft *shhhh-shush* of the balcony door sliding open behind him.

He froze.

"Don't tell me you're dead already," Gina's voice on the voice-mail message said, "I'm gonna be so annoyed, because I'm downstairs right now."

Shake saw it then, the leather carry-on next to the desk. He smiled.

"It was either this or box up all my clothes, wasn't it?" he said. "Stick them on the curb?"

"Shut up and kiss me," Gina's voice behind him said.

He shut up, turned, and kissed her.

"The maid let you in?" he said.

"She was very accommodating. I speak French, you'll remember."

"I remember." He kissed her again.

"I need a shower," she said. "And I'll let you join me if you beg. Hey! What are you doing?"

He had her by the wrist and was pulling her toward the door.

"We have to get out of here," he said. "Right now."

"What? Why?"

"Trust me," Shake said, "you don't want to know."

Chapter Thirty-Five

Shake, Gina had to say, looked like hell on toast—rumpled and unshaven and exhausted, too thin, a rime of dried sweat on the collar of his shirt. But he was still Shake, his eyes clear and wry, his smile going straight to the center of her chest and giving her heart a little tap.

Gina supposed she didn't look her best either, not after twenty-plus hours on airplanes.

"Trust me," he said, "you don't want to know."

"You mean you don't want to tell me."

"Yeah."

He snap-checked the hall, both ways, then hustled her out of the room, down the stairs, across the lobby. They jumped into one of the cute little open-air moto-carts that Gina had taken from the airport.

"Go," Shake told the driver.

"Where?" the driver said.

"Anywhere. Just drive around. But not around here."

The driver shrugged, and off they went. Shake took a deep breath. He let it out slowly.

"You better look like such shit because you've been pining away for me," Gina said.

"I look like shit?"

"Well?"

"Yes, I've been pining away for you. Like crazy."

"I don't believe you."

He kissed her again, a long time. "Well?"

A breeze blew the scent of jasmine over them. The late-afternoon light gave the river a golden, romantic glow.

Gina was so stupidly happy to see Shake, at such peace to sit squeezed up against him again, his rumpled and sweat-rimed self, that she could barely keep from laughing.

"What about you?" Shake said. "Have you been pining away for me?"

"Yes."

Which wasn't a lie. It wasn't! Gina's pining had just taken a different form from Shake's, that was all. You could even argue, she argued, that her devotion was even more powerful than his. She'd faced temptation, after all, and walked away from it.

He was looking at her.

"That's a lot of thinking you're doing," he said, "for one little yes."

"If you've been pining away for me," she said, "then why didn't you ask me to come with you in the first place? I was so mad at you. You should have begged me to come with you."

Gina loved Shake's smile best, but his baffled frown—that crease between his eyebrows—came in a close second.

"I thought you'd be mad at me *if* I asked," he said. "Are you serious? You *wanted* me to ask you to come?"

"Of course I wanted you to ask. So start talking, partner. What's going on?"

He grimaced. "There's good news and bad news."

"Which means there's bad news and worse news." Up ahead a scatter of small, dark shapes rose from a tree, like confetti tossed in the air. "Are those . . . ? Those are *bats*."

"Yeah."

Gina shivered. "I hope that's the bad news."

"I wish."

He told her about Babikian taking over the negotiations for Lexy's release, promising to deliver $8 million in diamonds.

"You follow?" Shake said. He knew he didn't need to spell anything out for her.

"Yes, thank you very much," she said. "Babikidoodle or whoever doesn't have any diamonds. He wants the kidnappers to get pissed off and kill her."

"That way he's covered. He'll tell the Board back home he tried his best."

"And . . . wait. And he'll tell them *you're* the one who fucked it all up."

"Me and Dikran. That's why Babikian wants to take me out. So there aren't any conflicting accounts."

"He's a smart fella, isn't he? Speaking of the opposite of that, where is he anyway? Dikran?"

Shake didn't say anything, just watched a couple of monks in saffron robes on a scooter zoom around them.

"Oh," Gina said.

It didn't make her sad, at all, that there was one less murderous thug roaming the face of the earth. At the same time, though, death—anyone's death—was never a joke. It was easy to forget sometimes, but every life was a real life, just as rich and deep and full of memories as your own.

"Did you know they all become monks?" she said. "Or most of

them, Cambodian guys. They do the monk thing for a couple of years when they're young, and then they go back to their normal life. It's a way they show their commitment to the faith."

"I didn't know that," Shake said.

"I read a book on the plane."

"He wasn't that bad a guy. Dikran wasn't."

"Are you serious?"

Shake leaned into her. He pressed his nose against the top of her head.

"I just want to breathe you for a while," he said.

"Okay."

Their moto-cart purred along through the balmy afternoon. Gina thought about Dominic. Flirting with him had been nice. And going to bed with him would have been nice, too. But it wouldn't have been *this*, it wouldn't have been Shake holding her tight and breathing her in. Not even close.

Their little moto-cart came to an intersection. The driver stopped at the light and glanced back at Shake.

"More, sir?" he said. "More just drive?"

"The airport," Shake said.

"The airport?" Gina said.

"You were right. I shouldn't have waited this long. Let's go home."

"Not the airport," Gina told the driver. "Just keep driving."

The driver nodded and pulled in to the intersection. Shake looked at Gina.

"I didn't come all this way just to turn around again," she said. "I'm not coming all this way and missing Angkor Wat, for example."

"And Lexy?"

"We'll try to save her skinny, bitchy ass first, I guess. If it's really that important to you."

There it was again, that baffled frown of Shake's that Gina enjoyed so much.

"Why?" he said. "Why are you doing this?"

"Because I want to see Lexy's face when she realizes *I* saved her. Oh, my God, it'll kill her. I'll be able to rub that in her face till the end of time."

Shake smiled. "And that's the only reason you want to stick around?"

"Why else?" she said.

She gave him her most innocent expression. He saw right through it. He better have.

"You know it might get a little dicey," he said.

"Oh, sweetpea," Gina said, "when has it ever been anything but?"

Chapter Thirty-Six

The goof left, and after a while he came back. He brought some *yaba*. Ramos stayed away from that sort of shit usually, any kind of meth, but the goof brought a little China White, too, and mixed that in with it. The three of them sat around and smoked, passing the burned foil back and forth, until the sun started to go down.

Ramos was worried about the Armenians. On the phone they hadn't put up any fight. They *wanted* to hand over the diamonds and collect their boss later. Maybe that was the way the Armenians did business, but it didn't make any sense to Ramos.

French didn't make any sense either. He wanted Ramos and the goof to pick up the diamonds together. Unless the Armenians kept their mouths shut, the goof would find out that the diamonds were worth eight million, not four.

"It doesn't make sense," Ramos had said to French when the goof went off to take a leak. "He'll find out about the extra four."

"If we make a stink, he'll be suspicious. Trust me, it won't be a problem."

Ramos hadn't said it would be a problem. Once he had the diamonds, he was going to put a bullet in the goof's head.

Or maybe he wouldn't. He kept thinking about the other guy, the Armenian from New Orleans. That guy said he could get Ramos off the hook with the Armenians. But Ramos couldn't count on that. He *could* count on the diamonds.

Más vale pájaro en mano que ciento volando, his brother always used to say. A bird in the hand is worth a hundred flying.

"Why don't they care?" Ramos said. "The Armenians. If we don't bring her with us?"

French reached for the foil. "Because they don't want to jeopardize this."

"Real talk," the goof said.

"It gives us a huge advantage," French said. "This ensures there won't be any funny business."

Did French think all this was funny? If he did, he was out of his mind.

"This isn't a joke," Ramos said.

"A joke? No. I mean we have the leverage. This way the diamonds *have* to be authentic."

"Okay."

"I need to take a leak," the goof said. He got up and left.

"So," French said. "When you took our girl her dinner earlier."

"Yeah," Ramos said.

"I'm just curious. If you . . . if she said anything to you."

"Like what?"

"Like anything."

She hadn't said anything. Ramos hadn't said anything. Ramos wouldn't have trusted anything she had to say.

"What time is it?" Ramos said.

The goof was back from the bathroom. "Six-thirty," he said.

"Let's go," Ramos said.

French followed them out to the Mercedes. "Remember," he said, then a lot of other things Ramos didn't listen to.

Ramos drove. The goof sat in the passenger seat. He held his piece in his lap, a big, bad Desert Eagle that was better for show than for shooting.

"Let's rock and roll," he said.

"Okay," Ramos said.

Ramos drove up the highway to 99. Dusk. Not too much traffic. On both sides of 99, in the little shacks up on stilts, kerosene lamps began to burn. A lot of the people in Cambodia were so poor they couldn't afford electricity. No plumbing in the shacks either. The people had to hike out into the fields when they needed to take a dump, even if it was the middle of the night.

Hijo de puta, Ramos hated the nights over here. They were darker than nights were supposed to be.

"Hey," he said.

"Hmm?" the goof said. He'd kept quiet the whole ride. Ramos hadn't thought he could do that.

"You're Cambodian."

"Half. And half Swedish."

"You believe in all that shit that Cambodians believe in?" Ramos said. "Ghosts, spirits. Coming back after you die and now you're somebody else."

"No way, bro. A little, maybe. My grandmother could tell the future. I shit you not. That's how she survived the KR. You know they killed a million people? My grandmother saved our whole family."

"How's that?"

"She saw what was going to happen before it did. Visions. Like, burning villages, blood on the walls. It was before I was born. My grandfather listened to her because he knew she could see the future. He was rich as balls because she could see the future. They landed in Paris two days before the KR took Phnom Penh."

"Huh," Ramos said.

The goof watched the rice fields go past.

"A million people," he said. "You want to believe in ghosts, bro, this is the place to do it."

Ramos wished he'd kept his mouth shut. He couldn't think of one time when keeping his mouth shut had been a bad idea.

"You down to make a deal, bro?" the goof said. "You and me?"

"Maybe."

"You know what I'm talking about?"

He was talking about cutting French out of the score.

"Yeah," Ramos said.

"Think about it."

Half of $8 million was $4 million. Ramos would clear that if he made a deal with the goof. He'd clear the same number if he put a bullet in the goof's head and stuck with French.

Or he could put a bullet in the goof's head and put a bullet in French's head and keep the whole $8 million for himself. He'd need to put a bullet in the woman's head, too, before he cut out, just to be safe.

Safe. Ramos knew that was off the table the minute the Armenians gave up the diamonds.

"Okay," he told the goof.

He saw the turn-in for the charcoal pit. He drove past a quarter klick, pulled off the road, and parked. The Mercedes was a pretty good car. Comfortable. When all this was over, Ramos was going to hate torching it.

The road was mostly empty. A couple of motorcycles, a couple of stray dogs trotting past with guilty looks. Dogs here walked right down the middle of the road, traffic buzzing all around them. Ramos didn't know how there were any stray dogs left in Cambodia.

"So now we just chill for an hour or so," the goof said. "And then . . ."

They both saw it, an SUV coming up the highway. It was the same big, black SUV Ramos had seen pick up the Armenian from New Orleans yesterday, outside the Friendly Fireplace.

"Is that them?" the goof said. "Shit. They're like an hour early."

"That's them."

"This is bullshit."

The SUV turned off the highway. Ramos started the Mercedes back up. He crossed the highway and followed the rutted dirt track the SUV had taken. It was more dark than dusk now, so he had to turn on his headlights. Not too far up the dirt track, they lit up what looked like an igloo, but made out of dirt instead of ice. The charcoal pit. The SUV was parked next to it. A guy with glasses leaned against the front bumper, arms folded.

"There he is," the goof said.

Ramos put on his mask. The goof put on his mask, French's mask. They got out of the car. Ramos left the headlights on.

"You're early," he told the guy with glasses.

"This is bullshit," the goof said.

He was twitchy. Ramos wished he'd put the Desert Eagle's safety on. The goof was liable to put a bullet in Ramos without even meaning to.

"Am I?" the guy in the glasses said. He had a big head like a piñata. "Well, I didn't want to be late for this, right? Traffic, roads. I didn't know how long it would take, exactly."

"You got the diamonds?" Ramos said.

"Sure. But who's your buddy?"

Meaning the goof.

"He's not my buddy," Ramos said.

"He's not? What is he? A hitchhiker you picked up on the way over?" He laughed. "Never mind. I'm just giving you shit.

My first rule, I gotta tell you, never pick up a hitchhiker who's armed."

He laughed again. Ramos heard someone else laugh, too, off to his left. Another guy with glasses stepped out from behind the charcoal pit. He was holding a shotgun, pointed between Ramos and the goof.

"Lose the gun," the guy with the piñata head said. "And tell your buddy to lose his, too."

If Ramos swung around and fired fast at the guy with the shotgun, he might get lucky. He had half a mind to try. It would be risky, though. The spread of a shotgun, at this distance, would take out both him and the goof, no problem.

"Lose the gun," the guy with the piñata head said again. "Last chance."

Ramos set his gun down.

"This is bullshit," the goof said, but he set his Desert Eagle down, too.

"You were supposed to come alone," Ramos told the guy with the piñata head.

"Don't worry, nothing's changed. We don't want any trouble. We want this to go down silky smooth."

Ramos didn't buy that. If he wanted this to go down silky smooth, he would have come alone. The second Armenian wouldn't be pointing a shotgun at Ramos and the goof.

"Okay," Ramos said.

"Here are your diamonds." The guy with the piñata head tossed a bag to Ramos. Ramos caught it. A black velvet bag, heavy, full of what felt like gravel.

"These are the diamonds?" Ramos said.

"That's it."

"Let me see," the goof said, and reached for the bag.

Ramos knocked his hand away. He pulled at the string that tied the bag shut and shook some of the diamonds into his palm. But they weren't diamonds. The bag really was full of gravel.

"What the fuck?" the goof said, looking over Ramos's shoulder.

The guy with the piñata head sighed. He was leaning against the bumper of the SUV again.

"Shit," he said. "You got me. I didn't think you'd check them right here. Did you think they'd check right here, Jeff?"

"I didn't," the other guy said. "Shit."

Ramos didn't know what the hell was going on. "Where are the diamonds?"

"I'm not trying to screw you over," the guy with the piñata head said. "Swear to God. It's just . . . the diamonds aren't here yet. I don't have them yet. But they're on the way. You have to give me some more time. I want to make this happen. I don't want you to get bent out of shape or anything."

Ramos was confused. What did the guy mean, that he thought Ramos wouldn't check the diamonds? Was he crazy?

The goof whispered something Ramos couldn't hear because of his mask.

"What?" Ramos said.

"I said what do we do now?" the goof whispered, louder.

Ramos didn't know what to do. He didn't know why he was still holding the bag of gravel. He dropped it.

"How much time you need?" he said.

The guy with the piñata head glanced at the second guy. Surprised.

"What?"

"How much more time you need?" Ramos said. "To get the diamonds?"

"Well . . . I'm not sure. A couple of days."

"Maybe a week," the second guy said.

"Yeah. Maybe a week. You understand how these things go, right?"

The guy with the piñata head didn't wait for Ramos to answer. He opened the door of the SUV and climbed up behind the wheel. The other guy made his way over, keeping his shotgun on them, and climbed in on the passenger side.

"Talk it over, hash it out." The guy stuck his piñata head out the window to say it. "Give us a buzz when you make a decision."

Before Ramos could tell him they didn't have his phone number, he hit the gas. The SUV blasted past, and the two Armenians were gone.

Chapter Thirty-Seven

So Gina wanted to stay and try to save Lexy. Shake was happy she was on board, but it didn't mean the boat had stopped sinking.

"What do you have?" she said.

He told her everything. He wanted to make sure she knew what she was getting into.

"We need to find out where she is," Gina said when he finished.

Shake agreed. "That's our best bet."

"But that's all you know?"

"That's it. Lexy told me she's a twenty-minute drive from the place they grabbed her. At least I think that's what she told me. Quinn's buddy I told you about, Ouch, he's checking it out, but I haven't heard back from him. She's somewhere quiet. Somewhere secluded."

Gina frowned. "She could have been *slightly* less helpful, I guess."

"She had to be careful. We didn't have much time, then Dikran went apeshit."

"Take me through it again, everything she said. Every little thing."

Shake took Gina through the first part of the conversation, up to the moment when Ramos first chimed in from the sidelines.

"Wait," Shake said. Lexy had been trying to say something when Ramos cut her off. So much had happened afterward, so fast, that he'd completely forgotten about that moment until now. "She asked me if I remembered what she always said. About life. How life is like a . . ."

"Like a what?"

"Give me a second."

They drove past a collection of stupas. Shake realized it was where Ouch's second-string thugs had jumped him. Almost unbelievable to consider, but getting jumped by those thugs had been one of the high points of his trip to Cambodia; everything since had been a wild career downhill.

"Life is full of hills and valleys," he said. "That's what Lexy used to say sometimes. You know, with a lot of ups and downs."

"It's probably more profound in Armenian."

"I can't believe I forgot she was trying to tell me that."

"Don't feel bad, pumpkin. So which is it, do you think? Is she on a hill or in a valley?"

"Flip a coin."

Gina tapped her fingers against her lips and thought about it. "I think we're looking for a hill," she said. "And there's something about the hill, right?"

"Something unusual."

"Or why would she mention it?"

"Yeah. So we're looking for an unusual hill a twenty-minute drive from the place they grabbed her? A secluded area."

"But 'unusual hill' is kinda vague, don't you think?" Gina said. "We need more to go on."

Shake knew it. He tapped their *tuk-tuk* driver on the shoulder.

"The Golden Moon Hotel. You know where that is?"

The driver nodded with somber disappointment. He was probably getting used to this, just cruising around town with the fare piling up.

"The Golden Moon Hotel?" Gina said. "Would you like to explain?"

"No," Shake said. "I don't even want to try."

THE RECEPTION DESK was empty again. Shake led Gina around back to Mitch's bungalow. He knocked.

"Why are you grimacing?" Gina said.

"Am I?" Shake guessed he was grimacing because he knew there was a possibility that Mitch would open the door wearing nothing but her toe rings.

"So who is the woman again?" Gina said.

"I told you. A woman who might be able to help us."

"That's a suspiciously skimpy description."

Shake caught himself grimacing again. The door opened. He was relieved to see that Mitch was fully dressed, in a Scooby-Doo T-shirt and a tie-dyed sarong.

She must have recognized the relief on Shake's face. She laughed.

"You thought I'd be starkers again, didn't you?" she said.

Shake winced. Gina smiled.

"Hi!" she said to Mitch. "I'm his wife, and I would love to hear more about that."

"Far out! It's brilliant to meet you!"

Mitch gave Gina a hug. Gina hugged back, watching Shake the whole time.

"He told me so much about you!" Gina said.

"He didn't want to see me starkers," Mitch said. "Last time he kept asking me to put on some clothes."

"In my defense," Shake said.

Mitch let Gina go and stepped back, to better regard the spot above Gina's head.

"I dig your aura," Mitch said. "Quite spicy. It's like . . . it's like a funky salsa band on a street corner in Havana. But some Ibiza nightclub, too."

"Thank you," Gina said. "I have absolutely no idea what you're talking about."

Mitch laughed again. "Yeah, occasionally I . . . oh."

She'd glanced at Shake's aura and done a sharp double take. Holy hell, Shake thought, how much trouble could one guy carry around? Maybe reincarnation *was* real and this version of him was now paying the price for a dozen nice, quiet lives he'd led in the past.

"I've no bloody idea what *that* is," Mitch said, frowning.

Shake realized she wasn't looking at the spot above his head after all but at a spot a foot or so to the left of it. Fantastic. Now his trouble had trouble.

"Never mind that," he said. "Mitch, you have a map of the area? A road map."

"I think so. Come on in."

They followed her inside. Queenie came padding out of the kitchen. When the dog saw Shake, she lowered her head and snarled.

"I thought she liked me now," Shake said.

"Queenie, chill," Mitch said.

She grabbed the dog by the collar and tugged her back into the kitchen. Gina was looking at all the postcards on the wall.

"Don't ask," Shake said.

Mitch returned from the kitchen and rummaged around in a desk drawer. She pulled out a map.

"Will this work?" she said.

"Let's see."

Shake spread the map out on the coffee table and located the spot where Lexy had been grabbed. He'd made sure to clock the kilometer marker when Tom Gone had driven him back to town after the second meeting with Ouch. He pointed to Road 67.

"You know what the speed limit is here?" Shake asked Mitch. "On this road?"

"Sixty, I think."

"Kilometers?"

"Yeah."

Shake did some rough calculations in his head. He moved his finger a few inches south along 67. That put him near a place called Preah Dak.

"I think my friend might be somewhere around here." Shake didn't want to come right out and ask Mitch if maybe she could use her psychic powers to figure out where Lexy might be. He figured it was better for team morale if Gina thought just Mitch was nuts, not both Mitch *and* Shake. "You know if there are any unusual hills around here?"

Mitch studied the map. "There aren't many hills in Siem Reap. But hold on. If you keep going a bit and turn east on National Highway 6, you'll come on Preah Ko."

"Preah Ko?"

"It's another temple, but not famous like Banteay Srei or Angkor. It's on a hill. Kind of an oddish hill? Some people say it looks like a turtle sticking its head up out of the mud."

Shake looked at Gina. Gina shrugged.

"Better than nothing, I guess," she said.

"Can you find us another map?" Shake asked Mitch. "One that shows us the place you're talking about?"

"Sure, but why don't I just go with you? Maybe I can help you find out if your friend's nearby."

"How?" Gina asked. "Do you have X-ray vision?"

Shake couldn't tell yet what Gina thought about Mitch. He thought it was a little ominous she'd let the naked thing slide by so easily.

"Not exactly," Mitch said. "It's more like . . . d'ya know how occasionally you can sense if someone is looking at you, even though your back is turned? It's a good moon tonight, some wicked astral currents, so maybe I can pick up a vibe."

Gina laughed. "I like you. But oh, my God, you are just completely batshit crazy, aren't you?"

"I like you, too!" Mitch said. "I'd love to read your past lives. I bet they're a trip."

"My current life has been a trip," Gina said. "I'm not exaggerating."

"Do you have a car?" Shake asked Mitch.

"Jacques has one. He won't mind if I nick it for a few hours. And . . ." Mitch was looking again at the spot to the left of Shake's usual trouble spot. "I'm sorry, but it's just so weird. There's this sort of presence next to you that wasn't there before. This really sort of . . . volatile presence?"

Why not? Shake thought. He'd lost his capacity to be surprised by news like this.

"We've got to get going, Mitch," he said. "We don't have much time."

"Right."

She headed off to get the car keys. Gina folded up the map and fanned herself with it.

"You understand now?" he said. "About her being naked? That's just the way she is. You don't have to worry. There was no kind of sexual thing going on."

"Oh. I know that," Gina said. "I wasn't worried."

Shake was relieved. Then puzzled. He waited for Gina to explain. She didn't. She switched the map to her other hand and kept fanning herself.

"It's kinda steamy in Cambodia, isn't it?" she said. "To state the obvious."

"You weren't worried?"

"About what? About her? Of course not."

Shake smiled. Gina was good. She was the best.

"You weren't worried because you trust me so much?" he said. "Or because I'm just some middle-aged dude and, you hate to break the news to me, not every woman I pass on the street wants to throw herself at me?"

She smiled back at him. "Listen," she said. "Not that I don't have complete faith in your Cambodian girlfriend's special hippie-dippy powers."

"I'm all ears," Shake said.

"I think we should split up. Divide and conquer."

"What do you mean?"

"Maybe Babikian will lead us to Lexy. If he's meeting with the kidnappers. You said you know where he's staying, so I'll go there and sit on him."

"No. No way."

"See where he goes. It's worth a try."

"It's too dangerous."

"He doesn't know me. And I won't get close."

"No."

She put her hands on Shake's face and rotated it toward her.

"If we're gonna do this together," she said, "we're gonna do this together."

Mitch returned, jingling car keys.

"Ready?" she said.

"Why not?" Shake said.

Chapter Thirty-Eight

Shake told Gina where the villa was and gave her a brief description of Babikian: big head, lots of teeth.

"You'll know him when you see him," Shake said, hoping she'd never have the opportunity.

"I'll be careful."

"Be very careful. Please."

She gave him a quick kiss. "You married me for a reason."

The car Mitch had nicked for a few hours was a 1997 Corolla. She drove it like she was trying to set the tires on fire. The road heading north was pitted with potholes, cluttered with dogs and bikes and carts stacked high with firewood, but Mitch aired the Corolla out. The palm trees by the side of the road whipped past until they were just one palm tree, stretched out like taffy, a blur.

Shake held on tight. He promised he'd never complain about his international driving students back in Bloomington.

"Sorry?" Mitch said.

"What?" Shake said.

"You just said something. I didn't hear it."

"I didn't say anything. Hole."

She glanced over at him and frowned, puzzled. "Are you sure?"

"*Hole.*"

Mitch whipped the Corolla around a pothole the size of the car. She glanced at him again.

"This is very weird," she said.

"Yeah," Shake agreed.

About a mile later, she slammed the brakes and sent them skidding into a small parking lot by the side of the road. On the other side of the lot was an old, ruined temple. The handful of squat sandstone towers looked like pineapples, or maybe hand grenades. Behind the temple was the hill Mitch had told him about. Not much of a hill, but at the top was a distinctive rock outcropping—an old guy with a real honker, sniffing the breeze.

"Up?" Shake said.

"The temple first," Mitch said.

"Whatever you say."

They walked over to the temple. No one else was around, just an old Cambodian woman sweeping the pathway with a broom made from twigs. Mitch put her palms together and bowed her head. The old woman beamed, set her broom aside, and did the same thing back.

"Nobody really comes here," Mitch said. They followed the pathway as it wound between the sandstone hand grenades. "Preah Ko is a bit of a lesser temple. So all the tourists go to Angkor Wat or Ta Prohm. Have you been to Angkor yet?"

She was taking her time now that she was out of the car, walking so slowly that Shake had to keep stopping and waiting for her to catch up.

"Not yet," he said.

He didn't want to rush her. If he was gonna let her do her thing, he had to let her do her thing. But . . . *shit*. Shake had no idea how much time he had left. For all he knew, Babikian had already made his play and the kidnappers had put a bullet in Lexy's head.

"So . . . anything yet?" he said.

Mitch was looking up at the reliefs on the side of a tower. The detail, everywhere, was spectacular. Buddhas and three-headed snakes, a demon sinking its teeth into a galloping horse. Each tooth had been individually, lovingly carved into the stone.

If this was a lesser temple, Shake wanted to see the greater ones.

"I'm having such a hard time," Mitch said. "I don't understand. I keep getting this kind of interference. Like when you're trying to have a conversation in a restaurant and the table next to you is really loud? And sort of . . . well. Sort of aggro?"

"Aggro?"

"Aggressive. Belligerent. Like not the kind of people you'd really want to sit next to. And . . . wait."

"What?"

"Do you hear that? Like a string quartet?"

Shake started to say that she was the one who could pick up that sort of thing, not him, but then he heard it, too. Violins, a cello.

In the grass on the other side of the temple, across from the exit, they found four Cambodians sitting and playing classical music. Two guys with violins, a woman with a bigger violin, another woman with a cello. Both of the women were missing a leg, from the knee down. The guys were missing both legs.

"Old land mines," Mitch whispered to Shake. "They're still everywhere, all over the countryside."

They listened to the rest of the song. It was slow and sweet and kind of spooky, like the tips of a woman's fingers brushed across your bare ribs. When the musicians finished playing, Shake dropped a five-dollar bill into the wooden bowl next to the cello player. The cello player gave Shake a nod and started in on a new song.

"Let's climb the hill," Shake told Mitch. He could see the beginning of a path that led up it.

"Why don't I go on ahead first. Have a few minutes by myself." She was looking at the spot next to him again.

"You think I'm the problem?" Shake said. "With the interference?"

"I don't know. I just want to see."

Shake shrugged. He stayed where he was and watched Mitch take the path up the hill. The jungle swallowed her. He waited through another sad, spooky song from the amputee musicians, then followed.

It took him about ten minutes to reach the top of the hill. He found Mitch standing on the rock outcropping, gazing over the tropical forest, green on top of green, that spread out in every direction.

Shake couldn't understand how the kidnappers could be holding Lexy anywhere near this hill. There *was* nothing near this hill, just a pocket here and there of jumbled stone the color of old charcoal, the ruins of old temples.

Mitch slapped at a mosquito and left a smear of blood on her neck. She cocked her head, and the bells attached to her dreads tinkled.

"What is it?" Shake said.

"I'm not sure. It's not really an exact science, is it? Especially something like this. This is even wonkier than dreams. It's like you throw a paper airplane and try to catch it at the same time."

"Just put me in the ballpark."

She pointed west, into the setting sun. "I'm getting a bit of a vibe about that spot."

"What spot?"

"See the roof?"

Shake shielded his eyes against the glare of the setting sun. He saw it now, maybe a quarter of a mile away as the bat flies, part of a roof and a wall—a yellow house, almost hidden by the trees.

"Yeah," he said.

She turned to him.

"You know, I really think it *is* you," she said. "That interference? Like someone who's really angry."

"What are they angry about?"

"I don't know. Some of what I'm hearing isn't in English, I don't think. And not Khmer."

"So do you think she's in there?" Shake said, squinting at the house.

"I really don't know. I'm sorry."

"Don't be sorry. I'm the one who dragged you out here." He was about to turn away when he noticed something. "The top window on the far right. What do you see?"

"What do I see? Yeah. Right."

Shake couldn't be completely sure, but it looked as though the dormer window on the right was boarded up. None of the other windows were boarded up. That didn't mean anything, necessarily, but it was all he had.

"I'm gonna check it out," he said.

"Is that safe?" Mitch said.

Shake didn't bother answering the question. He called Gina.

"You okay?" he said.

"Of course. I'm at the villa. Well, I'm parked down the street. My *tuk-tuk* driver's named Peachy. That's his real name."

"They probably think our names are crazy."

"Says the guy named Shake."

"No sign of Babikian?"

"Not yet."

Shake was relieved. "Good. Forget him and get out of there. I might have found where they have Lexy."

"So what's the plan?"

"I'm gonna check it out and go from there."

"Is Summer of Love there with you?"

"Yeah," Shake said. "She found the place."

"Good for her. Ask her to do me a favor and pinch your left arm. As hard as she can."

"What?"

"And tell me if your vision's blurred. I want to see if you've had a stroke."

"I didn't say it was a good plan."

"Trust me. It's not even a plan."

Shake admitted she was right. A real plan didn't include the phrase "go from there."

"I'll play it safe," he said. "But these guys are amateurs. And the one guy might flip on his partner, push comes to shove."

"This is the guy who almost shot you, right?"

"He didn't shoot me. That's a good sign, don't you think?"

"You're golden, pumpkin."

But Gina didn't tell him to back off. She knew that the clock on Lexy was ticking.

"I'll talk to you later," he said. "Forget Babikian and get out of there."

"Okay."

Shake ended the call. He decided to exhaust all options before he set out for the house in the jungle and called Ouch's number.

A click. A voice barked something in Khmer.

"Ouch?" Shake said.

"Shay?"

"Did you find out anything?"

"No, Shay. I have not been sexy food."

"All right. I think I know where the kidnappers have her. Maybe."

"You know where she is?" Ouch said.

"Yeah. The temple called . . ."

"Preah Ko," Mitch said.

"Preah Ko," Shake told Ouch. "There's a big yellow house off by itself about a quarter of a mile west of there."

"A yellow house?"

"Yeah. One of the windows is boarded up. I know that's not a lot to work with."

"Where are you now, Shay?"

"I'm up the hill from Preah Ko. I'm gonna go check the house out."

"I will be there in ten minutes, Shay. Wait for me."

Shake didn't love that idea. He thought one guy snooping around might be more sexy food than Ouch and his dead-eyed bodyguard crashing in and blowing everyone away.

"I'm gonna go in solo," Shake said, "on the down low to make sure she's really there. My friend Mitch is here. She'll meet you at the temple and point out where the house is. If I need you, I'll call."

"A yellow house, you say. Are you sure?"

"Mitch will point it out to you. But hang back, and I'll call if I need you."

"Mmm."

Shake decided to take that as a yes. He killed the call.

"Wish me luck," he told Mitch.

Chapter Thirty-Nine

After Ramos and Bjorn left to collect the ransom, French decided to wait ten minutes before he went upstairs to free Alexandra. He mixed himself a martini and carried the chessboard from the kitchen back into the parlor. He wanted to make sure Ramos and Bjorn were really gone, that they didn't return to the house for some unexpected reason.

French wasn't waffling. He'd made his choice. Of course, sure, he continued to consider the possibility that it was the wrong choice. But he wasn't Sylvia Plath in *The Bell Jar,* immobilized with indecision as each of the beautiful figs in front of her turned black. No. He'd made his choice and would stick to it, come what may. He remembered the line from the Auden poem: "Each to his own mistake; one flashes on."

He studied the chessboard but found it hard to concentrate. The dark bishop was in a pickle. But if French moved his knight *here* . . .

Was it a mistake to free Alexandra? French was trading $3 million for the wispy promise of . . . what, exactly? He didn't trust Alexandra. He'd be a fool to trust her. So what made him think she'd honor her pledge to him? Ramos claimed that Alexandra hadn't said a word to him when he brought her dinner earlier, but was he lying? What if she'd offered him the same deal that she'd offered French? What if . . . ?

Stop, French told himself. He drained his martini and checked his watch. He was surprised to discover that twenty minutes had passed. *Go,* he told himself. He stood.

The attic was an oven. Sweat dripped from his forehead onto his fingers as he fumbled with the key to the padlock.

"Calmly," Alexandra said softly.

"I know. Yes."

Finally the padlock snapped open. French pulled the chain free. He unlocked the cuffs around Alexandra's ankles and helped her to her feet.

"And now my hands," she said.

"Let's just get you downstairs, first."

"But . . ."

French didn't think he could explain to her why he didn't want to uncuff her hands. He wasn't sure he understood it himself.

"Everything's fine," he said. "It's really okay."

She hesitated, examining him, then nodded. He led her down the stairs and into the parlor. He checked his watch and relaxed. He had plenty of time. It wasn't even eight o'clock yet. Ramos and Bjorn hadn't even met with the Armenians yet.

He led her to the sofa. She sat, reluctantly.

"Jeremy," Alexandra said. "Free my hands. We must hurry."

"Everything's fine. We have plenty of time. My associates won't be back for another forty-five minutes, at a minimum. They're picking up the diamonds."

"Diamonds?"

"Yes. I didn't tell you. A new person is handling the negotiations on your end. He's paying us with diamonds."

French glimpsed it in her eyes again, that flash of lightning that cut through the otherworldly gray and illuminated a black granite peak.

"We must go now, Jeremy. *Now.*"

He moved across the room to the chessboard and touched his finger to the tip of the dark bishop's miter.

"Let me run an idea past you," he said.

"Jeremy."

"What if there's a way here for us to have our cake and eat it, too? I haven't thought this through completely yet, but what if we wait until I have the diamonds in hand. And then, I don't know . . ."

No, French hadn't thought it through at all. He realized there was no way to avoid the decision he had to make: the diamonds or Alexandra.

He needed more time. He tried to remember the famous lines from "Prufrock." Something something "time." For the life of him, French couldn't recall it, a poem he'd known by heart since the first year of grad school.

All that came to mind, at the moment, was a poem by Dr. Seuss he'd learned as a child.

"This reminds me," French said. "When I was eleven years old, I was on the sixth-grade basketball team. I wasn't bad, actually. I had a certain grace. But I suppose I was . . . I was too cerebral for sports, I suppose. I remember one game, at the end of the game, the coach sent me in and—"

"*Jeremy,*" Alexandra said, her voice somehow both soft and sharp.

He looked up from the chessboard. "Yes?"

"Please. I must help you understand. This new man who makes a deal with you now? His name is Ruben Babikian, and he wishes to be *pakhan.* He will not pay you or your associates one penny for my life."

"Really? He seemed genuinely . . . I don't know."

"If I was in his place, I would do the same. There are no diamonds, Jeremy. You must free me before your associates return."

He set the key to her handcuffs on the chessboard, on an ebony square. After a moment of thought, he slid the key to a maple square.

"How do I know I can trust you?" he said.

"You cannot know this," she said. "But you must act. If you do not free me, *now,* we will both die."

Before French could answer, he heard the front door bang open. He went blank for an instant. It was as if he'd been reading a book and accidentally skipped a page.

Ramos stormed into the parlor and saw Alexandra. He stopped. Stared.

"The fuck is going on?" Ramos said.

It was only a quarter till eight. It was only a quarter till eight! Ramos and Bjorn should still be up the road from the charcoal pit, waiting for the Armenians to arrive.

"Why is she down here?" Ramos said. He noticed the handcuff key on the chessboard and picked it up. "What's this?"

"I can explain," French said. He slipped his other hand into the pocket of his blazer and gripped the handle of his gun.

"Forget it," Ramos said. *"Shit."*

He started pacing. He grabbed a bottle of Bombay from the cabinet and took a long swig. When he set the bottle back down, he missed the edge of the cabinet. The bottle hit the rug with a hollow *bonk.*

Something was wrong. The only other time French had seen Ramos this frazzled was after the Zoom with the Armenians. And he seemed even *more* frazzled now.

"What's going on?" French said. "Why are you back so soon?"

"Hijo de puta."

"And where's Bjorn? Is he—"

"He had to take a fucking leak."

"Why didn't you meet with the Armenians?"

Ramos paced back to the cabinet. He couldn't find the bottle of Bombay, so he grabbed a bottle of Johnnie Walker.

"We did," he said.

"You did? Look at me, Mason."

Ramos, as he chugged the scotch, had his eyes on Alexandra. She ignored him. She had her eyes on French. He knew what she was trying to tell him.

Shoot him.

"So do you have them?" French said. "The diamonds?"

"No. The guy didn't have the diamonds. He tried to give me a bag of rocks."

"What?"

"He said he needed more time. To bring the diamonds in."

What? French tried to determine if Ramos was lying. Maybe he really did have the diamonds and was planning to steal them from French. But no. Ramos was dense, not stupid. If he wanted to steal the diamonds, why would he return to the house? Why would he put on this performance?

"Jeremy," Alexandra said quietly.

"So they still intend to pay the ransom?" French asked Ramos.

"The Armenians are trying to fuck us."

"Not necessarily. Let's stop and think this through. There's a lot at stake here."

"Think it through?" Ramos turned to French. "Are you out of your mind?"

French realized that Ramos had his gun in his hand. French hadn't seen him draw it.

"Mason," French said. "Just calm down."

"There's nothing to think through," Ramos said. "This is over.

We have to end this. We have to end this now and get the fuck out of here."

He strode across the room toward Alexandra. French couldn't speak or move. He felt trapped outside the moment, no longer a character living in the first-person present but a retrospective narrator gazing back on events that had already happened.

Ramos stood over Alexandra. She regarded him coolly, regally.

"Why do you wait?" she said.

He lifted his gun, but . . . only to stick it back in his waistband. He knelt in front of her. Their faces were as close as lovers, only a foot between them.

"I do this," he said, looking her in the eye, "you'll do what you can for us?"

She nodded. "I will."

"What . . . what are you doing?" French said.

"Letting her go," Ramos said. "This is over."

"But . . ."

He reached around behind her. French drew the gun from his pocket. He aimed it at Ramos. "Stop," he said.

Ramos looked up at French. He started to say something, and French fired. The bullet struck Ramos in the shoulder and the impact jerked him sideways, as if Ramos were shrugging with annoyance.

The surprise on his face seemed strangely mild, French thought, given the circumstances.

He fired again. Ramos slumped forward, one arm flung wide and his head cradled in Alexandra's lap. She gazed down at him, and French, still outside the moment, still a retrospective narrator, thought how remarkably the pose captured Michelangelo's famous pietà of Mary holding the body of Jesus.

And then Alexandra looked up at him.

"You are a fool," she said.

Chapter Forty

Shake sent Mitch back to the temple parking lot to wait for Ouch and followed a path down the back side of the hill. At the bottom of the hill, the path ended abruptly. Shake didn't love the idea of hiking a quarter of a mile through the Cambodian countryside, especially not after seeing up close what land mines could do. He turned off his phone's ringer and started walking.

The going wasn't too rough. Lots of trees and vines, but not what you'd call real jungle, and plenty of moon to see by. It took Shake about ten minutes to reach the house. It was a sprawling old French Colonial mansion, the paint blistering and the roof shedding shingles, the garden around it gone wild.

Shake crouched in the garden about a hundred feet away. The dormer window he'd spotted from the top of the hill was definitely boarded up. That still didn't prove anything, though. He needed to get inside and take a look around.

The lights were on at the front of the house. In back, where Shake was, the windows were dark. He hoped at least one of them was unlocked.

Staying low, he crept through the jungle of a garden. He wasn't worried about land mines now, but snakes. When he reached the house, he saw that the closest window was wide open.

Shake checked the room inside—a bedroom, dark and empty—and then pulled himself through the window. He edged into the hallway, also dark and empty. From the far side of the house, he could just make out the murmur of voices, or maybe a TV. The attic, if he had his bearings right—

A door behind him opened, flooding the hallway with light. Shake turned as a Cambodian guy stepped out of a bathroom. The guy was wearing a little hat like something an organ grinder's monkey might wear and holding a big-ass .44 Magnum in his hand. He saw Shake and stopped, surprised. Shake was surprised, too, but recovered fast. Before the guy could lift his gun, Shake hit him in the nose with the heel of his hand, as hard as he could. The guy's head snapped back and smacked against the doorframe. He dropped the gun and slid down the wall, dazed.

Shake picked up the gun and pointed it at the guy.

"Quiet," he whispered. "You understand?"

The guy's eyes were watering with pain, and his little hat had been knocked cockeyed. It was hanging off the side of his head, pinned to a hank of his hair.

He nodded. "Don't shoot. Please."

"What's your name?"

"Bjorn."

"Bjorn?" Shake said.

"Yes. Please. It wasn't me. I just did what they said."

"Listen to me, Bjorn. Okay? I am gonna shoot you, unless you tell me exactly what I need to know."

The guy, Bjorn, nodded again. "Anything."

"Where are the others?"

"The sunroom."

"How many?"

"Two."

"And where's the woman?"

"I'm not sure. She's with them, I think."

Shake took out his phone to call Ouch, but the crack of a gunshot—on the other side of the house—stopped him.

"Oh, shit," Bjorn said. "Please don't shoot. I'll give you money. It wasn't me."

Another gunshot. Shake knew he didn't have time to wait for backup. He grabbed Bjorn by the arm, yanked him to his feet, and shoved him down the hallway.

Up ahead he heard a voice. A woman's voice. Lexy. Shake felt a wave of relief.

"You are a fool," he heard her say.

Using Bjorn as a human shield, the gun jammed into his ribs, Shake pushed into the room. Lexy sat on the couch, the body of a man draped across her lap, leaking blood onto the Oriental carpet. It was Ramos, Shake realized, the ex-con who'd tracked him down outside Mitch's bungalow.

Across the room from Lexy stood a tall blond guy with a ponytail. He had a gun, still pointed at Ramos. When he finally noticed Shake and Bjorn, he blinked.

"I shot him," he said.

"I see that," Shake said. "Why don't you put down the gun?"

"What?"

The guy with the ponytail swung his gun around and pointed it at Shake. Shake ducked behind his human shield as far as he could get.

"Put down the gun," Shake said, "or I shoot your buddy here. Bjorn."

The guy with the ponytail was blinking like crazy. Shake remembered that from the Zoom call.

"I don't care," the guy with the ponytail said.

"Dude!" Bjorn said. "You dick!"

The guy with the ponytail kept the gun on Shake but addressed Lexy. "I'm not a fool, Alexandra."

Lexy didn't answer. Shake glanced over at her. She had a thoughtful expression on her face.

"Hey, Lexy?" Shake said. "Want to pitch in here?"

She ignored Shake. "What is your real name, Jeremy?" she asked.

"His name's French," Bjorn said. "French Byrnes, and this whole thing was his idea, I swear. He's—"

"Shut up," Shake said, and jammed the gun hard into Bjorn's ribs.

"French," Lexy said. "Remember what I said to you. Yes? About the past. It holds no power over us. What choice you make next, that alone determines the future for you. For all of us."

The guy, French, closed his eyes and took a deep breath, making it a big dramatic performance. From the corner of his eye, Shake saw Lexy slide her hand out from beneath the body on her lap. In her hand was a gun. Shake recognized it—Ramos's gun.

"Let me just say," French said, and then Lexy shot him.

THE GUNSHOT HAD barely faded when Shake heard gravel churn in the driveway outside. Car doors thumped. A few seconds later, Ouch entered the room, followed by Mitch, then Tom Gone and the two Cambodian guys who'd jumped Shake in the Buddhist cemetery. All three of them were carrying AK-47s. Mitch, when she noticed the two dead bodies, gasped and put a hand over her mouth.

"Hello, Shay," Ouch said.

Shake was happy to see him but even happier he no longer needed him.

"Looks like we're all good here," he said. Well, Shake and Lexy were all good. It was going to be a different story for Bjorn. Shake guessed Ouch was either going to teach him a lesson or make him one.

"I will take this from you now, Shay," Ouch said. Shake handed over Bjorn's gun. "And please go sit with Miss Ilandryan."

Shake walked over to the couch. A pair of handcuffs, one cuff unlocked, dangled from Lexy's wrist. Ramos had decided to set her free after all, but then his partner had shot him. Go figure.

"You okay?" he asked her.

Lexy shoved Ramos off her lap. The body thumped to the floor.

"Now, yes, thank you."

Ouch said something in Khmer. Tom Gone came over and collected Ramos's gun from Lexy.

"You, too," Ouch told Mitch, "joint discovery if you do not mind, please."

Joint discovery. *Join the others.*

Lexy smiled at Mitch. "I think we are acquainted, yes?"

"Mitch, from your hotel," Shake said. "She helped me find you."

"I am grateful."

"No worries," Mitch said. And then she frowned at Shake. "It's still there. That presence that's been following you around."

"Where is Dikran?" Lexy asked Shake.

Shake wasn't paying attention to either one of them now. Ouch's guys, he'd realized, were pointing their rifles at him and Lexy, not at Bjorn. Who'd slunk over to stand next to Ouch.

Shake didn't understand what was happening here, or why.

"Ouch," he said. "We're all good here, right?"

"Oh, Shay," Ouch said. "I am afraid not."

Shake glanced at Lexy. He could see she didn't understand what was happening either.

"What's the problem?" Shake said.

Ouch gave Bjorn a smack on the back of the head, knocking the miniature hat crooked again.

"Here is the problem," he said.

Bjorn stared down at his flip-flops.

"This wasn't my fault, Daddy," he said. "I swear."

Chapter Forty-One

Silence," Ouch said, and gave his son another smack on the back of the head.

His son. His *son*. Shake had one simple thought: *Oh, shit*.

"Ouch . . ." Shake said.

"Oh, Shay," Ouch said, "do you have children? They drive you crazy! When you told me about the yellow house, I was very upset. Because I knew then—my stupid son!"

"It was all their idea, Daddy. I just—"

"*Silence.* Or I will tell Tom Gone to take you to the roof and throw you away. Now. Explain."

"It was a good plan, Daddy. I heard you talking about this tourist from America who was such a big deal, so I thought . . ."

Ouch scrubbed his face with the palm of his hand. Tom Gone had a stick of Juicy Fruit waiting for him when he was done.

"My stupid son," Ouch said. "How can you be so stupid?"

"It was an awesome plan, Daddy! But they didn't bring the ransom. They were supposed to pay us the ransom tonight."

"How much?" Ouch said.

"Eight million dollars. Eight million dollars' worth of diamonds."

Ouch brightened. "Yes?"

"But there weren't any diamonds, Daddy! They gave us a bag full of rocks."

So Shake had been right about Babikian. Ouch looked over at Lexy. She shrugged.

"Could you *please* shut up for one second," Mitch whispered to Shake.

"What?" Shake whispered back, surprised.

She sighed. "Not you."

Ouch was frowning, putting together the pieces. It didn't take him long. He gave his son another smack.

"My son has put me in a very difficult situation," he said.

"I will be grateful to you," Lexy said. "You understand this, yes? My organization will not hold you or your son responsible for anything that has happened here."

Ouch nodded. "With due respect, Miss Ilandryan, I do not think you can make this promise. Your organization sent rocks for you, not diamonds. Yes? So. I must consider my reputation, the safety of my son. I must consider the cost by feet."

The *cost-benefit*. Ouch popped in another stick of Juicy Fruit. Shake could see that he'd made up his mind. He was going to apply the simplest solution to his dilemma, the safest one, and get rid of everyone on the wrong side of the room.

"Of course," Lexy said. How she managed to remain so serene in these kinds of circumstances always amazed Shake.

"Ouch," Shake said. "Please. Just—"

"Yes, yes, the bloody diamonds!" Mitch said.

Shake and Ouch turned to her. She blushed.

"I'm sorry. It's just . . . that's what I keep hearing now. It's on and on about, 'Yes, diamonds. Yes, diamonds.' I don't know why."

"What?" Ouch said, confused. "Who is saying this?"

"There aren't any diamonds, Daddy," Bjorn said, "I swear. Because right after we picked up the ransom, I was going to shoot that one and steal them."

He pointed to Ramos. Ouch nodded his approval.

"Maybe you are not so stupid after all," he said.

Yes, diamonds. Shake couldn't believe he hadn't thought of this earlier. "Wait a second," he said.

Ouch clapped his hands together. His guys, Tom Gone and the other two, raised their AK-47s.

"I'm sorry, Shay," Ouch said. "I am afraid we are all finished here."

"Babikian does have the diamonds," Shake said. "He wants Ms. Ilandryan out of the way, but he also wants the eight million dollars. You understand what I'm saying?"

That had been Babikian's move all along: take delivery of the diamonds but then never pay the ransom. When he got home, he'd tell the Board that the kidnappers had double-crossed him. He'd take over the top spot in the organization and keep the diamonds for himself. A win-win.

"Yes, diamonds, yes, yes, yes," Mitch said. She put her hands over her ears. "I can't even hear myself think."

"Mmm," Ouch said.

"Now those diamonds can be yours," Shake told Ouch. "Eight million dollars. That changes your cost-benefit, right? And Ms. Ilandryan is in charge of her organization again. An organization that's very grateful to you."

Ouch was intrigued. Shake could tell.

"But tell me this, Shay. Where is this man who has the diamonds? He is not here. They are not here. So how does this help me?"

"I might know where he is," Shake said. "Let me make one call."

Ouch considered. Finally he nodded. Shake took out his phone.

He saw Gina had called three times while his ringer was off. The last time he talked to her, Shake had told her to forget about Babikian.

He tapped her number. After a couple of rings, Gina picked up.

"Please," Shake said before she could say anything, "tell me you didn't listen to a word I said."

Chapter Forty-Two

Gina had stayed right where she was, of course, parked down the lane from Babikian's villa. She hadn't come all the way to Siem Reap just to be the supportive wife, the cheerleader on the sideline. If there was action to be had, she was going to have some.

Ten minutes after she solemnly promised Shake that she'd bail on Babikian, the villa gate opened and a black Escalade slid out. Gina pointed to it, and Peachy, her *tuk-tuk* driver, feathered in behind, a real pro. The Escalade led them to the airport.

"I listened to every word you said," Gina told Shake. "I weighed them very carefully."

She heard his sigh of relief. "So do you have him? Babikian?"

Gina had been forced to buy a ticket to Bangkok to get through security, but now from across the concourse she had a perfect view of Babikian. He sat in the airport bar, scrolling through his phone and sipping what looked like a piña colada.

"I've got him," Gina said. "He's at the airport. Lexy is gonna reimburse me two hundred and eleven dollars, by the way, for a ticket to Bangkok."

"The airport? Shit."

"I tried calling you. He's got to be on either the flight to Bangkok or the one to Hong Kong."

"When?"

"They both board in about ten minutes."

"Can you slow him down?"

Gina rolled her eyes. "Do you know what I'm doing right now?"

"Are you rolling your eyes?"

"Yes. And yes, I can slow him down, thank you very much."

"Do it, please."

There was a tightness to his voice, a rough, scratchy edge that Gina had never heard before.

"Everything cool on your end?" she said.

"It's cool. I love you."

For sure, now, Gina knew his end wasn't cool. But she wasn't going to be a baby and fall to pieces. She needed to get to work.

"I love you," she told Shake, and hung up.

She walked across the concourse to the airport bar. Babikian was sitting at a table by himself. Gina thought she *might* be able to lift his passport, but probably he had it in the inside pocket of his suit coat, and his suit coat was fashionably tight and buttoned. The pick would be tougher than anything she'd tried in years.

Oh, well. She had plenty of other tricks up her sleeve.

Babikian had drained his piña colada and was starting to stand when Gina dropped into the chair across from him.

"Hi," she said.

Babikian looked at her and smiled. Zowie! Shake hadn't exaggerated when he said the fella had teeth.

"Not interested," he said. "Sorry. Whatever your game is."

She had to read him fast. What floated his boat? Gina wished now that Shake had told her more about him. She decided to go with the old tried-and-true. Almost every guy she'd ever met had one big, throbbing weakness. His ego.

"If you want to play a game, I have a game for you," she said. "But you won't win it. That's my warning to you."

"You're not a hooker," he said.

"No. I'm a firm believer that sex should never be transactional."

"You're in the wrong place if you're a hooker. Do you know what a girl costs here? Like thirty dollars for the night. I'm talking about a girl who looks like a supermodel. Miss Cambodia probably costs thirty dollars a night."

"I sell cell-network software solutions to the governments of developing nations that don't need them and can't afford them. And right now I'm so bored I could die."

He glanced at his watch and sat back down. "What kind of a game?"

"I'm gonna ask you five questions," Gina said. "All you have to do to win, you just have to give a wrong answer each time."

He studied her, trying to sniff out the catch.

"There's no catch," Gina said. "Cross my heart. Five wrong answers and you win."

"What do I win?"

"Anything you want. 'Cause you're not gonna win."

He studied her some more. "You're flying to Hong Kong tonight?"

"Yes."

"Then I want you when we get there. You spend the night with me."

"No dice. I told you, I'm not a hooker. And I thought I made clear my position on transactional sex?"

"What are you worried about? You said I wasn't going to win."

Gina knew it wasn't really sex or her that Babikian was after. He was the kind of man who got off on making a woman do whatever the woman said she didn't want to do. If Gina had mentioned she never, ever ate shellfish, Babikian would want to take her out to dinner at an oyster bar.

She pretended to think it over. "Fine. But if I win . . . *when* I win, I want liquid assets."

"How much?"

"Twenty grand."

"You're crazy."

"So you do think I'm gonna win," she said.

He checked his watch again. "Twenty grand. So that's your hustle."

"Shall we get started? But first you have to promise you've never played this game before. You have to be sporting about this."

"I've never played it."

"Promise."

"I promise."

A guy who could have been Babikian's little brother—his head maybe a scootch smaller and a suit not quite as expensive—made his way across the bar to them. He ignored Gina.

"We're boarding in five minutes," he told Babikian.

"All right. I'm gonna win a quick bet first."

The little brother looked consternated, but he kept quiet.

"First question," Gina said. "Your answers should be totally wrong, so I know they're wrong. What was your most beloved childhood pet?"

Babikian deliberated. "Polar bear."

"We're boarding in five minutes," Little Brother said again.

"Then I've got five minutes, don't I? Jeff?"

"Yeah, Jeff," Gina said.

Jeff gave her a look, daggers, and slunk over to the bar.

"Next question," Babikian said.

"Okay. What's your favorite flavor of ice cream?"

A beat. "Mashed potatoes and liver."

Gina leaned across the table. She locked eyes with him.

"What one thing," she said, "do you want more than anything else in the world?"

He didn't react, but she thought she saw a ripple of movement at the bottom of his dark eyes.

"I want to stay right where I am," he said. "I want to be the guy in the background for the rest of my life."

Gina leaned back and laughed. "Not bad. That's usually a tricky one. Okay. Are we on number three or four now?"

Babikian made an exasperated face. Thinking, probably, *Stupid bitch.*

"We're on question four now. You're running out of—" He realized she'd nailed him, and how. "Wait . . ."

She smiled. "*That* was question four. 'Are we on three or four?' And I'm happy to say your answer is correct!"

"No," he said. "Damn it. You cheated. You—"

"I was pissed when it happened to me, too," Gina said. She'd thrown a shot glass at his head, the guy long ago who'd suckered her with the Five Questions. "Now, about that twenty grand."

Babikian, really pissed, shoved himself away from the table and stood. Little Brother was making his way back to the table.

"We're gonna miss the flight, man," he said. "We've got to roll."

Babikian came around the table so he could stand over Gina. He leaned close, his hot piña colada breath in her face, letting her know that he had six inches and fifty pounds on her and could make her eat shellfish anytime he wanted to. "Check's in the mail, sweetheart."

"Don't be a sore loser," she said. "Let's play again, double or nothing. Maybe you'll win this time."

He kicked his chair out of the way and strode off, Little Brother falling in behind him. Gina watched them jog down the concourse. A couple of gate agents, down at the far end, frantically waved them on. Babikian and Little Brother reached the gate. The agents smiled. Little Brother handed over his boarding pass and passport. Babikian reached into his suit coat's pocket and . . .

Gina flipped open Babikian's passport and snuck a peek at his photo. Nobody took a good passport photo, did they? She wondered why that was.

She was heading for the exit when four Cambodian soldiers went hustling past her, down the concourse toward Babikian's gate. Gina called Shake.

"Hi, pumpkin," she said. "Did you just send in the cavalry?"

"Ouch did," Shake said. "He has friends in high places."

The Cambodian soldiers surrounded Babikian. They pointed their machine guns at him and started yipping. Gina couldn't hear from this distance what Babikian was saying. It looked like he was complaining. Then threatening. Then one of the soldiers punched him in the stomach with the butt of his machine gun, and Babikian dropped to his knees.

"Well, then," Gina told Shake, "your boy's not going anywhere now."

AFTER HE TALKED to Gina, Shake had to hold his breath for a few more minutes, until Ouch's phone rang and his guys at the airport checked in.

It was a short call. Ouch smiled when it was over. He put his phone away and clapped his hands together.

"There are diamonds!" he said. "I think we have a sexy food conclusion, Shay!"

An ache of sweet, debilitating relief spread over Shake. He sat down before he fell down.

Lexy, on the other end of the couch, reached for him. Shake took her hand and gave it a squeeze. Neither of them spoke. Words, at a time like this, couldn't even come close.

Chapter Forty-Three

On the ship to America—in the heat and the filth and such terrible waves that Alexandra thought the ship would be turned upside down—she and Dikran had talked of death.

"When I die," he said.

"You will never die, *jigyars*. You are too strong."

"When I die, do not bury me."

"No?"

"Burn me there, wherever I fall, and let my dust choke the throats of my enemies!"

She smiled now, thinking of it, thinking of him. Oh, Dikran. How was it possible that a voice so loud could ever be silenced?

"So he wanted to be cremated?" Shake said. "You're sure?"

They stood on the banks of the river in Siem Reap. Four of them: Alexandra, Shake, Gina, and the woman from the hotel. Mitch. She had brought incense with her, and a big, ugly dog almost as big and ugly as Dikran.

"I thought he would've wanted a blowout," Shake said. "A casket with a lot of bling. Strippers and Armenian folk music and maybe a virgin sacrifice or something."

Alexandra smiled. Here was another impossibility come to pass, that Dikran and Shake would become friends. Perhaps not friends, but not enemies. Perhaps still enemies, but not enemies as much as before.

"I am sure," she said.

She stepped to the edge of the water with the box. Mitch lit the incense.

"I'll say a few words, shall I?" Mitch said.

"What can you say?" Alexandra said. This woman did not know Dikran. Who did? Only Alexandra.

Mitch closed her eyes. She spoke to the sky.

"Somebody misses you," she said. "Somebody misses you so much."

Alexandra flicked a tear from her cheek. She took the powder of Dikran in her palm and spread it on the water. Powder and bits of bone, tooth. He did not sink. This made Alexandra happy. She watched the current carry Dikran away, into the twilight shadows.

She climbed the bank to Gina.

"You came to Cambodia to stand by your husband," Alexandra said. "I understand this. But still I am grateful to you."

"I just need to be reimbursed two hundred and eleven dollars at some point," Gina said. "No rush."

Alexandra smiled. "We could be friends, I think. In a different world."

"Far, far away."

Shake was heading toward them. Alexandra and Gina both waved to him. *Go, we are busy talking.*

"Got it," he said, and went to gaze at the river.

"May I ask you a question?" Alexandra said to Gina.

"Sure."

"When I met you the very first time. You are no longer the woman you were then. Would you agree?"

"You can change your life, too, if that's what you're asking."

Alexandra touched a finger to Gina's earring and admired it. Gina's earrings were not expensive, yet elegant.

"Is that what I ask?" Alexandra said.

"I did it. So I'm pretty sure you could do it. Between you and me . . ."

"Yes?"

"Nothing. I was on the verge of giving you a compliment but restrained myself in the nick of time."

"Ah. Well."

Alexandra gave her a kiss, one on each cheek, and then walked over to Shake.

"Were you guys talking about me?" he said.

"Of course."

He laughed. "I didn't think so."

"Thank you, my friend. You know that I am in your debt."

"I've lost track after all these years. Who owes what."

"Perhaps this is for the best. Perhaps this is the definition of friends?"

The ugly dog had wandered close to them. She growled at Shake, until Mitch pulled her away.

"Sorry!" she said.

"That dog liked me for a while," Shake said. "I don't know what happened."

Alexandra knew he had something else to say to her but searched to find a way. She did not mind the wait. She breathed in the fresh air. Never again would she take this for granted, the possibility to take fresh air into her lungs whenever she wished.

"I'm sorry, Lexy," Shake said at last. "I know what Dikran was to you."

She gave him a kiss, one on each cheek.

"Good-bye, my friend," she said. "Until next time."

Chapter Forty-Four

Shake and Gina stayed in Cambodia for a couple of extra days so they could visit Angkor Wat. Ouch, who insisted on picking up Shake's hotel bill, approved.

"Good, good," Ouch said. "I am certain you will injure it very much."

They did enjoy it, but Shake didn't really relax until their plane out of Siem Reap was in the air.

"So what do you think happened to Babikian?" Gina asked him after the flight attendant brought around the warm nuts.

"No clue," Shake said. He'd known better than to ask Lexy about it. Maybe Babikian was already dead. Maybe he was in the process of wishing he were dead. Or, hell, maybe he was still Lexy's number two and Lexy had given him a raise for showing initiative. It wouldn't surprise Shake.

"I forgot to tell you," Gina said. "Mitch told me that in a past life I was a Viking warrior."

"Sounds about right."

"I didn't believe that spooky woo-woo shit before. But now that I know I was such a badass, I'm all about it."

Shake thought about his last conversation with Mitch, when she dropped them off at the airport. She'd lifted her sunglasses and looked at him.

"Don't tell me," he said. "My aura."

"No. Your aura's all sorted. It's blending now, and not so darkish green."

"But?"

Mitch was looking a couple of feet to his left, at the presence she said had caused all the psychic interference for her. The presence that wouldn't shut up about the diamonds and had, if you thought about it, saved Shake's ass.

"It's not so aggro now," Mitch said, "but it's still there."

Shake supposed he could live with that.

"Thanks for everything," he'd said. "Have a good life or two."

THEY LANDED IN Indianapolis at five o'clock in the afternoon and made it back to the house a little after seven. They were both exhausted, but Gina told Shake they had to stay awake until bedtime in Bloomington. She knew from experience that it was the only way to beat jet lag.

"We can beat jet lag tomorrow," Shake said.

"I have an idea. We'll go have a picnic."

"I just want to sleep."

"A picnic at Bottoms Up Quarry. We can watch the sunset. Don't refuse me."

He sighed but nodded. "Never."

He put a six-pack in the cooler, and Gina grabbed a blanket. They stopped by the organic market for some jamón ibérico sliced so thin you could see through it, then drove a few miles out of town. They parked at the derelict stone-cutting plant, where the trail started. From there the quarry was just a five-minute stroll through the woods.

The sun was so low in the sky that the long blades of their shadows reached the entire length of the golden stone shelf. Gina spread out the blanket. They'd explored a bunch of the abandoned quarries in the area, including the one where *Breaking Away* had been filmed, but Bottoms Up was their favorite. Even drunk-ass college kids considered it too dangerous for quarry jumping—the limestone walls slanted away from the water, seventy feet below—so Shake and Gina usually had the place all to themselves.

The beer was cold, the stone beneath the blanket still warm from the afternoon sun. The light was amazing.

This is home, Gina thought. How weird was that? How awesome?

She got up and walked to the lip of the quarry. From this high, in this light, the water far below was a deep, inky indigo. It was like she was looking up instead of down, into the vast mysterious reaches of outer space.

Shake stayed back on the blanket. She knew he didn't like heights. He said it was because he was from New Orleans and had grown up below sea level.

"No more adventures," he said. "What do you say?"

"Yes."

He thought for a second. "Yes, no more adventures?"

"Yes. Not for a while at least."

"Good," Shake said. "Unless you're thinking a different kind of one."

She guessed where he was going with this.

"Well, you're not getting any younger," she said. "You don't want to be so old you can't play catch with little Casey."

"Is little Casey a boy or a girl?"

"I'm good either way. I just like the name."

"Well, then . . ."

His voice trailed off. Gina turned to see why. A guy came limping out of the woods. Gina didn't recognize him at first. His hair was a mess, and the suit looked like he'd pulled it out of a Dumpster.

Dominic. The casino boss.

She felt a warning tingle at the base of her skull, even before she saw the gun in his hand.

"Well, well," Dominic said. "What have we here?"

He'd been staking out their house, she realized, and had followed them here.

Shake had seen the gun, too. He stood.

"Hey," he said, nice and friendly. "Can we help you with something?"

Dominic lifted the gun and pointed it at Gina. He glanced over at Shake.

"So this is your husband?" he said.

"Hello, Dominic," Gina said.

"You two know each other?" Shake said.

"It's an interesting story," Gina said.

"I screwed your wife," Dominic said. "Last week. Sunday night."

"Liar." Gina hesitated, then looked over at Shake. She decided she might as well get this over with. "We made out for like two seconds."

"You made out with him," Shake said.

"I was going to tell you about it at some point."

"At some point?"

"Listen, I'm so sorry, buttercup. Okay? I got bored, and I was mad at you for going off without me and . . . there's other shit, too, that has nothing to do with you. But, see, the main thing is, I made out with him for like two seconds and then I realized I didn't want anybody but you. No. I realized I already knew that."

Dominic limped a couple of steps closer. Gina, backed up to the edge of the shelf, had nowhere to go but a long way down.

"Do you know what you did to me?" Dominic said.

"You deserved it," Gina said. "Don't be such a sissy. Your knee's going to be fine."

Shake was off to Dominic's right. He reached for his beer bottle—the best weapon at hand, Gina guessed—but Dominic swung the gun over.

"Stay right there."

"Just getting a drink. Okay?"

Shake reached for the bottle again. Dominic fired. The bullet slapped off the stone a few feet from Shake.

"I see you move one more time, I'm gonna kill you, too."

"You don't want to kill anybody," Shake said. "Spend the rest of your life in stir? You won't like it. I've been there."

"So have I." Dominic turned the gun back on Gina. "Answer my fucking question."

"Is this about the twenty grand?" she said. "For God's sake, Dominic. I left you most of your money."

"You stupid bitch," he said, "that wasn't my money. That was a casino account."

"So? Fine. Put down the stupid gun, Dominic. I'll give you the money back. All's well that ends well."

She saw something in his eyes, stormy and wild, that she hadn't noticed before: desperation.

"You don't fucking understand," he said. "They thought I stole it. The people I work for. So they started poking around."

Gina would have laughed if there hadn't been a gun pointed at her face. Even so, she almost did.

"You mean you *were* stealing from them? And that's how they found out?"

"If they track me down, I'm a dead man. I've been living in my car for three days."

"Take it easy," Shake said. "We can help you out."

"Shut up. I don't want your help."

Gina's heel slipped—the rock along the lip of the quarry was broken and crumbling—and she almost lost her balance.

"Can't run from me now, can you?" Dominic said. "You ever heard of karma? What goes around comes around."

Gina took a peek over her shoulder. She could jump. She'd run the hurdles in high school and still had plenty of spring left in her step. But even if she managed to clear the quarry wall and the boulders lined like blunt teeth along the water's edge, even if the water was deep enough that she didn't break her neck, where would that leave Shake?

"Let's play a game, Dominic," she said.

That threw him. He'd rehearsed this moment a few hundred times. And every time there'd been a lot of Gina crying and begging.

"I don't think you understand what's about to happen here."

"You're just scared you'll lose. C'mon. Here's the game. I'm going to ask you five questions, and if you answer them all wrong, you win. There's no catch, I promise."

Shake glanced over at her. Gina could read his mind and knew what he was thinking. *You got a plan, I hope?*

Gina hoped he could read *her* mind.

"If I win," she told Dominic, "you let us go."

He laughed, hoarse and harsh. "Why the fuck would I do that?"

"Because if *you* win," Gina said, "you can do whatever you want with me."

"I'm gonna do that anyway."

"Yes, but . . ." Gina had never been able to cry on cue, so she bit the inside of her cheek hard. Her eyes began to water. "Please. At least give me a chance. I'm begging you."

Gina waited to see if he understood what she was offering him: more time to enjoy her suffering.

"If I win," he said, "I kill your husband, too."

"What? No. That's not—"

"I kill him first, so you can watch. That's the only way I'll play."

Gina bit the inside of her cheek again. The tears were rolling now.

"But if I win, you'll let us go," she said. He wasn't going to let either one of them go, whether he won or lost. She'd realized that a few minutes ago. But she needed him to lose. "Okay?"

"What's the game?"

"Five Questions. You just have to get the answers wrong. Make sure I know the answers are wrong. But tell me before we start if you've ever played the game before."

Dominic shook his head. "I've never played. Get started."

"Okay. First question. What was your most beloved childhood pet?"

He was zeroed in on her just like Babikian had been, trying to work out the catch.

"A monkey," he said.

"Next question. What's your favorite flavor of ice cream?"

"Motor oil."

"What's the one thing, I mean the *one* thing, you want more than anything else in the world?"

She'd lowered her voice so he'd have to tilt his head closer. Gina couldn't risk a glance at Shake. She could sense, from a subtle shift in the light and shadow, that Shake had moved a step to his right. Maybe.

"I want all this to be over," Dominic said.

Gina shook her head. "That's too vague. How am I supposed to know if . . . ? Never mind. Okay. Wait. Which question are we on now?"

"This is number—" Dominic stopped himself. He laughed again. "That's it? You thought it would be that easy?"

"I didn't—"

"Nineteen. That's the answer to your question. We're on number nineteen."

Gina felt her stomach float upward, like when an elevator you're riding in drops too fast.

Well, she pretended to feel that way.

"You cheated," she said. "You knew that was coming. Seriously, have you played this game before?"

"No," Dominic said. Pleased with himself, despite everything.

Gina waited to see if he'd figure it out for himself. He didn't.

"That was the fifth question," she explained. "'Have you played this game before?' And since your answer was correct, I win."

His scruff of a goatee twitched. Guys who tripped up on question five got even more pissed off than the ones, like Babikian, who tripped up on number four. They thought they'd won. They were already savoring the spoils of their own cleverness.

"Stupid bitch," Dominic said. "You really thought I was gonna let you go if you won? Tell me you did and make me laugh."

Gina glanced over at Shake. Just as she'd hoped, he'd eased his way to the very edge of the quarry shelf.

"You ready to do this, sport?" Gina said.

"No," Shake said.

She took another quick peek over her shoulder. Seventy feet was a whole lot of feet.

"Really kick off and get as clear as you can," she said.

"Got it."

"Love you and all that."

"Back at you."

"Are you listening to me?" Dominic asked Gina. He was about to pull the trigger of the gun. "You're gonna die right now, right here."

"Sure hope not," Gina said.

Together she and Shake turned, crouched, and leaped.

Chapter Forty-Five

Shake kept waiting to hit something, water or rocks. But he just kept falling, falling. It seemed like he might fall forever. He could hear Gina screaming. Maybe he was screaming, too. He heard a gunshot.

And then he hit the water. Feetfirst, but still the impact knocked the wind out of him. The water was cold and black. He couldn't see Gina. He kicked off his shoes, blew out a breath, and followed the bubbles back to the surface.

Gina bobbed up a second later. She was laughing.

"That was kind of fun!"

They'd missed the rocks by about ten feet.

"I disagree," he said.

He heard another gunshot. The echo pinged around between the limestone walls of the quarry. Shake wasn't too worried. It was almost dark now, and the guy, high up on the edge of the shelf, had a bad angle on them. Shake was glad he only had the Glock, and not something with more reach.

"Under," he told Gina, and pointed to the rocks at the bottom of the opposite wall.

She took a deep breath and dove beneath the water. Shake did the same. They frog-kicked to shore and pulled themselves up onto the rocks. The guy didn't have any angle now. Shake pulled Gina behind a big boulder just to be safe.

They could see the guy moving around, trying to line them up.

"He better be careful," Gina said.

He was too close to the edge of the quarry. Every now and then, his foot would slip, skidding through the loose rubble until he caught his balance.

He was way too close to the edge. He was going to kill them if it killed him. They saw his foot slip again. He tried to recover, but his other foot slipped, too, and he lurched forward like he'd been shoved from behind.

Down he went. Shake watched him tumble, his head banging against the side of the quarry, a finger plinking every key on the piano. He looked away before the guy hit the rocks at the bottom of the wall.

SHAKE AND GINA were still soaked from their swim, and the temperature had dropped about ten degrees now that the sun had gone down. One of the cops went off to see if she could find them a couple of blankets.

"So," Shake asked Gina. "Anybody else you wanted to tell me about at some point? Anybody else you almost slept with recently?"

"I told you. I didn't really almost sleep with him."

"I heard you."

"How mad are you?"

"We can talk about it later."

"Do we have to?"

She was shivering. He put an arm around her and pulled her close.

"No."

The cop brought them blankets and a thermos of hot coffee. Shake realized he knew her. She was the cop who'd been behind Shake in her Dodge Charger, way back when, making Jawad, Shake's Thursday-afternoon driving lesson, so nervous.

"Just a few more questions," the cop said, "and then we'll get you out of here."

"No problem," Shake said.

"You guys have had quite a night."

Shake smiled. Gina was smiling, too.

"We plan to take it easy," he said, "here on out."

Acknowledgments

I'm deeply grateful for my agent, Shane Salerno. He is the first person I'd call if I ever found myself entangled abroad in a dangerous and shadowy underworld. The Story Factory, including Ryan Coleman, never lets you down.

The good folks at William Morrow and HarperCollins would probably get a call too. Thank you especially to Liate Stehlik, Emily Krump, Tessa James, and Jessica Lyons.

Trish Daly!

Maureen Sugden copy-edited this book with her usual skill, grace, and good humor.

Thank you to the readers who over the years sent me belligerent emails asking me when the hell the next Shake book would be out. Your enthusiasm for my characters is hugely appreciated.

The best part about being a crime writer is that you become part of the crime-writing community. I've met some of my absolute favorite people in the world here (they know who they are, I hope), and I'm so grateful for all the writers, readers, reviewers, bloggers, marketers, and booksellers I've had the good fortune to know.

My wife, Christine, deserves all the credit for everything, and then some.

About the Author

LOU BERNEY is the multiple award–winning author of *Dark Ride, November Road,* and *The Long and Faraway Gone,* as well as *Gutshot Straight* and *Whiplash River.* His short fiction has appeared in publications such as *The New Yorker, Ploughshares,* and the Pushcart Prize anthology. He lives in Oklahoma City and teaches in the MFA program at Oklahoma City University.

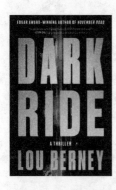

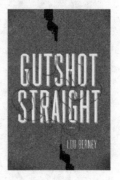